實用 船藝與海技英文

 方信雄｜著

五南圖書出版公司 印行

前言

　　鑒於坊間有關海員與航海英文著作甚多，然內容頗多不是脫離現今航運實務，就是實務上罕用詞彙，亦即未能跟進當前航海與船員實務進展。觀其原因除了著者既非航海科班出身，或不具備航海本業背景外，亦有雖具航海與船務經歷但已淡出職場有年所造成的。

　　其次，由於海上貿易運作與航儀全面電腦化，使得許多傳統海運實務相關用詞成為罕用詞，甚至已完全不再被業界引用。以電子海圖（ECDIS）的問世為例，大部分航海人員原本賴以為生的助導航設施（Aid to Navigation）一夕之間成為過往古董文物。最典型的現象就是新一代的駕駛員幾乎不會觀測燈塔，因為只要觀測雷達就可測定船位，何需費時辨別燈塔的所在與燈質。連帶的使得有關燈塔相關術語漸被海員淡忘。不容否認的，當前此等專有名詞充其量僅能說是航海知識，而非影響航行安全的主要關鍵。

　　眾所周知，海上環境瞬息萬變，船舶管理階層或船舶操縱者可以從容地本著自身的知識、經驗對橫置於前的困難、險阻或是發展中的危險狀況做出平靜、適當的回應，以化解危機或降低損害至最低程度，而此種難以下定義的職人專業工藝與技巧，即傳統航海上所稱之「優良船藝」（Good Seamanship）。

　　基本上，船上所有甲板作業實務皆屬「船藝」（Seamanship）範疇。「船藝」可以被視為一種基本船舶手（工）藝（Craft），係指經由多年海上工作經驗的傳承、練習與鍛鍊而成的專業技巧。它是一種代代傳承而下的技巧，無法單憑納入標準工序或經由課堂上傳授即可習得者。海員具備「優良船藝」與否絕對是一家航運公司經營成功的最主要關鍵因素。可惜隨著科技的發達，海事人力速成的趨勢，使得往昔產學界標榜專業技術的「船藝」一詞，幾已被眼前船上日常例行性繁雜事務的「船務」所取代，連帶的使得技術含量較高的「海技」亦被日趨

忽視，因而造成當前船員基本功與海事關鍵技術存有很大改善空間的現象。為避免此一負面趨勢的持續發展，本書特以被當前職場淡忘的「船藝」一詞取代含括營運業務的「船務」，進而將編撰內容聚焦於船舶日常運作實務，以及船舶航行暨操縱領域。

海運事業乃最典型跨國產業，因而無論管理者或從業人員，如何精準使用工作詞彙常是整體船務運作成敗的主因，因此本書主要針對海員與岸際船務有關人員之日常業務需要做考量，並以精簡與實效並重為編纂要旨。

不容否認的，筆者自身本非英文科班出身，英語文的程度仍有待加強，今膽敢僅憑藉服務航海界數十寒暑的職場工作心得與教學經驗編纂此書，純出自拋磚之圖，尚祈各方賢達、師長、先進不吝指教，期以提升我國航海同行的船用英文實力。

目錄

第六章　船務管理　233

第七章　海事文書　253

第一章 船藝與海技英文的職場背景

　　船舶運轉不僅在地理上跨國界，船員編制更採多元國籍船員混乘制，故而船舶內部管理與外部的船岸間溝通皆須依賴有效的聯絡與語言表達能力。跨國界溝通當然需要共通的語言與文字，始能充分理解溝通對方的企圖與需求。當前國際海運社會已達成以英文為共同工作語言的共識，因而一定程度的英文語言能力與書寫能力已是當前管理級船員或岸際管理幹部必須具備的職場能力。

第一節　海上航行主要通訊語言與設備

　　眾所周知，英文已成為國際貿易、法律、外交、航空與海運等不同領域的通用語言，故而國際海事組織（IMO）乃積極促成海事專業英文說法與寫法的標準化，並自2001年11月起採用標準海事聯絡語法（詞組）（The IMO's Standard Marine Communication Phrases, SMCP），其目的是要所有從事與船舶有關業務的人員，不論其母語是否為英文，僅能使用標準措辭與語法，以確保通訊旨意的精準傳達。很遺憾的，除了教育與訓練背景的差異外，因為未具強制性規定，筆者長期從職場上的觀察發現，幾乎所有海員與介入海員事務的陸岸人員都依舊樂於使用屬於他（她）們自己版本的英文會話。似此，船與岸或是船與船之間未能使用標準聯絡用語與詞彙，焉能確保通訊品質。

　　除了上述通訊語言外，最重要的當屬通訊設施，而目前船上使用最為普遍的語音通訊（Voice Communication）設備就是特高頻無線電話

（Very High Frequency, VHF）。依據國際電信聯合會之無線電頻率劃分表，VHF是指頻帶由30MHz到300MHz的無線電電波。

　　有關VHF被廣泛使用於船舶上之緣由為一九六六年六月十六日英國籍油輪Alva Cape與美國籍蒸汽機油輪Texaco Massachuetts在紐約港Bayonne Bridge西側的Bergen Point外，因兩船使用VHF聯繫的不當而釀成撞船的大禍，並造成三十四名船員被燒死，以及嚴重的海水污染。如此重大的海難事故發生於首善之港的紐約對美國是何其大的打擊，終促使美國國家運輸安全局（NTSB, National Transportation Safety Board）積極著手調查，並於一九六九年做出航行於美國水域之船舶應加強船舶與船舶間的無線電話通訊的迫切性建議。直至一九七一年八月四日尼克森總統始簽定船舶駕駛臺與船舶駕駛臺之間的無線電話通訊法案（Vessel Bridge-to-Bridge Radiotelephone Act）。雖此一法案僅適用於美國水域，但卻引起主要沿海國間的爭議，因為國際間已有國際海上避碰規則（COLREGS）作為船舶避碰的依據，故而利用VHF聯絡做成船舶避碰協定的正當性與合法性頗受質疑。然無論如何，由於美國的強勢主導與後續又接連發生數起類似海難，最後終促使國際海上人命公約（SOLAS）亦通過VHF的設置與使用相關規定。

　　另一方面，由於不當使用VHF已被國際海法界普遍認定為不適當的航海行動（Inappropriate navigational action）或怠忽職守（Inaction）的案例，亦即負責航行者若有不當使用VHF的事實，則其所受的譴責與過失程度理應加重。再者，不論兩船在VHF的通話是否包括達成航行上的協議，其通話的內容極可能作為日後判定肇事船舶之間所應負責任比重之依據。可見不當使用VHF絕對是海員不適當行動或疏忽的一種，故而吾人對於通話時的遣詞用字與行動企圖的一致性焉能不謹慎為之。

一、使用頻道

　　原則上，VHF的第16頻道（Channel 16）為通用頻道，旨在傳送一

般的訊息。故船舶一旦與沿海國岸台（或其他船台）建立聯絡後，必須依沿海國電臺規定（或船台建議），轉換到其他作業頻道，如第12頻道以收聽航行訊息。全世界的海岸無線電話站台，經常變更頻道以傳送航行相關資料，此乃為避免第16頻道被占用或過於吵雜。在此情境下，可能使用到的語句有：

- You must keep radio silence in this area on channel 16 ...

（在此區域內第16頻道必須保持靜默。）

【註1】

此例句旨在要求海員避免在此頻道交談。因為第16號頻號是指定用做「呼叫」及「緊急」時所使用之頻率，不得做一般例行性或拖延時間式的使用。例如沿海國的海岸電臺的廣播常用Channel 16籲請附近船舶注意並轉至其他工作頻道。

- Taiwan Coastguard, Keelung: All ships. This is Taiwan Coastguard, Keelung. A situation report follows on channel two three. Out.

（基隆海巡署：所有船舶！這裡是基隆海巡署，狀況報告隨後將在第23號頻道播出。）

【註2】

接收到此信文的船舶必須依照例句中的說明，將VHF頻道改為23號，以便接收海岸電臺廣播的內容。

　　「第16頻道」在無線電呼叫上可以唸成「Channel Sixteen」，亦可說成「Channel One Six」。兩者雖說法不同，但其意義卻相同。

　　因此，利用VHF通話時應注意事項如下：

1. 隨時保持守聽第16頻道。
2. 使用雙頻道守聽功能，以守聽其他需要收聽之頻道。
3. 在以第16頻道發出訊息以前，應確定有無「Mayday」之遇難信號或其他應優先予以發送的安全信號。
4. 建立以第16頻道僅用於「聯絡頻道」之觀念，然後再轉換至另一

頻道通話，以免干擾到其他更加緊急訊息的收發。切記不可使用第16頻道閒聊無關航行安全事項，否則極可能因漏聽重要安全相關訊息，進而導致危險，更甚者造成生命財產之損失。

必須強調的是，儘管國際海運社會一再要求所有海員使用「標準海事通訊用語」，但實務上，本於海上職場背景與船上的傳統習慣，在船舶運作過程中難免出現日常職場行話，而非都使用「標準海事通訊用語」。在某種程度上，講行話正是專業與技藝的展現，更是「巷仔內ㄟ」、「匠人」、「職人」（Seaman-like）的特質。因而本書除了無線電通信外，在適當情節處都會加註職場實務用語，以免讀者與職場實務脫節。

【註3】海上使用無線電話的紀律

IMO建議：遇有任何緊急狀況時，第16頻道的其他用途，均應立刻停止。

同時在使用第16頻道呼叫以前，應小心確認當下是否有其他船台呼叫遇難信號「Mayday」的緊急狀況。有許多人命及財產即是因此一頻道遭受外來之干擾致漏收信文而損失的。吾人應切記當有緊急狀況時，僅能傳播與此一緊急狀況有關之消息，而不應再納入其他之情報。

二、船藝與海技英文的職場背景

除了前項所述，船舶對外的語音通訊外，一般船舶內部管理經常使用的職場英文更應是管理級幹部務必具備的基本管理技能。尤其眼前船舶多屬多元國籍船員混乘的編制，如未能精準的在適當場合，使用正確的語言詞彙表達自身的企圖，不僅難行承上啟下之效，更可能釀成原可避免的困擾，小從無謂爭議，大至引發嚴重業務損失乃至重大事故，皆有可能。故而努力練習提升英文表達能力，絕對是管理級幹部加強自身職場能力無可迴避的必修功課。

第二節　海運大環境的演變

- The global economy is heavily dependent on the safe and efficient movement of ships.

  （全球經濟嚴重依賴船舶安全與有效的運作。）

- Shipping and maritime navigation of the 20th and 21st centuries are burdened by lots of contradictions related to technological, economic and organizational development. These contradictions become apparent through an insight into maritime accidents recorded in the last and early this century.

  〔二十世紀與二十一世紀的海運業與海上航行（人員）承擔著許多關於技術的、經濟的與組織發展的矛盾。而從觀察上一世紀至本世紀初的海事紀錄即可得知，此一矛盾變得愈趨明顯。〕

- This is an age of extraordinary technological change. Perhaps today's developments are akin to the 19th century's Industrial Revolution, where industrial change eventually affected culture and thought.

  （這是一個航海技術上大改變的時代，或許今天的發展正如同十九世紀大革命一樣，亦即工業革命與變化終將影響職場文化與人們的想法。）

- The maritime world is a fascinating mixture of straightforward tasks in a complex world.

  （海運世界是由複雜環境中許多單一任務所組成的迷人組合。）

- The sea is still the same dangerous place but since the days of sail, the inevitable march of progress has forced the industry to acknowledge new challenge, dangers and lifestyles while at the same time reducing accident rates and introducing safer working practices throughout.

（自從帆船時代起，大海即一直充滿著相同的風險，迫使業界無可避免地，始終在邁向降低事故率與引進更安全的工作實務的同時，去認知新的挑戰、危險與價值觀或生活方式。）

• Maintaining a safe navigational watch is a combination of a myriad of tasks.

（保持安全航行當值是許多工作的結合。）

• In view of the circumstances changed and prejudice of national marine policy, mariner had becoming really a rare species in our country.

（由於海運大環境的改變與國家海洋政策的偏頗，造成海員在我們國家成爲稀有人種。）

• There will be bigger and more complex ships, increased speed, greater port efficiency, more regulations and above all a far higher demand for public accountability in the maritime industry. The IMO has taken a clear stand on the duties of the maritime community, on its responsibility for the environment.

（船舶愈造愈大愈複雜，船速變快，提升港口效率，以及制定更多的法規，尤其賦予海運業對於公共責任的更高要求。國際海事組織對於海運社會保護環境的責任採取非常明確的立場。）

• As ships get bigger and safety margins get smaller, you need a professional way of manoeuvre.

（船舶愈造愈大，安全邊際就變得愈小，因而愈需專業的操船方法。）

- Language barriers on foreign ships continue to be a serious obstacle to the safe navigation of these vessels in pilotage waters.

  （外國船舶的語言障礙仍然是引航區內其他船舶航行安全的嚴重妨害。）

- Since effective information exchange is vital to safe navigation, safety is compromised on those vessels where the pilots are unable to communicate with the crew.

  〔因為有效的資訊交換對於安全航行最為重要，而在那些引水人與船員無法溝通的船舶上，船舶安全常被（語言障礙）妥協掉。〕

- The only practical way to improve operation relationship is to improve communication between pilots-masters-officers of the watch. This can be by one common language internationally.

  〔改善（駕駛臺團隊）作業關係唯一實際可行的方法就是改善引水人、船長、當值駕駛員之間的溝通聯絡，而此只有藉由一種共同的國際語言達致。〕

- Everyone in the responsibility chain in shipping has to be vigilant and alert to any indication for developing slackness in safety standards in shipping.

  （在海運責任鏈中，每一個環節中的每一個人都負有對海運的安全標準朝鬆懈發展保持警戒與提出預警的責任。）

- What the pilot sees in the operational environment is totally different picture to what a port state control surveyor or inspector may witness when the ship is static alongside a berth.

  （引水人在操船環境下所看到的船舶，可能與港口國管制官員所看到泊靠於碼頭上的靜態船舶的狀況是完全不同的。）

- We need to recognize that these external parties are more likely to demand higher standards of competence and practice in the future than they do now.

  （我們必須體認到所有外部團體一定會不斷要求我們提供更高標準的能力與實務標準。）

- For hundreds of years the marine navigator has played a pivotal role in promoting economic development and the wealth of nations.

  （幾百年來，海員在提升國家經濟發展與繁榮上扮演了重大角色。）

- International awareness of the need to protect the environment has increased in recent years. Accordingly, MARPOL has been updated by numerous amendments with the aim of further reducing operational and accidental pollution from ships.

  （近年來國際社會對環境保護的警覺性日趨升高。所以國際防止海洋汙染公約爲了進一步降低船舶操作與事故所造成的汙染，一再修訂條款。）

第二章　常用詞彙

1. **Abaft** (*adv*) 在船艉、向船艉、在……的後面
   Toward the stern.
   （面對船艉方向。）

2. **Abandon ship** (*vt*) 棄船
   The captain issued the order to abandon ship because she is sinking.
   （由於船舶正在下沉中，船長下令棄船。）

3. **Adrift** (*adj/adv*) 漂浮、漂流
   In a drifting condition, at the mercy of wind and tide.
   （受制於風與潮流的作用，處於漂流狀態下。）

4. **Advance** (*n*) 循原航向向前移動的距離
   When altering course, the distance that a ship advances in the direction of original course, measured from the position whore the wheel is put over to position where she is pointing to her new course.
   （當船舶轉向時，船舶循原航向移動的距離，此距離自開始用舵點量起，至船舶轉向到新航向止。）

5. **Advection Fog** (*n*) 平流霧
   A kind of fog which caused from the horizontal shifting of a warm-wet air to a cold water surface or ground.
   （由於濕暖空氣水平流經較冷的地面或水面，氣團底層降溫至露點，水汽凝結而成，一般範圍較廣，持續時間較長，不分晝夜，以春夏較多。）

6. **Affluent** (*n*) 支流
   A tributary river or brook.
   （較大河流的支流或小溪流。）

7. **Aft** (*adj*) 船艉的、朝向船艉的

   Toward the stern of a ship.

   （面對船艉的方向。）

8. **After-Peak** (*n*) 艉尖艙

   A compartment just forward of the stern post.

   （位於艉柱正前方的隔間。）

9. **After Perpendicular** (*n*) 艉垂標

   The vertical line through the intersection of the load water line and the after edge of the stern post.

   （指一條經過由艉柱的後緣與滿載水線交點的垂直線。）

10. **Age of the Moon** (*n*) 月齡、月的盈虧

    The interval in days and decimals of a day since the last New Moon.

    （自前一次新月起算之日數時間間隔。）

11. **Age of the tide** (*n*) 潮齡

    The interval between the occurrence of New or Full Moon and the next spring tide at any given place.

    （在任何特定地點，新月或滿月與下一次大潮之間的時間間隔。）

12. **Agonic line** (*n*) 零磁偏差線

    A line joining point on the earth's surface where is no magnetic variation.

    （指地球表面上一條通過所有磁偏差為零的各地點的線。）

13. **Aground** (*n*) 擱淺

    Resting on the bottom.

    （船舶擱置在海底上。）

14. **Alongside** (*adv*) (*prep*) 靠泊

    A ship is alongside when side by side with a wharf, jetty, or another ship.

（指船舶傍靠於碼頭、突堤或其他船舶。）

15. **Alternating light** (*n*) 變色光、更迭光

A light which shows different colours in succession on the some bearing.

（在某一方向以兩種或兩種以上顏色的燈光交替連續發光的導航燈光。）

16. **Amidship** (*s*) (*n*) 船舶舯部

In the longitudinal, or fore-and-aft center of a ship. Halfway between stem and stern.

（船舶的縱向中心；船艏與船艉的正中間點。）

17. **AMVER** (*n*) 自動互助船舶救援系統

Automated Mutual-Assistance Vessel Rescue System.

（「AMVER」一詞，最早本來是指「大西洋商船緊急通報系統」。）

18. **Amplitude of the tide** (*n*) 半潮差、潮汐振幅

The different between mean tide level and high or low water.

（平均潮面與高或低潮面之間的高度差距。）

19. **Anchorage** (*n*) 錨地

Water area which is suitable and of depth neither too deep nor too shallow, nor in a situation too exposed, for vessel to ride in safety.

（係指水深不會太深，不會太淺，也不會過於曝露，適於船舶安全停泊的水域。）

20. **Anticyclone** (*n*) 反氣旋

Area of relatively high barometric pressure around which wind circulation is clockwise in N hemisphere, and anticlockwise in S hemisphere. General associated with fine and settled weather.

（在北半球氣壓相對較高的區域，在其範圍內風向會呈順時鐘方

向旋轉。在南半球則呈逆鐘向旋轉。多半伴隨著良好與穩定的天氣。）

21. **Aphelion** (*n*) 遠日點

The time or position at which a planet is farthest from the Sum.

（行星做繞日運動時，當其在運行軌道上離太陽最遠的時間或位置，源自拉丁語「aphôlium」。）

22. **Apogee** (*n*) 遠地點

The point in the orbit of the Moon which is farthest from the Earth.

（指月亮在其運行軌道上離地球最遠的點。）

23. **Apron** (*n*) 碼頭岸肩

The portion of a wharf or quay lying between the waterside edge and the sheds, railway lines or roads.

（指碼頭水際邊沿與倉庫、鐵路或公路之間可供作業的碼頭區域。碼頭岸肩的寬闊度為影響碼頭作業效率高低的主要因素之一。）

24. **Approaches** (*n*) 趨近水路

The waterways that give access or passage to harbours, channels.

（可以進、出或穿越港口、水道的水路。）

25. **Archipelago** (*n*) 群島、列島

A sea studded with many islands. A large group of islands.

（遍布許多島嶼的海面；島嶼群。）

26. **Arc of Visibility** (*n*) 能見弧

The sector, or sectors, in which a light is visible from seaward.

（從外海觀測，可以看到燈光的弧度區。）

27. **Area to be avoided** (*n*) 避航區

A routeing measure comprising an area within defined limit in which navigation is particularly hazardous and which should be avoided by all ships, or certain classes of ship.

（包括一個含有明確界限，航行於其間特別危險，所有船舶或某類型船舶需要迴避的水域之航路措施。）

28. **Artificial harbor** (*n*) 人工港

A harbor where the desired protection from wind and sea is obtained from moles, Jetties, breakwaters.

（一個藉由人造堤岸、突堤或防波堤遮擋風與浪的港口。）

29. **Astern** (*adv*) 向後、在船艉方向

Signifying position, in the rear of or abaft the stern.

（表示在船艉後方的某位置。）

30. **Awash** (*n*) 適涸岩

A shoal, rock or other feature is termed awash when its highest point of the feature is within 10 cm of the level of the water.

（指外形的最高點介於水面10公分內的淺灘、暗礁或其他地形等。）

31. **Awash at high water** (*n*) 高潮時可見

May be just visible at MHWS or MHHW.

（可能只有在平均大潮高潮或平均最高高潮時始可看見者。）

32. **Azimuth** (*n*) 方位角

The angle between the meridian and the vertical circle passing through a celestial body.

（子午線與通過某一天體的垂直圈之間的角度。）

33. **Azimuthing Control Device/Propulsion systems** (*n*) 360°全方位推進系統

With two or three thrusters, ships are able to turn a full 360° in ever-more tight circles, which is increasingly important for ship handling operations in harbors. They are all slightly different from each other. Fundamentally, from a Ship Handler's point of view, is that actually operating the pod to manoeuvre the vessel follows the same principle for whatever type of azimuthing system is installed.

（船舶若裝有二具或三具360°全方位推進器，如新式郵輪，船舶就可在原地進行360°迴轉，此可提升船舶在港內的操縱性。雖廠牌不同有些微差異。基本上，從操船者觀點來看，就是所有廠牌實際上都是利用操作一根操縱桿以相同的原理操縱船舶。）

34. **Backing** (*n*) 風向逆轉

The wind is said to back when it changes direction anticlockwise.

（當風向改變的方向呈逆時鐘方向時稱之。）

35. **Backwash** (*n*) 反沖浪

Waves reflected from obstructions such as cliffs, seawalls, breakwaters, &c.,

〔從懸崖、峭壁、堤岸、防波堤等障礙物反射（沖）而來的波浪。〕

36. **Ballast** (*n*) 壓艙物

Any weight carried solely for the purpose of making the vessel more seaworthy. Ballast may be either portable or fixed, depending upon the condition of the ship.

（用以增加船舶適航性的任何重物。依據船舶的狀況，壓艙物可以是固定的，亦可以是可移動的。但一般商船多指可壓入或排出艙櫃的海水；小遊艇除增加穩定度外，或有利用水泥塊置於船艏或船艉部調整俯仰差者。）

37. **Bar** (*n*) 沙洲

A bank of shore debris, such as sand, mud, gravel, or shingle, near the mouth of a river or at the approach to a harbour, causing an obstruction to entry.

（鄰近河口或進出港口的航路，由砂石、泥土、砂礫或鵝卵石堆積而成的沙洲淺灘，致造成船舶進出的阻礙。）

38. **Barge** (*n*) 駁船

A craft of full body and heavy construction designed for the carriage of cargo but having no machinery for self-propulsion.

（一艘設計用以運送貨物，但未配置自力推進機器的方型，且結構巨大的船舶。）

39. **Bay** *海灣*

A comparatively gradual indentation in the coastline, the seaward opening of which is usually wider than the penetration into the land.

（指地形和緩凹入海岸線，而且近海側的開口通常比深入陸岸的部分寬，規模比同為海灣的「Gulf」小。）

40. **Bay plan** (*n*) 貨櫃船的櫃位圖

A schematic diagram of container bays within a container vessel. The bays represent vertical divisions of the entire stowage area and are numbered from bow to stern.

〔貨櫃船內的貨櫃積載排列示意圖。「Bay（列）」代表整個裝櫃區內的垂直間隔，自船艏編數依序起算至船艉。〕

41. **Beach** (*n*) *海灘*

Any part of the shore over which shore debris, such as mud, sand, shingle, pebbles, is accumulated in a more or less continuous sheet.

（指由陸上碎屑殘礫，諸如泥土、沙、礫石或鵝卵石等連續或間斷堆積而成的部分海岸。）

42. **Beacon** (*n*) *信標、導航標物*

A mark constructed of metal, wood, concrete or masonry, or a combination of these material, erected on or in the vicinity of dangers or on shore, as an aid to navigation. Beacons are often surmounted by topmarks or have incorporated in them distinguishing marks or shapes, which are termed daymarks. They sometimes exhibit lights and may be fitted with radar reflectors.

（指一個由金屬、木頭、水泥或石頭，或是由這些材料組合而成的標誌，豎立在危險物上或其附近或岸上，作爲助導航設施使用。信標通常會在其頂部設置「頂標」或其他藉以供人易於辨別的標誌物或各種形狀物，此稱爲日標。信標有時會顯示燈光或裝置雷達反射器以提升其功能。）

43. **Beam** (*n*) 船寬；橫梁

The extreme width of a ship; The athwarship members of the ships' frame which support the deck.

（船舶的最大寬度；支撐甲板的船舶肋材的橫向構件。）

44. **Beam, On the Beam** (*n*) 正橫

An object is said to be on the beam, or abeam, if its bearing is approximately 90° from the course being steered.

（當一物體或目標，其方位與本船行駛的航向約呈90°時，稱該目標位於正橫。）

45. **Beam sea** (*n*) 橫浪

The condition where the sea and swell approach the ship at right-angles, or nearly so, to the line of the keel.

〔當波浪或湧浪以90°或接近90°的方向趨近船體（龍骨線）的狀況稱之。〕

46. **Belay** (*vt*) 〔將繩子〕挽住

To secure or make fast (a rope, for example) by winding on a cleat or bitts.

（利用將纜繩捲繞於纜樁上以制止受力的纜繩滑脱的方法。）

圖2.1　將纜繩「挽」在繫纜樁上

47. **Bell-buoy** (*n*) 鐘浮

A buoy fitted with a bell which may be actuated automatically or by wave motion.

（指一浮標其上裝有號鐘，可自動發聲或經由波浪搖晃啓動而發聲。）

48. **Berth** (*n*) 船席；操船水域

The space assigned to or taken up by a vessel when anchored or when lying alongside a wharf, jetty.

（被指定用來作爲船舶泊靠碼頭、突堤或錨泊的空間。）

To give a wide berth. To keep well away from another ship or any feature.

（應有足夠寬裕的船舶操縱空間，以便遠離他船或地形地物。）

49. **Bight** (*n*) 寬闊且和緩彎曲的海灣

A crescent-shaped indentation in the coastline, usually of large extent and not more than a 90° sector of circle.

（海岸線呈新月型凹陷，而且凹陷的圓弧通常不會超過90°。）

50. **Bilge** (*n*) 船底兩舷的彎曲部、船舭

The rounded side of a ship where it curves from the flat bottom plates to the vertical shell plating.

（指介於船底平板船殼和船舶兩舷垂直船殼底部之間的彎曲船體部。）

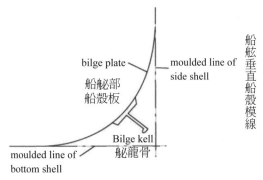

bilge plate
船舭部
船殼板

moulded line of
side shell

船舷垂直船殼模線

Bilge kell
舭龍骨

moulded line of
bottom shell

圖2.2　船舭部船形構造示意圖

51. **Bilge keel** (*n*) 舭龍骨

Longitudinal angles welded and riveted bock to bock on the bilge of a vessel, to check the ship's tendency to roll.

（用焊接或鉚接於船舶兩舷舭部的連續性縱向角材，用以減緩船舶的橫搖趨勢。）

圖2.3　舭龍骨

52. **Boatswain** (*or Bosun*) (n) 商船的水手長

53. **Boatswain's chair** (*or Bosun's chair*) （專供懸吊作業的單人跳板。）

圖2.4　單人跳板

54. **Bollard** (*n*) 繫纜樁

A post firmly embedded in or secured on a wharf, jetty, &c., for mooring vessels by means of wires or ropes extending form the vessel and secured to the post.

（一支穩固固定或崁入碼頭、突堤的柱狀物，用來讓自船舶送出的纜繩或鋼纜繫固於其上，以固定船舶。）

55. **Boss** (*n*) 螺旋槳的軸套、套筒

The part of the propeller to which blades are attached. Also the aperture in the stern frame where propeller shaft enters.

（屬螺旋槳的一部分，俥葉附著其上。亦指位於艉肋材上供螺旋槳軸穿過的套筒。）

56. **Breadth Extreme** (*n*) 最大寬度

The maximum breadth measured over plating or planking, including beading or fenders.

（從一舷船殼板橫向量至另舷船殼板的最大寬度，包含舷外的裝飾物或碰墊。）

57. **Break bulk ships; General cargo ships** (*n*) 雜貨船

Ships that carry a wide variety of cargoes in many different types of containers.

（指運送許多不同包裝型式的各種貨物的船舶。）

58. **Breakers** (*n*) 碎浪花

Waves or swell which have become so steep, either on reaching shoal water or on encountering a contrary current or by the action of wind, that the crest falls over and breaks into foam.

（當波浪或湧浪的坡度過於陡峭時，無論在抵達淺水區或遭遇逆向流，或因風的作用，波峰就會墜落，進而破碎成泡沫。）

59. **Breaking sea** (*also known as "white horses"*) (n) 碎浪、白浪

The partial collapse of the crests of waves, less complete than in the case of breakers, but from the same cause.

（成因如同碎浪花一樣，只不過只有部分波峰墜落。）

60. **Breakwater** (*n*) 防波堤

A solid structure, such as a wall or mole to break the force of the waves, sometimes detached from the shore, protecting a harbor or anchorage, alongside which vessels usually can not lie.

（一個用來保護港口或錨地的實體結構，諸如海牆或堤岸，用來破除波浪的力量。有時候不與陸岸連結，船舶通常無法靠泊在防坡堤上。）

61. **Breast Line** (*n*) 橫纜

Mooring line leading approximately perpendicular to ship's fore and aft line.

（纜繩自船上送出的角度與船舶艏艉線幾成直角的繫纜。）

62. **Broach to** (*n*) 船身打橫

To be carried inadvertently broadside on to the sea, when running before it.

（船舶順風行駛時由於操舵不當或其他原因致使船身打橫而呈舷側

受浪的狀態。）

63. **Bulk cargos** (*n*) 散裝貨

Commodities such as grain, oil, coal and fertilizers carried without containers.

（諸如穀類、油品、煤炭及肥料等毋須包裝即可運送的貨物。）

64. **Bulk carrier** (*n*) 散裝船

Ship that carry cargoes such as grain or sulphur in bulk.

（指運送諸如穀類或硫磺等散裝貨物的船舶。）

65. **Bunkering** (*vt*) 加油

The process of fueling a merchant marine vessel.

（商船添加燃油的過程。）

66. **Bulkhead** (*n*) 艙壁

A partition in a ship which divides the interior space into various compartments.

（船上用以分隔內部空間成為各不同艙間的隔板。）

67. **Bullnosed Bow** (*n*) 球形船艏

Bow with large rounded bow point underneath water line.

（船艏水線下部有大型突出圓艏的結構。）

68. **Bulkhead Collision** (*n*) 防碰艙壁、避碰艙壁

A watertight bulkhead approximately 25 feet aft of the bow, extending from the keel to the shelter deck. This bulkhead prevents the entire ship from being flooded in case of collision.

（大約位於船艏後方25呎處，自龍骨向上延伸至船艏樓甲板的艙壁。此艙壁主在防止船舶碰撞時船舶整體浸水。）

69. **Bulwark** (*n*) 舷牆

The upper section of the frames and side plating, which extends above and around the upper deck.

（船舶肋材與船殼板沿著主甲板向上延伸的最上緣部分。）

70. **Bow** (*n*) 船艏部

The fore end of a ship.（船舶的前端）

71. **Buoys** (*n*) 浮標

Floats of standard colours and shapes moored as aids to navigation, particularly for marking fairways and detatched dangers, they may carry topmarks, be fitted with reflectors, exhibit light and sound bells, gongs, whistles.

（繫固於特定地點以標準顏色與形狀標示作為助導航用的浮體，特別是用作標識航道與孤立危險物的浮標，可能設置有配置反射器、顯示燈光與號鐘、鑼、汽笛的頂標。）

72. **Cable** (*n*) 鏈 $\approx$ 185.3184 m

A nautical unit of measurement, being one tenth of a sea mile.

A term often used to refer to the chain cable by which a vessel is secured to her anchor.

（航海用度量單位，約等於十分之一浬；亦常用於指稱連結船舶錨具的錨鏈。）

73. **Camber** (*n*) 拱高、梁拱、曲弧度

A slope upwards toward the center of a surface, as on a deck amidships for shedding water.

（自外向中心呈向上傾斜的表面，如船舯甲板自縱向中心線向兩舷側呈向下傾斜狀以利排水。）

74. **Cape** (*n*) 岬、海角

A piece of land, or point, facing the open sea and projecting into it beyond the adjacent coast.

（一塊自鄰近海岸線向開闊海域突出的陸地或尖端。）

75. **Cast** (*vt*) 使改變航向

To turn a ship to a desired direction without gaining headway or sternway.

（在不增加船舶前進或倒退速度的情況下，將船舶轉向所期望的方向。）

76. **Causeway** (*n*) 堤道、砌道

A raised roadway of solid structure built across low or wet ground or across a stretch of water.

（為穿越濕地或淺水而建築的實體結構的高地堤道。）

77. **CBM** (Conventional Buoy Moorings) (*n*) 傳統式浮筒繫泊

The usual method of mooring craft in enclosed waters with mooring buoys forward and aft.

（指通常在封閉水域內利用前、後繫泊浮筒將船舶繫泊的方法。）

78. **Cells** (*n*) 貨櫃格槽

Constructed areas and spaces to accommodate containers inside a ship.

（貨櫃船船艙內設計用以裝載貨櫃的結構區域與空間。）

79. **Channel** (*n*) 航道

A comparatively deep waterway, natural or dredged, though a river, harbour, strait, or a navigable route through shoals, which affords the best and safest passage for vessels or boats.

（指河川、港口、海峽中相對較深的水道或是穿越淺灘的可航行通道，可以是天然亦可是人工挖濬的，其可提供船艇最佳的安全通路。）

80. **Characteristic of a light** (*n*) 燈質

This term denotes the property of it appearance by which it is distinguished.

〔用以表示供作辨識用的燈（塔）光的特質。〕

81. **Circular radiobeacon** (*n*) 循環型無線電標杆

A radiobeacon which transmits the same signal in all directions.

（可作360°發送相同信號的無線電標杆。）

82. **Chart Datum** (*n*) 海圖水深基準面

The level below which soundings are given on charts and above which are given the drying heights of features which are periodically covered and uncovered by the tide.

（海圖上用以表示其下水深，以及受潮汐影響定期浮出與淹沒的地形物在其上高度的水平面。）

83. **Charter party** (*n*) 租傭船契約

A Charter party is a document of contract by which a shipowner agree to lease, and the charterer agree to hire, a vessel or all the cargo space, or a part of it, on terms and conditions <u>set forth</u> in the charter party. Shipowners and charterers may, and usually do, have clauses deleted, changed, added or amended to suit a particular case.

（租船契約乃是船東同意出租船舶，而租船人也同意租用整艘船舶，或所有裝貨空間，或只租用其中一部分，雙方依據租船契約<u>載述</u>條款與條件所簽訂的契約文件。船東與租船人通常會依特定情況刪除、變更或增添契約條款。）

【註1】

If your vessel is chartered it is of the utmost importance had you read the charter party carefully, especially the added clauses, until it is thoroughly understood. It is advisable to have the officers read it as a matter of information and it will do no harm to discuss it with them, especially with the chief officer.

（如果您的船舶已被出租，首要之務就是詳讀租船契約，特別是附加條款，直至徹底了解為止。最好亦請船副詳讀，並了解租船資訊，而且要與之坦誠討論，尤其是大副。）

84. **Civil Twilight** (*n*) 民用曙光

The period of the day between the time when the Sun's center is 6° below the horizon and sunrise (morning twilight), or between the time of sunset and that when the Sun's center is 6° below the horizon (evening twilight)

（太陽中心在水平線下6°與日出時的時間間隔，稱作晨曙光；或是太陽中心在水平線下6°與日沒時的時間間隔，稱作暮曙光。）

85. **Claw off** (*vt*) 使船轉向上風

To best or reach to windward away from a lee shore.

（使船轉向上風以遠離下風岸。）

86. **Clear berth** (*n*) 安全泊位

The area within the circle in which an anchored vessel may swing which is clear of other ships or obstruction.

（指可供錨泊船舶遠離他船或障礙物安全迴旋的圓形水域面積。）

87. **Clipper Bow** (*n*) 飛剪型船艏、內斜型船艏

A bow with an extreme forward rake, once familiar on sailing vessels.

（船艏有突出傾斜向外的構造，如同帆船船艏一般。）

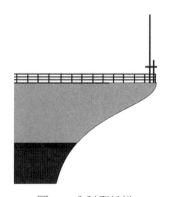

圖2.5　內斜型船艏

88. **Coast** (*n*) 海岸

The meeting of the land and sea considered as the boundary of the land.

（陸地與海洋的交會處，可視為陸地的界線。）

89. **Coasting** (*vt*) 沿岸航行

Navigation from headland to headland in sight of land, or sufficiently often in sight of land to fix the position of the ship by land feature.

（在陸地目視可及時，船舶自某陸岬或海角航向另一陸岬或海角；或是當陸岸近到足以讓航行者利用陸岸特徵或地形測定船位時稱之。）

90. **Coastline** (*n*) 海岸線

The extreme limit of direct wave action. The landward limit of the beach.

（波浪可直接沖擊所及的極端邊界；海灘向陸際延伸的盡頭。）

91. **Coastwise traffic** (*n*) 沿岸／近海航行船舶

Is that which sails round the coast, and to sail coastwise means coasting as opposed to keeping out to sea.

（指沿著海岸線航行，而不駛向大海的船舶。）

92. **Coastwise Trade** (*n*) 沿岸或近洋航業

Trade between ports of one country.

（專營國內各港口之間的航運業務。）

93. **Cocked hat** (*n*) 定位三角形

The triangle formed by the intersection of three lines of bearing on the chart.

（海圖上三條方位線交叉形成的三角形。）

94. **Cofferdam** (*n*) 堰艙、隔離艙

A small space left open between two bulkheads as an air space to protect another bulkhead from heat, fire hazard or collision.

（在兩艙壁之間留下較小空艙，以保護另一艙間免受熱流、火災與碰撞浸水之害。）

95. **Cold front** (*n*) 冷鋒

Line in which cold air inserts itself beneath a mass of warm air.

（一條冷氣團沿著該線插入暖氣團下方的線。）

96. **Confluence** (*n*) 匯合點

The joining together of two rivers or streams.

（兩條河川的匯合處。）

97. **Confused sea** (*n*) 混淆浪、亂浪

The disorderly sea in race. Also when waves from different direction meet, due normally to a sudden shift in the direction of the wind.

（急速而來的不規則海浪；又當風向突然改變方向時，造成來自不同方向的波浪相遇。）

98. **Conical buoy** (*n*) 圓錐形浮標

A cone-shaped buoy moored to float point up.

（繫固於特定地點的圓錐形浮標。）

99. **Conspicuous object** (*n*) 顯著目標

A natural or artificial mark which is distinctly and notably visible from seaward.

（從海上明顯易見的自然或是人造的標誌。）

100. **Container ship** (*n*) 貨櫃船、中國大陸稱集裝箱船

A vessel devoted to the carriage of specialized containers at sea.

（專供海上運送制式貨櫃的船舶。）

101. **Contour** (*n*) 等高線、等深線

A line joining points of the same height above, or depth below, the datum.

（連結基準面上相同高度各點之線，或基準面下相同深度各點之線。）

102. **Controlling depth** (*n*) 控制水深、可航最小水深

The least depth available for navigation, which controls the draught of vessels using the particular area or channel.

（可供航行的最小深度，用來管制使用特定水域或航道船舶的吃水。）

103. **Coriolis force** (*n*) 柯氏力、地球自轉偏向力

An apparent force acting on mass of air or water in motion, due to the rotation of the earth, causing deflection of wind and currents, to the right in the N hemisphere and to the left in the S hemisphere.

（作用於運動中的空氣或水質點的慣性力。因為地球逆時針運轉，造成風與水流的偏向，使得北半球的風向右偏轉；南半球則相反，受到逆時針的偏向力向左偏轉，偏北風漸轉為西至西北風，而偏南風則逐步轉為東至東南風。）

104. **Continental shelf** (*n*) 大陸棚、大陸礁層

A zone adjacent to a continent and extending from the low water line to a depth at which there is usually a marked increase of slope towards oceanic depth. Conventionally, its edge is taken as 200m, but it may be between about 100 and 350m.

（指接連在海岸之外，坡度最平緩的海底，每公里的深度增加不過1～2公尺。大陸棚的寬度各地不一，有窄於1公里者，也有寬達1,000公里以上者。依照慣例，它的外緣水深多採200公尺左右的地方，但可能介於通過此地帶後100～350公尺間，海底坡度都會突然變陡，過此以下，便是大陸坡。）

105. **Continental slope** (*n*) 大陸坡

The slope seaward from the shelf edge to the beginning of a continental rise the point where there is a general reduction in slope.

（大陸坡指從大陸棚外緣向海一側較陡地下降到深海底的斜坡。大陸坡上界水深多在100～200公尺之間；下界水深一般在1500～3500公尺處。）

106. **Continental rise** (*n*) 大陸隆

A gentle slope rising from the oceanic depths towards the foot of the continental slope.

（大陸隆是指從較深的海洋深度向大陸坡外緣底部的斜度和緩地帶。）

107. **COSPAS** (*n*) 前蘇聯的遇難船舶搜索衛星系統

Space system for search and distress vessels.

（是一種專門為搜救遇難船舶而設立之太空系統。）

108. **COSPAS-SARSAT system** (*n*) 衛星輔助搜救系統

A satellite-aided search and rescue system based on low-altitude near-polar-orbiting satellites and designed to locate distress beacons transmitting on the frequencies 121.5 MHz and 406 MHz

（利用低高度繞極軌道衛星，鎖定遇難船舶求救信標發送頻率為121.5 MHz 和 406 MHz 的求救信號，進行搜救的衛星系統。）

【註2】
COSPAS-SARSAT是一種專門為搜救而設立之國際衛星系統。於1988年7月1日由加拿大、法國、俄國與美國等4國協議設立。其中，3顆遇險搜索衛星系統COSPAS（Space System for Search of Distress Vessel）衛星由俄國提供，而輔助搜救系統SARSAT）Search and Rescue Satellite-Aided Tracking）的3顆衛星則由美國所提供，共計6顆衛星。

109. **Creek** (*n*) 海、河、湖的小港灣

A comparatively narrow inlet, of fresh or salt water, which is tidal throughout its course.

〔指相對較小（位於海、河、湖）的淡水或海水小水灣，灣內始終受著潮流的影響。〕

110. **Customs clearance** (*n*) 結關

The documented permission to pass that a national customs authority grants to imported goods so that they can enter the country or to exported goods so that they can leave the country.

（海關所簽發允許進口物品入境或出口物品出境的准許文件。）

【註3】
實務上，出港船舶必須取得海關結關文件始可啓航，因此欲出港船舶呼叫引水站請求引水人時，引水站常會詢問：「Does your customs clearance processing complete?（貴輪取得海關結關許可證？）」

111. **Cut** (*n*) 相交、小運河

The intersection on the chart of two or more position lines.

An opening in an elevation or channel. Similar to a canal but shorter.

（指海圖上二條或二條以上位置線的相交；較一般運河短的小運河或小溝渠。）

112. **Cut tide** (*n*) 切潮

A tide which fails to reach its predicted height at high water.

（指一潮汐現象在高潮時未達到其預測高度。）

113. **Dries** (*n*) 週期淹露帶

Visible when the height of the tide is between the height specified and that at which the feature is awash.

〔當潮高介於指定高度與可以看到礁岩（或淺灘）頂部恰好浸水時之間的高度。〕

114. **Danger** (*n*) 危險、危險物

The term is used to imply a danger to surface navigation, opposed to submarine navigation.

（通常用來表示相對於水下航行，對水面航行所構成的危險。）

115. **Danger Angle (Horizontal or Vertical)** (*n*) 水平或垂直危險角

Angle subtended at the observer's eye, by the horizontal distance between two object or by the known height or elevation of an object, which indicates the limit of safe approach to an off-lying danger.

（由觀測者眼睛所測得兩目標之間的水平角度，或已知高度或海拔目標的垂直弧角，據此作為安全趨近或遠離已知危險物的極限認定。）

116. **Danger line** (*n*) 危險線

A dotted line on the chart enclosing, or bordering, an obstruction, wreck, or other danger.

（在海圖上用以圍住，或劃定一個障礙物、沉船或其他危險物的界線的虛線。）

117. **Date Line** (*n*) 國際換日線

The International Date Line, accepted by international usage, is a modification of the 180° meridian drown to include islands of any group on the same side. When the Date Line is crossed on an easterly (westerly) course the date is put bock (advanced) one day.

〔國際間基本上以180°經度線為換日線，又名國際日界線、國際日期變更線或國際日期線。顧及行政區域的統一，換日線並不完全沿180°的子午線劃分，而是繞過一些島嶼和海峽，使得其位於子午線的同一邊。例如由北往南通過白令海峽和阿留申群島、薩摩亞、斐濟、東加等島嶼到達紐西蘭的東邊。由西向東越過此線（從台北飛往紐約）日期需減一天；由東向西越過此線（從紐約飛往台北）日期需加一天。〕

118. **Datum** (*N*) 基準面

A horizontal plane to which heights, depths or levels are referred.

（用以作爲高度、深度或水平面的水平參考基準面。）

119. **Dawn** (*n*) 黎明、曙光

An indefinite time of day when it begins to grow light.

（每天當太陽開始發出亮光的一段不確定時段。）

120. **Daylight** (*n*) 白晝

An indefinite time of day, after dawn and before sunset.

（一天當中自黎明後至日落前之間的一段不確定時間。）

121. **Daymark** (*n*) 日間標誌

Large unlit beacon.

（不配置燈光的大型信標。）

122. **Deadweight** (*n*) 總載重量

The total weight of cargo, fuel, water, stores, passengers and crew and their effects that a ship can carry when at her designed full-load draft.

（船舶達到其設計最大吃水線時所能積載的貨物、燃油、淡水、司多、旅客船員及其個人攜帶物品的總重量。）

123. **Deadweight tonnage** (*n*) 載重噸位

A measure used to estimate a ships' cargo capacity.

（用來估算船舶實際可載貨重量的測量方法。）

124. **Deck Forecastle** (*n*) 艏艛甲板

A deck over the main deck at the bow.

（位於船艏部，高於主連續甲板的上層甲板。）

125. **Deck Poop** (*n*) 艉艛甲板

The raised deck on the after part of a ship.

（位於船艉部，高出主連續甲板的較高層甲板。）

126. **Deck Shelter** (*n*) 遮蔽甲板

A term applied to a deck fitted from stem to stern on a relatively light superstructure.

（指從船艏至船艉設於相對較輕的上層建築物上的甲板。）

127. **Deep Tank** (*n*) 深艙

These usually consist of ordinary hold compartments, but strengthened to carry water ballast.

（通常由一般的貨艙所構成，但都會強化結構以適於作爲壓艙水艙使用。）

033

128. **Deep water route** (*n*) 深水航路

A route within defined limits which has been accurately surveyed for clearance of sea bottom and submerged obstacles as indicated on the chart.

（一條經過精確測量海底深度，並在海圖上標出水中障礙物，且具有明確邊界線的航路。）

129. **Demurrage clause** (*n*) 滯期費條款

The Clause states that if the charterer does not complete loading or discharging in the laydays allowed by the charter party, he must pay for the delay at the stipulated sum per day.

（租船契約的滯期費條款會載明如果租船人未依租船契約規定的工作天數完成裝或卸貨，則需償付依照契約載明每天應付的滯期金額。）

130. **Departure** (*n*) 橫距

The East-West component of a rhumb line track.

（恆向線航法航跡上的東西向要素。）

131. **Depth** (*n*) 水深

Vertical distance from the sea surface to the sea bed, at any state of the tide.

（在任何潮汐狀態下，從海面上到海底之間的垂直距離。）

132. **Dew Point** (*n*) 露點

Lowest temperature to which air can be cooled without condensation of its water vapour.

（指在固定氣壓之下，空氣中所含的氣態水達到飽和，但其水蒸氣不會凝結時所需要降至的溫度。）

133. **Diaphone** (*n*) 霧笛

A fog signaling instrument using compressed air.

（利用壓縮空氣發出霧號的器械。）

034

134. **Diesel generator** (*n*) 柴油發電機

The diesel generators work by burning fuel to produce linear motion, then transform the linear motion of pistons into a rotational motion by crankshaft and then transmit to the load.

（指以柴油為燃料，利用氣缸內活塞往復運動，再推動曲軸旋轉以輸出電動勢的發電設備。）

135. **Direction light** (*n*) 指向燈

A light showing over a very narrow sector, forming a single leading. This sector may be flanked by sectors of greatly reduced intensity, or of different colours or character.

（一盞僅在某非常狹窄的水平弧度角內顯示的燈光，形成單一的引導方向。此一燈光弧度的兩側邊界可能顯示大幅降低強度，或不同顏色，或不同燈質的光弧作為區隔。）

136. **Directional radiobeacon** (*n*) 指向無線電標杆

A radiobeacon which transmits two signals in such a way that they are of equal strength on only one bearing.

（指在同一方位發送二種相同強度之信號的無線電標杆。）

137. **Discoloured water** (*n*) 變色的海水

Areas where discoloration of the water exists, possibly indicating a shoal or other danger, but which may be duo to biological.

（某一水域如發現海水變色，可能表示有淺灘或其他危險物存在，或是因爲水中生物使然。）

138. **Displacement** (*n*) 排水量

The weight in tons of the water displaced by a ship. This weight is the same as the total weight of the ship when afloat.

（船舶所排開的水以噸爲計算單位的重量。此一重量等同於船舶浮於水面上的總重量。）

139. **Diurnal inequality** (*n*) 日潮不等

The inequality, either in the heights of successive high waters or in the intervals between successive high or low water.

（無論在連續二個高潮的潮高，或是連續二個高潮或低潮間的時間間隔不等均稱之。）

140. **Diurnal springs** (*n*) 全日潮大潮

Tides of greatest range associated with the Moon's maximum declination as opposed to spring tides associated with phases of the Moon.

（相對於因月象變化所產生之大潮，太陰赤緯達到最大時產生最大潮差之潮汐。）

141. **Diurnal stream** (*n*) 日潮流

A tidal stream which reverses its direction once during the day.

〔一天內只改變一次（反）方向的潮流。〕

142. **Diurnal tide** (*n*) 全日潮

A tide which has only one high water and one low water each day.

（指每天只有一次高潮與一次低潮的潮汐現象。）

143. **Dock** (*n*) 船渠

An area of water artificially enclosed in which the depth of water can be regulated.

（指一經人工圍堵的水域，並藉由閘門管制水域內的水深，大多設於潮差較大的內河型港口。）

144. **Doldrum** (*n*) 赤道無風帶

Comparatively windless zone, along equator, that separates the prevailing winds of north and south Latitudes.

（沿著赤道相對無風的地帶，其分隔了南、北緯的盛行風帶。）

145. **Dolphin** (*n*) 繫船柱

A built-up mooring post, usually of wood, erected on shore or in the water, to which vessels may secure clear of quays.

（組合型繫纜柱，通常由木柱製成，豎立在岸上或水中。船舶可遠離碼頭將船繫固其上。）

146. **Double Bottom** (*n*) 雙層船底

A tank whose bottom is formed by the bottom plates of a ship, used to hold water for ballast, for the storage of oil, etc. A term applied to the space between the inner, and outer bottom skins of a vessel.

（由船舶底部船板作為槽櫃的底部，用以積載壓艙水、油料等；船舶內底及外底結構之間的空間。）

147. **Double Tide** (*n*) 雙潮

A tide, usually in the vicinity of an amphidromic system, which, due to a combination of shallow water effects, contains either two high water or two low water in each tidal cycle.

（指一通常存在於無潮體系附近的潮汐現象，因為結合淺水效應，每一潮汐週期包括兩個高潮或兩個低潮。）

148. **Downstream** (*n*) 下游、順流

In general, in rivers or river ports, whether tidal or not, the direction to seaward.

（通常在內河或內河港，無論有無潮流，向海一側的方向稱為下游。）

149. **Draft** (*n*) 水呎

The depth of a vessel below the waterline measured vertically to the lowest part of the hull, propellers or other reference points.

（船舶在水線下的深度，即從水線垂直向下量至船殼、螺旋槳或其他基準點的最低處之間的距離。）

150. **Draft Marking** (*n*) 吃水標誌

The measurements on a ship's hull indicating its depth in the water.

（船殼上用以標示船舶浸水深度的量度標誌。）

151. **Drag** (*n*) 流錨 (vt) 拖、曳；拖動

A ship is said to drag if the anchor will not hold her in position. Commonly used by seamen to describe the retardation of a ship caused by shallow water.

〔如果一艘船舶的錨具無法將船固定在其錨泊的位置時稱爲流錨；亦常被船員用來敘述當船舶航行在淺水區時會造成船舶有拖曳（阻礙）難行的現象。〕

152. **Dredge** (*vt*) 疏浚：挖掘

To deepen or attempt to deepen by removing material from the bottom.

（用挖泥船等設備自海底移除海底物質以增加水深。）

153. **Dredge** (*n*) 疏濬

A vessel used to deepen water. The process of deepening water.

（一艘用來濬深水深的船舶；濬深水深的過程。）

154. **Drag Sweep** (*vt*) 耙平

To tow a wire or bar set horizontally beneath the surface of the water to determine the least depth over an obstruction or to ascertain that required minimum depth exists in a channel.

（藉由在水面下拖曳鋼索或水平棒柱以測量海底障礙物上方的最小水深，或確認航道必須具備的最低水深的狀況。）

155. **Drift** (*vt*) 漂流

To move along with the current, tidal stream, or wind, or under the influence of all of these.

（指船舶或物體隨著洋流、潮流，或風，或是所有這些因素的混合作用影響而漂移。）

156. **Drift current** (*n*) 風吹流

A horizontal movement in the upper layers of the sea, caused by wind.

（由於風的作用造成上層海水做水平向移動。）

157. **Drilling rig** (*n*) 鑽井平台

A moveable floating platform used to examine a possible oil or natural gas field.

（用來探勘可能油源或天然瓦斯田的可移動漂浮平台。）

158. **Drizzle** (*n*) 細雨、毛毛雨

Precipitation of very small rain drops.

（指非常小的雨點降水。）

159. **Dry Docks** (*n*) 乾船塢

A dock into which a vessel is floated, the water then being removed to allow for the construction or repair of ships.

（指船舶可以駛入，並可浮泛於其中的船渠，再藉由關閉渠門排開水體以利進行船舶維修或造船。）

160. **Drying heights** (*n*) 乾涸高度

Heights above chart datum of features which are periodically covered and exposed by the rise and fall of the tide.

（指海上隨著潮汐的漲落定期被淹沒或露出的礁岩或障礙物，其外形高於海圖基準面的高度。）

161. **DSC (Digital Selective Calling) system** (*n*) 數位選擇呼叫系統

A technique using digital codes which enables a radio station to establish contact with, and transfer information to, another station or group of station, and complying with the relevant recommendations of the International Radio Committee. (CCIR)

（利用數位電碼使得無線電站台可以依據國際無線電委員會的相關建議與中繼台或其他船、岸台建立聯繫。）

162. **Dumping ground** (*n*) 傾倒區

An area similar to a spoil ground.

（類似廢土或泥沙堆積場的水域。）

163. **Dune** (*n*) 沙丘

A ridge or hill of dry wind-blown sand.

（由乾燥風吹積而成的隆起脊狀小沙堆。）

164. **Dyke or Dike** (*n*) 堤、溝、壩

A causeway or loose rubble embankment built in shallow water.

（築於濕地或淺水的堤道、砌道或碎石堤岸。）

165. **Ebb tide** (*n*) 落潮

A loose term applied both to the falling tide and to the outgoing tidal stream.

（同時使用於正在降落中的潮汐現象，以及水平流向大海的潮流的不嚴謹說法。）

166. **Eddy** (*n*) 漩渦、渦流

A circular motion in water. A horizontal movement in a different direction from that of the general direction of the tidal stream in the vicinity, caused by obstructions such as islands, rocks.

（水中的循環運動。從水域附近的潮流的通常方向開始做不同方向的水平移動，一般都是由諸如島嶼、礁石、突堤的阻礙水體的流動

所造成的。）

167. **EPIRB (Emergency Position-Indicating Radiobeacon)** (*n*) 應急指位無線電示標

A station in the mobile service, the emissions of which are intended to facilitate search and rescue operations.

（可以發射信號以便於搜救作業的移動發射台。）

【註4】

EPIRB所發出121.5MHz及406MHz之遇險警告信號，可以藉由COSPAS-SARSAT搜救系統的衛星傳至岸上的地面終端站（LUT），再利用衛星收到的遇險信號頻變計算出遇險船舶的位置，並將其結果傳至任務管制中心（MCC），MCC將所接收的資訊加以處理後，再傳送給搜救協調中心（RCC），當RCC收到遇險信號時，會設法與遇險船舶通信，並依距離的遠近而決定，由RCC或遇險船舶附近的船舶來展開搜救。

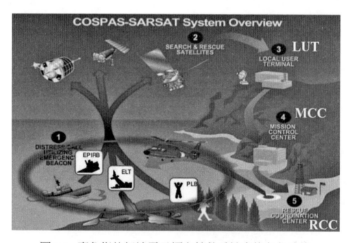

圖2.6　應急指位無線電示標在搜救系統中的角色功能

168. **Equator** (*n*) 赤道

Is that great circle of the earth that lies midway between the poles.

（地表上位於兩極中間的大圈。）

169. **Equilibrium Tide** (*n*) 平衡潮

The tide which would theoretically exist on the Earth in the absence of land masses and certain other stipulated conditions.

（指理論上存在於沒有陸塊或其他規定條件的地球上的潮汐。）

170. **Equinox** (*n*) 春分、秋分

Either of the two point at which the Sun crosses the Equator-or the dates on which these occurrences take place.

（太陽從北半球往南，或是從南半球往北越過赤道時的兩個點，或是此現象發生的日期。）

171. **Equinoctial Spring Tide** (*n*) 分點大潮

A spring tide occurring near the equinoxes.

（發生在春分或秋分時的大潮。）

172. **Established direction of Traffic flow** (*n*) 交通流的既定方向

A traffic flow pattern indicating the directional movement of traffic as established within a traffic separation scheme.

（在分道通航計畫中用來表示既定的船舶方向性運動交通流模式。）

173. **Estuary** (*n*) 河口；海口灣

An arm of the sea at the mouth of a tidal river.

（位於潮流河口的狹長海灣。）

174. **Even keel** (*n*) 平吃水

The state of a ship when her draught forward and aft are the same.

（指船舶的艏、艉吃水相等時的狀態。）

175. **Fairlead** (*n*) 導索器

A term applied to fittings or devices used in preserving the direction of a rope, chain or wire, so that it may be delivered fairly or on a straight lead to the sheave or drum.

（一種用來維持繩索、鏈條或鋼索導引方向的設置，以便將繩索或

鋼索正直的導引至纜機的滑車輪或絞纜鼓上。）

176. **Fairway** (*n*) 航道

The main navigable channel, often buoyed, in a river, or running through or into a harbour.

（在河道上，或是穿越及進出港口的主要航行水道，通常設置有浮標顯示航道界限。）

177. **Falling tide** (*n*) 退潮

The period between high water and the succeeding low water.

（高潮與接續的低潮之間的時間間隔。）

178. **Fathom** (*n*) 噚

A unit of measurement used for soundings. Equal to 6 feet.

（用以測量水深的度量單位，等於6呎。）

179. **Fathom line** (*n*) 等深線

Submarine contour lines drawn on charts, indicating equal depths in fathoms.

〔畫於海圖上的海底輪廓線，用噚（或公尺）表示相同深度各點的連線。〕

180. **Fender** (*n*) 碰墊

This term is applied to various devices fastened to or hung over the side of vessel for the purpose of preventing rubbing or chafing.

（泛指固定或繫著於碼頭旁或船舷作為防止磨擦的各種設備。）

181. **Ferry** (*n*) 渡輪

A boat, pontoon, or any craft, used to convey passengers or vehicles to and fro across a harbor, river.

（用以運送旅客或車輛往復地穿越港口或河川的船艇、駁船或任何載具。）

182. **Fin stabilizer** (*n*) 止搖穩定翼

The function of a <u>fin stabilizer</u>, found at the bottom part of the ship's hull, is to provide resistance to the excess rolling of ship in either direction.

（位於船舶兩舷船殼板底部的<u>止搖穩定翼</u>之功能是抑止船舶產生過度的橫搖。）

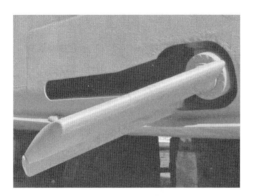

圖2.7　止搖穩定翼

183. **Fish haven** (*n*) 人工魚礁

An area where concrete blocks, hulks, disused car bodies, are dumped to provide suitable condition for fish to breed in.

（任何經人工拋置水泥塊、廢船、報廢汽車，以提供適於飼養魚類條件的水域。）

184. **Fish pound** (*n*) 魚塘

A barrier across the mouth of a creek placed to retain fish in the creek.

（一個設置於河口或海灣面對外海出口處利用柵欄將魚攔在小港灣內的養魚塘。）

185. **Fishing ground** (*n*) 漁場

Area wherein fishing craft congregate to fish; most particularly those areas occupied periodically by the large fishing fleets.

（一個漁船船隊群聚漁撈作業的水域；特別是指那些定期會被大型漁船隊占用的水域。）

186. **Fetch** (*n*) 風浪區

The area of the sea surface over which seas are generated by a wind having a constant direction and speed.

（因固定的風向與風速造成在海面表面上產生海浪的水域。）

187. **Fix** (*n*) 定位

The position of the ship determined by observations.

（利用觀測天體、岸形、地標所測得的船舶位置。）

188. **Fixed light** (*n*) 固定光

A continuous steady light.

（指一個連續穩定的燈光。）

189. **Fixed and flashing light** 定光聯合閃光

A fixed light varied at regular intervals by a single flash of greater brilliance.

（一個定光在固定時間間隔變換燈光爲加強亮度的單一閃光。）

190. **Fixed and group flashing light** 定光聯合群閃光

A fixed light varied at regular intervals by a group of two or more flashes of greater brilliance.

（一個定光在固定時間間隔變換燈光爲加強亮度的二個或以上的閃光。）

191. **Fjord** (*n*) 峽灣、海谷 [kk: fjord]

A long narrow arm of the sea between high cliffs.

（介於懸崖或峭壁之間狹長形海灣。）

192. **Flared Bow** (*n*) 弓形外展船艏

A bow with an extreme flare at the upper and forecastle deck.

（船艏艛與船艏主甲板處成極度外展曲線型的船艏。）

圖2.8　貨櫃船船艏甲板外展明顯以利裝貨

193. **Flashing light** (*n*) 閃光

A light showing a single flash at regular intervals. The period of light being always less than the period of darkness.

（指在固定時間間隔顯示單一閃光的燈光；在一個週期內，燈光顯示的時間常短於黑暗的時間。）

194. **Floating beacon** (*n*) 浮動標杆

A moored or anchored floating mark ballasted to float upright, and sometimes carrying a light or radar reflector.

（一個利用繫固或錨泊，並藉由壓重保持穩定的直立浮動標誌，有時候會裝置燈光或雷達反射器。）

195. **Floating crane** (*n*) 浮動吊桿

A crane mounted on a pontoon.

（裝置於駁船上的吊桿；常用於拋錨船舶，或傍靠於靠岸船舶的近海一側協助進行裝卸作業。）

圖2.9 大船利用浮動吊桿卸貨至駁船上

196. **Floating dock** (*n*) 浮動船塢

A watertight structure capable of being submerge sufficiently, by admission of water into the pontoon tanks, to admit a vessel.

（一個可藉由壓入海水至浮箱，並可下沉至足夠深度，允許船舶進入其間或其上方的水密結構物。）

197. **Flood channel** (*n*) 漲潮河道

A channel in tidal water through which the flood tidal stream flows more strongly, or for a longer duration of time, then the ebb.

（在受潮水域內漲潮流較落潮流強，或漲潮流的時間較落潮流長的河道。）

198. **Flood tide** (*n*) 漲潮

A loose term applied both to the rising tide and to the incoming tidal stream.

（同時使用於正在上漲中的潮汐現象，以及水平流向內陸的潮流的不嚴謹說法。）

199. **Flow** (*n*) 流水

The combination of tidal stream and current; the whole water movement.

（潮流與洋流的結合，表示水體的整體移動。）

200.**Flush Deck** (*n*) 平甲板

A deck running from stem to stern without being broken by forecastle or poop.

（自船艏至船艉未被艏艛或艉艛中斷的連續甲板。）

201.**Fog** (*n*) 霧

Condensed water vapor, which differ from clouds only in that it rise near the earth.

（指在接近地球表面的大氣中懸浮的水滴或冰晶組成的水汽凝結物。其與雲的差別在於霧只發生在近地表處。）

202.**Fog signals** (*n*) 霧號、霧中信號

Sound signals remitted in thick weather or low visibility as aids to navigation.

（在濃霧天候或低能見度時發出的聲音信號作爲助導航使用。）

203.**Following sea** (*n*) 順風浪

One running in the same direction as the ship is steering.

（指運動方向與船舶航行方向相同的海浪。）

204.**Forced tide** (*n*) 強制潮

A tide which exceeds its predicted height at high water.

（意指在高潮時的潮水超越其預期高度。）

205.**Ford** (*n*) 可涉水而過之處、淺灘

A shallow place where a river, may be crossed by wading.

（指河川水深較淺處，有時可以涉水而過。）

206.**Foreland** (*n*) 海岬、前陸、堤岸的前沿

A promontory or headland.

（海角或陸岬。）

207.**Foreshore** (*n*) 前灘、海灘

A part of the shore lying between high and low water lines of Mean

Spring Tides.

（介於平均大潮時的高、低潮線之間的部分沿岸區。）

208.**Forward** (*adj*) 船艏的、朝向船舶前部的

Toward the bow of a ship.

209.**Foul berth** (*n*) 有觸礁或撞碰危險的船席或泊位

A berth or anchoring position in which a ship cannot swing to her anchor or mooring without fouling another ship or on obstruction.

（指錨泊船舶若繞其錨具迴轉勢必會撞上其他船舶或障礙物的船席或錨位。）

210.**Foul bottom** (*n*) 沾滿貝殼或藻類的船底

The bottom of a ship when encrusted with marine growth.

（意指船舶底部覆蓋著海洋生物。）

211. **Foul patch or area** (*n*) 海底障礙物未清除區

A region of limited extent in comparatively shallow water, where the sea bed is strewn with wreckage or other obstructions making it unsuitable for anchorage.

（指在較淺水域的某一限制範圍內的區域，區域內散布著沈船殘骸或其他障礙物，故而不適於錨泊。）

212.**Freeboard** 乾舷

The distance from the water line to the top of the weather deck on the side.

（在船舷自露天甲板上緣量至水線之間的距離。）

213.**Free port** (*n*) 自由港、免稅港

A port where certain import and export duties are waived, to facilitate re-shipment to other countries.

（指一個為便於將貨物轉運至其他國家，對部分貨物免課徵進、出口稅的港口。）

214. **Freeing Ports** (*n*) 排水孔

Holes in the bulwark or rail, which allow deck wash to drain off into the sea.

（位於舷牆或圍欄上的小孔，以便將甲板上的積水排入海中。）

215. **Freshet** (*n*) 山洪、洪水

An abnormal amount of fresh water running into a river, estuary or the sea, caused by heavy or prolonged rain or melted snow.

（指豪雨、長時間降雨，或冰雪融化造成異常爆量的淡水流入河川、河口或大海。）

049

216. **Full and down** (*n*) 滿載

A ship loaded with its full amount of cargo, fuel, water, and stores. Also loaded down to its maximum load markings.

（指船舶艙間裝滿貨物、燃油、水與司多；同時載重量亦達到其最大載重標誌。）

【註5】
如純就貨物裝載而言，「Full and down」一詞係指船舶裝貨裝到容量與載重量都達到其最大量的狀態。此時當然要考量重量貨與容積貨的取捨比例，以及不同貨物的運費始能取得最大獲利。

217. **Gangway** (*n*) 舷門、舷梯

The opening in the bulwarks of vessel though which persons come on board or disembark.

（舷門指位於船舶舷牆上的開口，專供人員登、離船使用；舷梯則指位於船舶舷側供人員上下的梯子。）

218. **Gas free** (*n*) 清艙除氣

As referred to tanks, means free from dangerous concentrations of inflammable or toxic gases.

（將槽櫃或艙間內的危險有毒或易燃氣體排出的作業。）

219. **Girt** (*n*) 橫反拖

Of a tug, being towed broadside on through the water by her tow-rope.
（指一艘拖船因拖纜施力方向不當致拖船被拉成打橫的狀態。）

220.**GMDSS (Global Maritime Distress and Safety System)** (*n*) 全球海上遇險與安全系統

GMDSS is an internationally agreed-upon set of safety procedures, types of equipment, and communication protocols used to perfect the current global maritime communication support network needed to implement the search and rescue plan.
〔是國際海事組織（IMO）利用現代化的通信技術改善海上遇險與安全通信，建立新的海上搜救通信程序，以完善現行海上通信的全球性通信搜救網絡。〕

221.**Gradient currents** (*n*) 梯度流

Currents caused by pressure gradient in the water.
（由水中的壓力梯度造成的水流。）

222.**Gravel** (*n*) 砂礫

Coarse sand and small water-worn or pounded stones.
（粗砂與被水沖擊而成的較小石子。）

223.**Ground** (*n*) 供某種目的使用的場地

A portion of the earth's crust, which may be submerged or above water, e.g. Spoil ground, fishing ground.
（地殼的一部分，可以是淹沒在水中，或是突出水面，如廢土拋置場、魚場即是。）

224.**Ground tackle** (*n*) 錨泊屬具

The anchor, chain cables, and windlass.
（包括錨、錨鏈以及錨機的總稱。）

225.**GRT (Gross Registered Tonnage)** 總登記噸位

> 【註6】
>
> 總噸位以「單位（Unit）」做為表示其大小的陳述，而非一如其他的船舶噸位用「噸」作為單位，例如：「For a ship with a tonnage between 5,000 and 140,000 units of gross tonnage...（總噸位介於5,000至140,000單位的船舶……）」

226.**Ground swell** (*n*) 涌浪、岸濤（涌：水由下向上冒出來稱之）

A swell which, on reaching depths of less than half its length, becomes shorter and steeper) i.e. influenced by the ground.

（當湧浪抵達水深不及其長度一半的淺水區時，受地表的影響會變得比較短且陡直。）

227.**Group Occulting light** (*n*) 聯頓光

A steady light with at regular intervals a group of two or more sudden eclipses, the total duration of darkness being less than, or equal to, that of light.

（一個穩定的燈光在固定時間間隔內，燈光會發生二次或以上的突然滅失，而燈光全暗的時間會短於或等於明亮的時間長度。）

228.**Groyne** (*n*) 阻流堤、壩

A low wall-like structure, usually extending at right angles from the shore, to prevent coast erosion.

（類似低牆式結構物，通常自岸邊以直角向外延伸，藉由其阻擋水流進而改變水流方向以防海岸或河岸被侵蝕。）

229.**Gulf** (*n*) 海灣

Port of the sea partly enclosed by land, usually of larger extent and greater relative penetration than a bay.

〔指比「Bay（灣）」大且更深入陸地，或是被陸地包圍的海灣。〕

230.**Gust** (*n*) 陣風

A sudden increase in the velocity of wind of short duration.

（風速在短時間內突然增強。）

231.**Half-masted** (*vt*) 降半旗

On decoration-day and on occasions of national mourning the ensign only should be half-masted.

（在先烈紀念日或全國哀悼場合，國旗需降半旗。）

232.**Half Tide** (*n*) 半潮

The height of the tide half way between high and low water.

（指潮汐的高度恰好位於高潮與低潮間之一半處。）

233.**Half-tide rock** (*n*) 半潮礁

Formally used to describe rocks which are awash at about Mean Tide Level.

（通常用來敘述高度恰與平均潮面齊平的礁石。）

234.**Harbour** (*n*) 港灣

A stretch of water where vessels can anchor, or secure to buoys or alongside wharves, and obtain protection from sea and swell.

The protection may be afforded by natural features or by artificial.

（指可以供船舶錨泊，或繫泊於浮筒，或停靠於碼頭，並藉以避免遭受湧浪侵襲的一大片水域；港灣的保護設施可以是天然的地勢，也有由人造的。）

235.**Hatch cover cleat** (*n*) 艙蓋鎖緊扣

（鎖緊扣除可增加艙蓋的固著性外，更可增加艙蓋的水密性。）

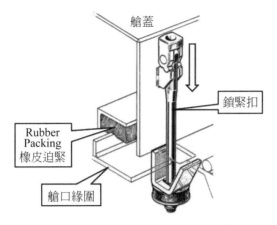

圖2.10 利用艙蓋鎖緊扣將艙蓋鎖緊

236. **Haven** (*n*) 港口

A harbor or place of refuge for vessels from the violence of wind and sea. In the strict sense it should be accessible at all states of the tide and conditions of weather.

（指可以供船舶擋風避浪的港口或處所。嚴格地說，它必須在各種潮汐狀況與氣象條件下都可以允許船舶進入者。一般都用於歐洲的港口名稱。）

237. **Hawse Pipe** (*n*) 錨鏈筒

The tube lining a hawse hole in a ship's bow.

（位於船艏具有管狀襯裡的錨鍊筒。）

238. **Head** (*n*) 海角、岬

A comparatively high promontory with a steep face.

（指具有較陡峭的表面且相對較高的海角。）

239. **Headline** (*n*) 船艏纜

Transporting wire or rope that is run from bow of a vessel to a position ahead when warping.

（當船舶欲絞靠碼頭或岸邊時，從船艏往船舶停泊位置前方送出的鋼索或纜繩。）

240. **Head sea** (*n*) 頂頭浪

A sea coming from the direction in which a ship is heading.

（來自船舶運動方向的波浪。）

241. **Heaving line** (*n*) 撇纜

Is a lightweight line which is used on board ship to establish a connection with people in another ship, or mooring line man on the shore.

（一條用以連結本船與他船船員或岸上帶纜人員的輕便繩索。）

圖2.11　船員手中的撇纜

242. **Heaving line knot** (*n*) 撇纜末端的繩結

Are used for adding weight to the end of a rope, to make the rope easier to throw.

（撇纜末端的繩結，用來聯結重物，以利撇纜的拋出。）

243. **Hectopascal** 百帕 (1hPa=100pdscal=1mb)

Unit of pressure used in meteorological work.

（用於氣象作業的氣壓單位。）

244.**Height** (*n*)（目標物的）高度

The vertical distance between the top of an object and its base.

（指一物體的底部至其頂部之間的垂直距離。）

245.**Height of the tide** (*n*) 潮汐高度

The vertical distance at any instant between sea level and chart datum.

（指任一瞬間海圖基準面至海平面之間的垂直距離。）

246.**High water** (*n*) 高潮

The highest level reached by the tide in one complete cycle.

（在一個完整潮汐週期中，海平面因潮汐作用達到最高水平時。）

247.**Higher High water** (*n*) 較高高潮

The higher of two successive high waters where diurnal inequality is present.

（指在日潮不等狀況下，兩個連續高潮中較高的一個高潮。）

248.**High Water Datum (or Datum for Heights)** (*n*) 高潮基準面、高度基準面

The high water plane to which elevations of land features are referred.

（作爲量測陸上目標物高度參考基準的高潮水平面。）

249.**High Water Full and Change** (*n*) 朔望高潮間隙

The average interval at any place between Moon's Transit and the next following high water on days of Full or Now Moon.

（任何一地在滿月或新月當天的月球中天與下一個高潮之間的平均時間間隔。）

250.**High Water Stand** (*n*) 高潮停潮

A prolonged period of negligible vertical movement near high water, this being a regular feature of the tides in certain localities while in other places stands are caused by meteorological conditions.

（在接近高潮時一段幾乎沒有垂直運動發生的較長時段。這是某些地方經常發生的潮汐現象。但是有些地方的停潮現象則是起因於氣象條件。）

251. **Hinterland** (*n*) 腹地

The land behind the coastline.

（指位於海岸線後方的陸地。）

252. **Holding ground** (*n*) 海底抓著力

The sea bottom of an anchorage is described as good or bad holding ground according to its capacity for gripping the anchor and chain cable.

In general, clay, mud and sand are good; shingle and rock are bad.

（敘述一個錨地的海底抓著力的優劣，主要依據其能讓船舶的錨具與錨鏈抓著與固定的程度決定。一般言之，黏土、泥土與砂子的底質較佳，礫石與礁岩底質較差。）

253. **Horn** (*n*) 汽笛

A fog signal using compressed air or electricity to vibrate a diaphragm.

〔利用壓縮空氣或電力振動膜（簧）片產生的霧中信號。〕

254. **Horse Latitudes** (*n*) 馬緯度

Zones of high atmospheric pressure with calms and variable breezes, which border the polar edges of the Trade wind areas in the N hemisphere.

（指海面平靜且和風風向多變的高壓區，其在北半球以貿易風的近北極側為界線。）

255. **Humidity** (*n*) 濕度

Moistness of atmosphere due to its vapour content.

（因大氣中含有水汽的含量所造成的濕度。）

256. **Hydrography** (*n*) 水道學、水道測量術

The science and art of measuring the oceans, seas, rivers, and other waters.

（指測量大洋、海洋、河川及其他水域的一門科學與技術。）

257. **Inherent vice** (*n*) 固有瑕疵

Quality changed in some cargoes which damages the commodity itself.

（某些貨物因品質變化致造成自身損害。）

258. **INMARSAT** (*n*) 國際海事通訊衛星

The organization established by the Convention on the INternational MARitime SATellite Organization.

（由國際海上衛星組織公約所建立的通訊體系。）

259. **International NAVTEX Service** (*n*) 國際航行警告和氣象預報電傳服務

The co-ordinated broadcast and automatic reception on 518 KHz of maritime safety information by means of narrow-band direct-printing using the English language.

（利用窄頻直接印字方式在518 KHz頻率協調發送與自動接收英文海事安全信息。）

260. **Inland** (*n*) 內陸

In the interior of the country, remote from the sea.

（位於一個國家遠離海洋的內陸。）

261. **Isobars** (*n*) 等壓線

Lines, on a meteorological chart, passing through all places having the same barometric pressure.

（在氣象圖上連結氣壓相同各點的線條。）

262.**Isobathic** (*n*) 等深線的

A line on a chart connecting points of equal underwater depth

（海圖上一條連接水面下深度相同各點的線。）

263.**Inland waterway** (*n*) 內陸水道

The navigable system of water comprising canals, rivers lakes, within the land territory.

（一國領土內包括運河、河川湖泊的水運航行系統。）

264.**Inlet** (*n*) 小港灣、澳

A small indentation in the coastline usually tapering towards its head.

（海岸線上微微內凹所形成的小港灣，通常愈往內陸寬度愈趨縮小。）

265.**Inshore Traffic Zone** (*n*) 近岸航行區

A routeing measure comprising a designated area between the landward boundary of a traffic separation scheme and the adjacent coast, not normally to be used by through traffic and where local special rules may apply.

（一個包含介於分道通航計畫的陸岸界線與鄰近海岸之間的指定區域內的航路規劃措施，通常不供一般船舶川航，而且常要適用當地特殊規則。）

266.**Isogonic** (*n*) 等磁偏差線

Of equal magnetic variation (declination).

（一條連結磁偏差相同各點的線。）

267.**Isophase light** (*n*) 等相光

A light with all durations of light and darkness equal.

（指一盞在整個週期內燈光的明、暗時間相等的燈光。）

268.**Jetty** (*n*) 突堤、渡埠

A structure generally of masonry, concrete, or wood, which projects usually at right-angles from the coast. Vessels normally lie alongside parallel with the main axis of the structure.

（通常爲石造、混擬土或木頭製成的結構體，期通常與岸線呈90°向外延伸。船舶通常與結構體的主軸線呈平行方向泊靠。）

269.**Kelp** (*n*) 海草、海藻

General name for large pieces of seaweed. Dead detached kelp floats on the water in masses.

（漂浮在水面上的大塊狀海藻的通稱。）

270.**Knot** (*n*) 節

One nautical mile (of 1852m) per hour.

（每小時一浬。）

271.**Lagoon** (*n*) 潟湖

The area of water enclosed by a barrier reef or atoll.

（由堡礁或環礁所包圍的一片水域；堡礁或環礁皆爲珊瑚礁群，故爲海洋環保首要標的。）

272.**Lake** (*n*) 湖泊

A large body of water entirely surrounded by land.

（由陸地完全圍繞的大片水體。）

273.**Lanby (Large Automatic Navigational Buoy)** (*n*) 大型自動航海浮標

A very large light-buoy, used as an alternative to a light-vessel, to mark offshore positions important to the Mariner.

（作爲替代燈船的大型燈浮，主在標誌離岸位置，對船員非常重要。）

274.**Landfall** (*n*) 初見陸地

The first sight or radar indication of land at the end of a passage.

（在航程終點時，用目視第一眼看到陸岸，或自雷達螢幕首次出現陸岸顯像的當下。）

275.**Landfall buoy** (*n*) 航程終點浮標

A buoy with a tall superstructure, marking the seaward end of the approach to a harbor or estuary.

（一個具有較高上層結構的浮標，用以標示船舶抵達港口或港灣的進出水道最靠近大海一端的起點。）

276.**Landing** (*n*) 登陸

A place where boats may ground in safety.

（可以讓船舶安全擱淺的處所。）

277.**Landmark** (*n*) 陸標

A prominent artificial or natural feature on land such as a tower or church, used as an "aid to navigation".

（陸上顯著的人造或自然的地形地物，諸如塔台或教堂，主要作爲助導航用途。）

278. **Lashing and shoring (choking)** (*n*) 綁紮撐墊

The method to stabilize cargo inside of a container or shup's cargo hold.

（固定貨櫃內或船艙內部所積載貨物的方法。）

【註7】
The fundamental and ultimate goal of delivering cargoes is to have them arrive safely at the destination. Therefore, securing cargoes onto the space they are put in is of utmost importance. The most common way of doing it is lashing and shoring/choking, in the right way.

貨物運輸的基本與終極目標就是將貨物安全送抵目的地。因此固定貨物是最重要的，最常用的就是綁紮、支撐與塞墊。

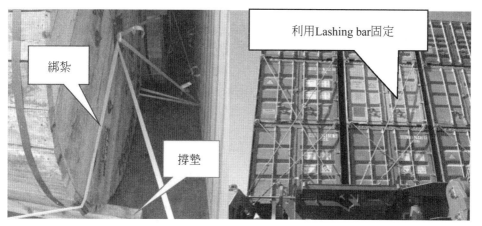

利用Lashing bar固定

綁紮

撐墊

圖2.12　貨櫃內部雜貨固定與貨櫃裝船綁紮的方法

279.**Latitude** (*n*) 緯度

The latitude of a place is its angular distance on a meridian, measured N or S from the terrestrial equator.

（一地的緯度乃是指其在子午線上的角距離，自赤道起始向北或向南量。）

280.**Laydays** (*n*) 工作或裝卸天數

When the vessel on a voyage charter is in port, the expenses of the shipowner continue. At the same time the loading or discharging is controlled by the charterer, who, if not held to a definite number of days to completed this work, can make the stay in port long and expensive for the shipowner. For this reason, the charter party will specify a definite number of days for loading or discharging cargo) or it may specify a certain number of tons per day to be loaded o discharged.

（當簽訂論程租傭的船舶停在港內時，船東的開銷支出持續發生。於此同時，船舶的裝卸作業則由租船人所控制。如果不明定完成裝卸工作的天數，可能造成船舶滯港過久與船東的支出增加。為此，租傭船契約上都會載明裝貨、卸貨的天數，或每天應裝載或應卸下貨載的頓數。）

281. **L-band EPIRB system** (*n*) L頻段應急指位無線電示標

A satellite EPIRB system operating in the 1.6 GHz frequency band through the INMARAST geostationary space segment.

（經由與地球旋轉同步的國際海事衛星發送1.6 GHz頻帶的衛星應急指位無線電示標系統。）

282. **L.B.P. (Length Between Perpendiculars)** (*n*) 垂標間距

The length of a ship measured from the forward side of stem to the aft side of the sternpost at the height of the designed water line.

（指在設計夏季載重線的高處，由船艏材前緣量至舵柱後緣間之水平距離。）

283. **Lee shore** (*n*) 下風岸

The shore towards which the wind is blowing.

（指風向吹襲一方的岸邊。）

284. **Leading light** (*n*) 導向燈

Light at different elevations so situated as to defined a leading line when brought into transit.

（利用前、後位處不同高度的燈光，當其被觀測者觀測成一直線時即可確定一船舶運動導引線。）

285. **Leading line (Range line)** (*n*) 導航線、疊標線

The line through leading marks intended to be used a navigational aid.

（指貫穿導向標誌的一條線，用作助導航使用。）

286. **Leading marks** (*n*) 導航標誌

Well-defined objects which, if kept in transit, will lead a vessel clear of dangers or in the best channel.

（指輪廓清晰的兩個明顯目標物，當觀測者保持兩目標成一直線的航向航行時，可引導船舶避開危險物或保持在安全航道。）

287. **Lee side** (*n*) 下風舷

The side of the ship or object which is away from the wind and therefore sheltered.

（指船舶或目標物不受風的一舷，也因而在該舷側可以得到良好遮掩。）

288. **Lee tide** (*n*) 順風潮

A tidal stream running in the same direction as the wind is blowing.

（指潮流流動方向與風吹方向相同的潮流。）

289. **Lee way** (*n*) 船位偏移

The amount of drift of a vessel to leeward of the course steered, due to the action of the wind.

（因風的作用，將船舶漂向與所航行之航向下風側之偏離量。）

290. **Lights** (*n*) 燈光

A comprehensive term including all illuminated aids to navigation, other then those exhibited from floating structures.

（廣義言之，包括所有能夠發光的助導航設施，但是從浮動結構物顯示者除外。）

291. **Lighthouse** (*n*) 燈塔

A distinctive structure from which a light or lights are exhibited as an aid to navigation.

（有獨特且具鑑別性，且能發出燈光作為助導航使用的建築物。）

292. **Light-buoy** (*n*) 燈浮

A buoy carrying a structure from which is exhibited a light.

（一個上方設有可以顯示燈光的浮動結構物；常常用於標誌航行水道。）

293. **Lights in line** (*n*) 邊界線指示燈

Two or more lights so situated that when in transit they define the limit of an area, or an alignment for use in anchoring. Unlike leading lights they do not mark a direction to be followed.

（兩個或以上的燈光被設於不同位置，當觀測者觀測此兩燈光成一直線時，用以界定某一水域的邊界，或作為船舶拋錨時的參考線。不似導向燈一樣，它並不用來指示船舶必須遵循的運動方向。）

294.**Light-ship** (vessel) (*n*) 燈船

A vessel anchored as a floating aid to navigation from which is exhibited a light.

（一般藉由展示燈光作為浮動助導航使用的錨泊船。）

295.**Line handlers** (*n*) 帶纜工

The shoreside personnel who handle the ship's line on the dock.

（在碼頭上協助處理船舶繫岸纜繩的岸上人員。）

【註8】
又稱Mooring Line Man

296.**Line-throwing Apparatus/Device/Gun** （撇纜槍）

【註9】
一般撇纜槍都是採用壓縮空氣推動的，因此稱為「氣動式撇纜槍（Pneumatic Line-throwing gun）」。

297.**List of Light** (*n*) 燈塔表

A booklet which stated all the datums, of lighthouse, light-vessel and light beacon in the world.

（一本專門記載全球各燈塔、燈船與燈標的所有資料的書刊。）

298.**L.O.A. (Length Over All)** (*n*) 全長、總長、船舶最大長度

The length of a ship measured from the foremast point of the stem to the aftermost part of the stern. (The full length of a ship)

（由船艏最前端量至船艉最末端間之水平距離，是為全長，亦稱總長。）

299. **Longitude** (*n*) 經度

The longitude of a place is the angular distance E or W of the Prime Meridian.

（某地的經度係指從格林威治子午線，亦即0°子午線向東或向西量至當地的角距離。）

300. **Long ton** (*n*) 長噸

A measure used to figure weight of cargo at 2,240 pounds per ton, as opposed to short ton or regular ton of 2,000 pounds.

（用以計算貨物重量的度量方法，每長噸等於2240磅，相對於短噸或標準噸的2,000磅。）

301. **Low Water** (*n*) 低潮

The lowest level reached by the tide in one complete cycle.

（在一個完整潮汐週期中，海平面因潮汐作用達到最低水平時。）

302. **Lower Low Water** (*n*) 較低低潮

The lower of two successive low water where diurnal inequality is present.

（指在日潮不等狀況下兩個連續低潮中較低的一個低潮。）

303. **Lunitidal Interval** (*n*) 月潮間隔

The time interval between the transit of the Moon and the next following high or low water.

（月球中天與隨之而來的高潮或低潮之間的時間間隔。）

304. **Main Ship Channel** (*n*) 主要航道

The channel having the greatest depth and easiest for navigation.

（指具有最大深度且適於航行的航道。）

305. **Main Steering Console** (*n*) 位於駕駛臺中央之主操控台

（位於駕駛臺兩舷翼側的操控台則稱爲「Wing Steering Console」。操船者在操控台可進行俥、舵、側推的控制。）

306. **Maneuvering speed** (*n*) 運轉速度

A vessel's reduced rate of speed in restricted waters such as harbors.

（船舶在限制水域，諸如港內，必須以較低的船速運轉。）

307. **Marina** (*n*) 遊艇碼頭

An area provided with berthing and shore facilities for yachts.

（提供遊艇停泊以及岸上設施的水域。）

308. **Mark** (*n*) 標誌

A fixed feature on land or moored at sea, which can be identified on the chart and used to fix a ship's position.

（位於陸上或繫泊於海上的固定形狀物體，可以在海圖上辨識，並供船舶定位使用。）

309. **Marsh** (*n*) 沼澤、濕地

Soft, wet land frequently flooded in rains and usually watery at all times.

（指柔軟濕地，在雨季常常淹水，故而經常呈現濕濕的狀態。）

310. **Mean High Water Interval** (*n*) 平均高潮間隙

The average time interval between Moon's Transit and the following high water.

（太陽中天與接續而來的高潮之間的平均時間間隔。）

311. **Mean Sea Level** (*n*) 平均海平面

The mean level of the sea throughout a definite number of complete tidal cycles, usually computed for periods of a month and of a year, and usually obtained from the average of hourly heights.

（指經由觀測一定數目的完整潮汐週期所得的水平面的平均值。觀

測時間範圍通常是一個月或一年的期間，如日平均海平面、年平均
海平面和多年平均海平面等等。一般驗潮站常用18.6年或19年期間
裡每小時的觀測值求出平均值，作爲該測站的平均海平面。）

312. **Mean High Water Springs** (*n*) 平均大潮高潮

The average (throughout a year when the average maximum declination of the Moon is 23.5°) of the heigests of two successive high
waters during those periods of 24 hours when the range of the tide is
greatest.

（當潮差達到最大的24小時期間內，二個連續高潮中潮高較高的一
個高潮的平均值；一年之中月球平均最大赤緯達到23.5°時的平均
值。）

313. **Mean High Water Neaps** (*n*) 平均小潮高潮

The average, of the highest of two successive high waters during
similar periods when the range of the tide is least.

（當潮差達到最小的24小時期間內，二個連續高潮中潮高較高的一
個高潮的平均值。）

314. **Mean High Water** (*n*) 平均高潮

The average of all high water heights.

（某地所有高潮潮高的平均值。）

315. **Mean Higher High Water** (*n*) 平均較高高潮

The average of the higher of the two daily high water, taken over a
long period of time.

（經過一段較長期間的觀測所取得每日二次高潮中較高一次高潮的
平均值。）

316. **Mean Tide Level** (*n*) 平均潮位

The average of all the high and low water heights only a long period
of time, usually computed for a year.

（觀測期間內高潮位及低潮位之平均值，亦即平均高潮與平均低潮之中間水位，故又稱為半潮位，通常以一年為觀測週期。）

317. **MAREP (Mariner Reporting system)** (*n*) 海事報到系統

The MAREP is a system used to enhance the navigational safety within specific areas through collecting amd utilizing essential ship information.

（專供收集並善用重要船舶情報，以提升特定區域內航行安全的系統。）

318. **Meridian** (*n*) 子午線

A Great Circle on the Earth's surface which passes through the terrestrial poles.

（地球表面通過南北地極的大圈。）

319. **Messenger** (*n*) 引繩

A light line used in hauling a heavier line (as between ships).

（船上用來連結並絞進笨重纜索，如拖船纜、鋼纜等的較輕細繩索。）

320. **Mirage** (*n*) 海市蜃樓

An optical illusion or distortion of appearance of objects due to abnormal refraction.

（因為異常折射所造成目標外觀的變形或視覺假象。）

321. **Mole** (*n*) 防波堤、堤埠

A concrete or stone structure, within an artificial harbour, at right-angles to the coast or the structure from it extends, alongside which vessels can lie.

（在人工港內建造的混擬土或石頭結構物，一般都與岸邊呈90°向外延伸，可供船隻傍靠。）

圖2.13　堤埠

322.**Monkey's fist** (*n*) 撇纜頭

To prevent personal injury, the "fist" should be made only with rope and should not contain added weighting material.

（為防止人員受傷，撇纜頭只能由繩索編結而成，不能包裹重物，如鐵塊或卸扣等。）

圖2.14　繩索編製的撇纜頭

323.**Monsoon** (*n*) 季風

The periodical trade winds of certain latitudes in the Indian Ocean and off Africa coast.

（在印度洋及非洲沿岸外海的某些緯度帶所吹襲的季節性貿易風。）

324.**Morse Code light** (*n*) 摩斯電碼燈

A light in which flashes of different duration are grouped in such a manner as to reproduce a Morse character or characters.

（一盞可藉由顯示不同長度閃光組合以產生摩斯字母碼的燈光。）

325.**Moor** (*vt*) 繫泊、被固定、被繫住 (*n*) 錨泊方法

To secure a vessel, craft, or boat by ropes, chains, etc., to the shore or on anchors.

（利用繩索或鏈條將一艘船舶、載具或艇筏繫泊在岸邊或固定於錨上。）

To ride with both anchors down laid at some distance apart, and the ship lying midway between them.

（利用船艏雙錨在分隔相當距離處拋下，讓船舶處於兩錨間之近中央處。）

326.**Moorings** (*n*) 錨具 (*n*) 繫留或繫船之設備、停船處

Gear usually consisting of anchors, cable, and a buoy to which a ship can secure.

（通常由錨、錨鍊與浮筒組成以供船舶繫泊的裝置。）

The mooring is the place in which a vessel may be secured.

（供船舶繫留或繫船之處所。）

327.**Mooring buoy** (*n*) 繫泊浮筒、繫船浮筒

A buoy of special construction which carries the ring of the moorings to which a vessel secures.

（一個設有供船舶繫固用的繫泊鏈環的特殊構造浮筒。）

328.**Molded Breadth** (*n*) 模寬

The greatest breadth of a vessel, measured from the heel of frame on one side to heel of frame on the other side.

（船舶的最大寬度；從一舷的肋材跟部量至另舷肋材的跟部。）

329.**Molded Depth** (*n*) 模深

The extreme height of a vessel amidships, from the top of the keel to the top of the upper deck beam.

（船舶舯部的最大高度，從龍骨的頂部量至主甲板橫梁的上緣。）

330. **Mooring line** (*n*) 繫纜

Cable or hawse lines used to tie up a ship.

（用以綁住船舶的鋼纜或纜繩。）

331. **Muster station** (*n*) 逃（求）生集合站

The place on a ship where passengers should assemble in the event of an emergency

（緊急情況時，船上旅客集合的地點。）

332. **MSI (Maritime Safety Information)** (*n*) 海事安全資訊

Navigational and meteorological warnings, meteorological forecasts, distress alerts and other urgent safety related information broadcast to ships.

（包括航行與氣象警報、氣象預報、遇難警報，以及其他傳送給船舶的緊急安全相關資訊。）

333. **Nature of the bottom** (*n*) 海底底質

The material of which the sea bed is formed, e.g. mud, stones.

（形成海床的物質，如泥土、石頭等。）

334. **NAVAREA** (*n*) 航行警告區

Short title of an area in the world-wind navigational warning service.
（用於風力航行警報服務的全球各區域的簡稱。）

335. **NAVAREA warning** (*n*) 航行警告區警告

Lang-range warning broadcasts issued by an area co-ordinate of the world-wind navigational warning service for his area and broadcast by powerful station or station to cover the whole of the area.

（利用發送功率可以涵蓋整個經協調的警告區的強力電臺播送有關風力的遠距航行警告資訊。）

336. **Navigable** (*adj*) 可航的、可供航行的

Capable of being navigated.

（指船舶可安全航行的水域或河道。）

337. **Navigation** (*n*) 航海術

The art of determining a ship's position and taking her in safety from one place another.

（利用測定船舶位置，並確保船舶能夠自甲地安全航行至乙地的技術。）

338. **Neap Tide** (*n*) 小潮

A tide of relatively small range occurring near the time of Moon's quarter.

（發生在接近上弦月或下弦月時潮差相對較小的潮汐。）

339. **Negative surges** (*n*) 潮升不足

Occasions when the level of the sea is lower than the predicted level. They are caused by meteorological conditions.

（當海平面的高度低於預期水平時的狀況，通常由氣象條件所造成的。）

340. **Negotiating** (*vi*) 越過、通過險要路段

Negotiating heavy traffic area.

（通過交通密集水域。）

341. **No Bottom sounding** (*n*) 測不到底的測深

A depth obtained at which the lead has not reached the bottom.

（探測水深時，在未探測到海底前，卻已達到測深設備作業極限時所測得的深度。）

342. **Nodal point** (*n*) 無潮點

The point of minimum tidal range in an amphidromic system.

（在無潮體系中潮差最小的一點。）

343.**Notice to Mariners** (*n*) 航船布告、航行通告、航海通告

Periodic publication notifying changes in, or additions to, previously published navigational data.

（用以通知改變或增添先前發行的航海資料的定期刊物。）

344.**Notice of Readiness** (*n*) 裝卸貨準備完成通知書

When on a voyage charter it is the master's responsibility to advise the charterer or his agent, n writing, as son as the vessel is in all respects ready to load or discharge. The date the notice is tendered, known as the "Reporting day".

（當船舶簽訂論程租傭後，船長有責任在船舶完成所有裝載或卸貨準備作業後，應盡速以書面告知租船人或其代理人；裝卸貨準備完成通知書提出的當天稱為「報到日」。）

345.**Nun buoy** (*n*) 菱形浮標

A buoy in the shape of two cones, base to base, and moored from one point so that the other is more or less upright.

（由兩個底部相連的圓錐形所形成的浮標，由於其係從其中之一尖點繫固，故而大多呈現近直立狀。）

346.**Obstruction** (*n*) 障礙物

A danger to navigation, the exact nature of which is not specified or has not been determined.

（對船舶航行構成危險，但並未詳述或確定其真正性質。）

347.**Occluded Front** (*n*) 滯留鋒

When a faster moving cold front overtakes a warm front they merge in what is called on occluded front.

（當移動速度較快的冷鋒超越前方的暖鋒並結合為一稱為滯留鋒。）

348.**Occulting light** (*n*) 頓光

A steady light with, at regular intervals, a period of darkness. The duration of darkness being always less than the duration of light.

（一穩定燈光在固定時間間隔燈光全暗一段時間，而燈光全暗時間經常比亮的時間短。）

349. **Offing** (*n*) 岸上能見的遠處海面

The part of the sea distant but visible from the shore or from an anchorage.

（從陸上或從錨地可以看到的遠處海面。）

350. **Oceanography** 海洋學

The study of the oceans especially of the physical features of the sea water and sea bed and of marine flora and fauna.

（專門研究海洋，特別是針對海水的物理特質、海床，以及海洋動植物的科學。）

351. **On-scene commander** (*n*) 現場指揮官

The commander of a rescue unit designated to co-ordinate surface search and rescue operations within a specified search area.

（搜救單位任命在特定搜索區內協調海面搜索與救助作業的指揮官。）

352. **On-scene communications** (*n*) 現場聯絡

Communications between the ship in distress and assisting units.

（遇難船舶與救助單位之間的聯絡。）

353. **Ooze** (*n*) 軟泥

Very soft mud, slime) especially on the bed of a river or estuary.

（非常軟的黏泥，特別是指沉積在河川或海口灣底床的軟泥。）

354. **Open water** (*n*) 開放水域

Water where in all circumstances a ship has complete freedom of manoeuvre.

（指在任何天候條件下船舶都具有完全操縱自由度的水域。）

355. **Offshore Renewable Energy Installations (OREIs)** (*n*) 離岸再生能源設施

356. **Offshore Wind Farms (OWFs)** (*n*) 離岸風力場

357. **Offshore Wind Turbines (OWTs)** (*n*) 離岸風力發電機

358. **Opening** (*n*) 開口

A general term to indicate a gap or passage.

（用以表示間隙、峽谷或通路開口的一般名詞。）

359. **Outfall** (*n*) 河口、出水口

A narrow outlet of a river into the sea or a lake, as opposed to the opening out at a mouth.

（相對於港口的開口，河川流入大海或湖泊的狹窄出水口。）

The mouth of a sewer or other pipe discharging into the sea.

（岸上汙水管或其他排泄入海的管線的出口。）

360. **Outfall buoy** (*n*) 出水口警示浮標

Buoy marking the position where a sewer or other pipe discharges into the sea.

（用以指示下水道或其他管線排泄入海處位置所在的浮標；強勁水流會影響船舶操縱，尤其是小型船舶。）

361. **Overfalls or Tide rips** (*n*) 激潮、逆流碎波

Turbulence associated with the flow of strong tidal streams over abrupt changes in depth, or with the meeting of tidal streams flowing from different direction.

（隨著強勁潮流流過水深急遽變化，或來自不同方向的潮流相遇所產生的亂流。）

362. **Parallel of Latitude** (*n*) 緯度平行圈

Small Circle on the Earth's surface parallel with the equator.

（地表上面與赤道平行的小圈；地表上不通過地心的圓皆稱小圈。）

363. **Partlow Circular Chart** (*n*) 冷凍貨櫃溫度記錄圖

（用以記錄冷凍貨櫃在運送與儲存過程中的溫度變化，以明各造之責任。）

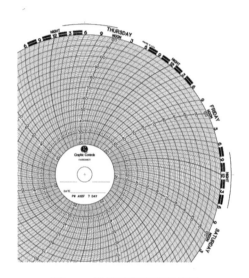

圖2.15　冷凍貨櫃溫度記錄圖

364. **Passage** (*n*) 通路、水路

A navigable channel, especially one through reefs or islands.

（指可航行水道，特別指穿過礁岩或島嶼者。）

365. **Passenger ship** (*n*) 客船

Vessels devoted primarily to the transport of persons

（專供運送人員的船舶。）

366. **Path** (*n*) 路線

The path of a ship is the route that is likely to be taken, the track being the route that has been taken.

（一艘船舶的路線係指其經常航行的航線，亦即其所採行航線的軌跡。）

367. **Pay off** (*n*) 船艏偏離風向

A ship pays off if her head falls away from the wind.

（指航行中船舶的船艏遠離風的來向。）

368. **Pebbles** (*n*) 小鵝卵石

Water-rounded material of from 4 to 64 mm in size.

（尺寸介於4到64公釐間，經由水流或海浪沖積成圓形的小石頭。）

369. **Peninsula** (*n*) 半島

A piece of land almost surrounded by water or projecting for into the sea.

（一塊幾乎被水體包圍或突出至大海的陸塊。）

370. **Perigee** (*n*) 月球近地點

The point in the Moon's orbit nearest to the Earth. When the Moon is in perigee the tidal range is increased.

（月球在其軌道運行最接近地球的一點。當月球在近地點時潮差會增大。）

371. **Perigee tide** (*n*) 月近點大潮

A spring tide, greater than average, occurring when the Moon is in perigee.

（大於平均值的大潮，發生在月球位於近地點時。）

372. **Perihelion** (*n*) 行星近日點

The point or time at which a planet is nearest in its orbit to the Sun.

（行星於其運行軌道上最接近太陽時之地點或時間。）

373. **Phase** (of the Moon) (*n*) 月象

The appearance at given time of the illuminated surface of the Moon.

（月球在特定時間所呈現出的光亮表面。）

374.**Pier** (*n*) 突堤碼頭、渡埠

A structure, usually of wood, masonry, or concrete, extending approximately at right-angles from the coast into the sea. The head, alongside which vessel can lie with their fore-and-aft line at right-angles to the main structure, is frequently wider than the body of the pier.

（指自岸邊以90°向海洋突出的木製、石製或混擬土所製成的結構。某些渡埠的近海端亦可以設計泊靠船舶，船舶的艏艉線方向通常與主結構成90°，而且較渡埠的主體寬。）

圖2.16　突堤碼頭

圖2.17　渡埠

375. **Pile** (*n*) 椿

A heavy baulk of timber or a column of reinforced concrete driven vertically into the bed of the sea or of a river.

（指垂直插入海底或河底的粗重木梁或強化混擬土圓柱。）

376. **Pilot boat** (*n*) 引水船

A boat which takes pilots to inbound ships and removes pilot from outbound vessels.

（專供載運引水人出海引領進港船，或接回出港船引水人的小船。）

377. **Pincer plier** (*n*) 老虎鉗

圖2.18　老虎鉗

378. **Pipe wrenches** (*n*) 管子鉗

圖2.19　管子鉗

379. **Pitch** (*n*) 船舶的前後向顛簸；螺距

Angular motion of a ship in the fore-and-aft plane.

（船舶在前後向平面上的角運動。）

A term applied to the distance a propeller will advance during one revolution.

（指船舶螺旋槳旋轉一圈所能推進的距離。）

380. **Pivoted beacon** (*n*) 可旋轉浮筒

A buoyant spar rising from a universal joint and sinker on the sea bed.

（利用萬用接頭與沉在海底的墜子相連接的漂浮圓材。）

381. **Plimsoll Mark** (*n*) 載重線標誌

The mark stenciled in and painted on ship's side, designated by a circle and horizontal lines to mark the highest permissible load water lines under different condition.

（用多條電焊線條與油漆標誌於船邊的標誌，由一個圓圈與多條水平線所標示，用以指明在不同狀況或季節下船舶所能裝載的最大允許重量。）

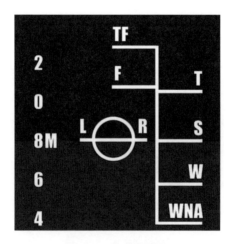

圖2.20　載重線標誌

382. **Point** (*n*) 小岬、小地角

A sharp and usually comparatively low piece of land jutting out from the coast or forming a turning-point in the coastline.

（通常指一從陸岸突向海面的尖銳而且較低的陸塊，常是船舶沿著海岸航行的轉向點。）

383. **Port** (*n*) 港口

A commercial harbor or the commercial part of a harbor in which are situated the quays, wharves, facilities for working cargo, warehouses, docks, &c.

（指商港或港口的商用營運區塊，設有碼頭、貨物裝卸設施、倉庫、船渠等。）

【註10】

一般「Harbor」多指天然港口，而「Port」則指人工港口，又一個「Harbor」內可以有好幾個「Port」，可見就面積而言，「Harbor」通常要大於「Port」。

基本上，「Quay」、「Wharf」、「Docks」都可稱作碼頭，但還是有下述的差別：

1. A quay is the built up on the bank of a harbor or dock where ships can moor.

   （「Quay」指建築在港口或船渠的堤岸上可供船舶繫泊用。）

2. A wharf is less substantial than a quay, and may be on the bank of a river.

   （「Wharf」的規模不如「Quay」大，有時設在河岸上。）

3. A dock is dug out and usually has gates so that the water level is kept up even though the tide has gone out. Access may only be at certain times of the tide. A dock is for mooring ships for cargo or passenger exchange, or sometimes repair.

   （「Dock」通常由人工挖掘並設有閘門，因而儘管退潮時渠內仍保有一定高度水平面，又因為船渠內水位穩定，故可提供船舶繫泊以裝卸貨物與上下旅客或從事維修作業。但是進出船渠常要等候適當的潮段時間。）

384. **Portable Pilotage Unit** (*n*) 攜帶式引航裝置

A Marine Pilot boards a vessel at sea bringing a backpack with tools for aid to navigation. In the backpack, you will normally find sensors and a laptop with navigational software. These sensors are portable, they have been carried onboard the vessel by the Pilot.

（引水人登船常帶有內建助導航工具的背包，背包內通常裝有GPS或其他航儀的感應器，以及有內建航行軟體的筆電；因為這些由引水人攜帶上船的感應器是可攜帶的，故而稱之。）

【註11】
前述感應器（Sensors）或天線（Antenna）可裝在駕駛臺翼側（Bridge wing）或駕駛臺上方最高處（Monkey island）。由於引水人預先將引航相關資訊灌入記憶體內，故而攜帶式引航裝置不僅因為其是重要的航行工具，同時也是引水人與船長或船員間的資訊、教學與聯絡溝通通信工具。

385. **Port Authority** (*n*) 港口主管機關

Persons or corporation, owner of, or entrusted with or invested with the power of managing a port. The agency that controls the maintenance and use of all the port's Facilities.

（指被授權、委託或投資管理港口權的個人、公司與業主；指掌管所有港口設施與保養的專業行政機關。）

386. **Port radio station** (*n*) 港務無線電臺

A radio stations normally operating in the VHF band through which messages can be passed to Port Authorities.

（一個通常利用VHF無線電頻帶操作的無線電臺，藉由其運作可將船舶資訊轉傳給港口主管機關。）

387. **Position line** (*n*) 位置線

A line on the Earth's surface represented on a chart on which a ship's position can be said to lie.

（在海圖上用以表示地表上船位所在的一條線；位置線可經由觀測天體、觀測岸上或海上固定目標、雷達測繪等方法取得。）

388. **Pratique** (*n*) 入港許可證

License to hold intercourse with the shore granted to a vessel often quarantine.

（允許一艘經過檢疫的船舶得以保持與岸上交流的許可證。）

389. **Precautionary area** (*n*) 警戒區

A routeing measure comprising an area within defined limits where ships must navigate with particular caution and within which the direction of traffic flow may be recommended.

（包含一個在明確界線內的區域之航路措施，船舶航行在此區域內務必特別提高警戒。通常會設定在該區域內交通流的建議方向。）

390. **Precipitation** (*n*) 降水

A deposit on the earth of rain, snow, hail and mist etc.

（雨、雪、雹與霧等降落至地表的天氣現象。）

391. **Prime meridian** (*n*) 本初子午線

The meridian from which longitude is measured.

〔穿過倫敦格林威治的經度線叫做本初子午線（0°經線），經度係以此子午線起向東或西度量。〕

392. **Prohibited Anchorage** (*n*) 禁止錨泊區

Used to indicate an area in which for some reason anchoring is not permitted.

（通常用以指示因為某些原因不允許船舶錨泊的水域。）

393. **Project depth** (*n*) 設計深度

The depth to which it is hoped to maintain an area or channel.

（預期保持某一水域或航道的水深。）

394. **Quadrature** (*n*) 上下弦月

A term applied principally to the Sun and Moon when their longitude differ by 90°.

（主要用來表示當太陽與月球經度相差90°時的月象。）

395.**Quarantine** (*n*) 動植物檢疫隔離

Isolation imposed on an infected vessel. All vessels are considered to be in quarantine until granted pratique.

（港口國對感染疫情的船舶進行隔離，所有抵港船舶都應進行檢疫直至取得檢疫完成證書始能放行。）

【註12】

「Quarantine」一詞源自拉丁字「Quadraginta」，意為「四十」。中世紀鼠疫流行時期，若懷疑船上貨物或旅客帶有致病源，港口主管機關會要求船隻在外海停泊四十天，確認安全後才放行進港，以防止旅客或貨物將傳染病帶入境內。眼前跨國運輸與旅行業務盛行，帶來傳染病的高風險與處理難度，因而維持此一機制的運作乃全球各沿海國的共識。

396.**Quarter** (*n*) 船側後半部、船舷部

A side of a ship aft, between the main midship frames and stern.

（船側後半部，介於船舯部肋材與船舷之間。）

397.**Quay** (*n*) 碼頭、埠頭

A solid structure usually of stone, masonry or concrete alongside which vessels may lie to work cargoes. It usually runs parallel along or nearly along the line of the shore.

（指利用石塊、混擬土建築在港口或船渠堤岸上的實體建築，可供船舶繫靠裝卸貨物使用。其建築排列方向大多與堤岸平行或近於平行。）

398.**Race** (*n*) 急湍、湍流

A fast-running stream, usually tidal, caused by water passing through a constricted channel or over shallows or by convergent streams, or in the vicinity of headlands. Eddies are often associated with races.

（指快速流動的水流，通常指潮流通過限制河道或過淺水域，或聚

合水流，或陸岬海角附近所造成的。湍流通常伴有渦流的產生。）

399. **Racon** (*n*) 雷控標

A radar transponder beacon which emits a characteristic signal when triggered by the emissions of ships' radar sets.

（指雷達應答器信標，當其接收到由雷達發射的脈衝波擊發時，可以發出獨特的信碼。）

400. **Rader conspicuous object** (*n*) 雷達顯著目標

Any object that can be distinguished readily on a radar screen.

（任何在雷達顯示螢幕上可以快速辨識的目標。）

401. **Radar reflector** (*n*) 雷達反射器

A device fitted to a buoy or beacon to increase the response to radar transmissions.

（一個裝在浮標或標杆上可以提升自船舶雷達所發射信號反應的裝置。）

402. **Radiation Fog** (*n*) 輻射霧

A kind of Fog which caused from radiation cooling in the night.

（由於夜間地面輻射不斷散熱，使得接近地面的空氣逐步冷卻，較潮濕的空氣很快便降溫至露點，形成無數的小水珠懸浮於空氣中。）

403. **Radio fog signal** (*n*) 無線電霧號

Special transmissions provided by a radiobeacon as an aid to navigation during periods of fog and low visibility.

（在霧季或低能見度時，藉由無線電標杆發射可作為助導航使用的特別信號。）

404. **Radiobeacon** (*n*) 無線電信標

A radio transmitting station on shore or at a light-ship, not necessarily manned, or light-buoy of whose transmissions a ship may take bearings.

（位於岸上或未佈署人員的燈船上的無線電發射台，或燈標上。船舶可藉由它的發射測得方位。）

405.**Ramark** (*n*) 雷達信標

A radar beacon which transmits independently, without having to be triggered by the emissions of ships' radar sets.

（一獨立發送信碼的雷達標杆，無須藉由船上雷達設備發射的脈波擊發。）

406.**Ram Bow** (*n*) 撞槌型船艏

A bow protruding underneath the water line considerably forward of the forecastle deck.

（船艏水線下部分明顯自艏艛甲板向前突出的船艏形狀。）

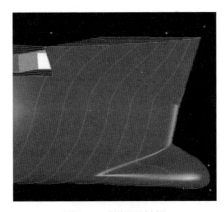

圖2.21　撞槌型船艏

407.**Range of the tide** (*n*) 潮差、潮距

The differences in level between successive high and low waters or vice versa.

（介於某一高潮與緊接其後的低潮之間的水平面高度差異，或是介於某一低潮與緊接其後的高潮之間的水平面高度差異。）

408.**Rapids** (*n*) 急流、湍流

The swift flow of water caused by a steep descent in a river bed.

（由於河床的坡度陡降所造成的快速水流。）

409.**Rate** (*n*) 潮流與洋流的速度

The velocity of tidal streams and currents.

410.**Rat guard** (*n*) 防鼠板

One of the circular sheet metal shields fastened to the mooring lines of a vessel to prevent rats from boarding or leaving it.

（指一片固著於船舶纜繩上的圓形鐵片，用來防止老鼠沿著繩索從船上跑上岸，或是沿著繩索自岸上爬上船。）

圖2.22 防鼠板

411. **Reach** (*n*) 直行水域

A comparatively straight part of a river or channel, between two bends.

（河川或航道中二個彎曲地形之間某段相對筆直的流域。）

412.**Rectilinear stream** (*n*) 直線潮流

A tidal stream which runs only in one of two general directions, with a period of slack water in between.

（僅在二個相反方向川流的潮流中間有一段憩潮。）

413. **Recommended direction of traffic flow** (*n*) 交通流建議方向

A traffic flow pattern indicating a recommended directional movement of traffic where it is impractical or unnecessary to adopt an established direction of traffic flow.

（在實際上不可行或無須採行既定交通流方向的水域中，用以指示船舶運動的建議方向的交通流模式。）

414. **Recommended track** (*n*) 建議航路、建議路線

A track shown on a chart, which all or certain vessels are recommended to follow. In a routeing system, it means a route which has been specially examined to ensure so for as possible that it is free of dangers and along which ship are advised to navigate.

（一條顯示在海圖上建議所有或某些船舶的航路。在航路系統中，其意味著該航路已經特別勘查，並盡可能確保遵循該建議航路航行的船舶可以避開危險。）

415. **Reefer container** (*n*) 冷凍貨櫃

Reefer containers are intermodal container that are used to transport temperature controlled cargoes such as fruits, meat, fish, seafood, vegetables across many miles and oceans.

（冷凍貨櫃乃指用來跨洋運送溫控貨物，諸如水果、肉類、魚、蔬菜等的複合運送貨櫃。）

While a reefer will have an integral refrigeration unit, they rely on external power, from electrical power points （"reefer points"） at a land-based site, a container ship.

（冷凍貨櫃內配置冷凍機，但須依賴來自岸端碼頭櫃場或貨櫃船提供的外部電源維持運轉。）

416. **Reefer plug** (*n*) 冷凍貨櫃插頭

Electrical power points at a land-based site.

（冷凍貨櫃的電源插頭；至於船上或岸上專供冷凍貨櫃使用的電源插座稱爲「Reefer Plug Socket」。）

417. **Reflector** (*n*) 反射器

A device fitted to buoys and beacons to reflect rays of light.

（一只裝置在浮標或標杆上方用以反射光線的設備。）

418. **Refuge harbor** (*n*) 避難港

An artificial harbor built on an exposed coast for vessel forced to take shelter from the weather.

（指建於曝露海岸線上的人工港，並藉以提供船舶被迫避開惡劣天候時的掩護。）

419. **Relative Humidity** (*n*) 相對濕度

Humidity of atmosphere when expressed as a percentage of the humidity of saturated air.

（大氣中的水蒸氣與在同溫度下飽和大氣的水蒸氣量的比例。）

420. **Reporting point (radio calling-in point, way point)** (*n*) 報告點、呼叫點、轉向點

A position in the approaches to certain ports where traffic is controlled by a navigation service at which ships entering or leaving report their progress as directed.

（在通往某些港口的航路上某一位置點，該點所在的船舶交通由航行服務中心管控，而且進入或離開該點的船舶應依指示報告其進程。）

421. **Restricted waters** (*n*) 限制水域

Areas which, for navigational reasons such as the presence of sandbanks or other dangers, confine the movements of shipping to narrow limits.

（某一水域基於航行考量，如沙洲或其危險的存在，限制船舶在限

定的範圍內運動。）

422. Rescue unit (*n*) 救援單位

A unit composed of trained personnel and provided with equipment suitable for the expeditions conduct of search and rescue operations.

（由經過訓練的人員組成，並配備適當設備以迅速執行搜索與救助作業的單位。）

423. Resolution (*n*) 決議案

A firm decision to do or not to do something.

〔（國際海事組織對海運社會作成）應作為與不應作為的明確決定。〕

424. Rhumb line (Loxodrome) (*n*) 恆向線

A line on the Earth's surface which makes a constant angle with the meridian.

（地表上一條與各子午線保持固定角度的線。）

425. Ride to the anchor (*n*) 錨泊

To lie at anchor with freedom to yaw and swing.

（讓船舶可以自由左右偏轉與繞圈洄游的錨泊狀態。）

426. Riding chain (*n*) 繫泊鏈

In permanent moorings, the chain cable that connects the mooring buoy with the ground chain.

（繫泊浮筒作業模式中，連接繫泊浮筒與橫臥於海床的底鏈之間之鏈條。）

427. Rise (*n*) 潮升

The level of High Water above Chart detum.

（指高潮水平面高出海圖基準面的高度。）

428. Rising tide (*n*) 漲潮

The period between Low Water and High Water.

（自低潮開始至高潮時的期間。）

429. River port (*n*) 河口港

A port that lies on the banks of a river.

（位於河岸上的港口。）

430. Roadstead (Roads) (*n*) 港外錨地

An open anchorage which may, or may not, be protected by shoals, reefs, &c., affording less protection than a harbour.

（位於港外而且欠缺淺灘、暗礁防護的開放型錨地，其提供的遮掩性較港口差。）

431. Roaring Forties (*n*) 咆哮四十、大西洋暴風雨帶

The belt in the oceans between 40°and 50° Nouth latitude, where there is unobstructed passage round the Earth for the prevailing westerly winds.

（指介於北緯40°與50°之間的西風盛行帶上環繞地球的暢通航路。）

432. Roll (*n*) 橫搖

The angular motion of a ship in the athwartship plane.

（船舶在橫向面的角運動。）

433. Rollers (*n*) 滾動巨浪

Swell waves sometimes grow in height as they move into shallow water to become destructive waves. Such waves are known as Rollers.

（當湧浪自大海進入淺水區時，其高度有時會增高進而變成破壞波，被稱為滾動巨浪。）

434. RORO (*n*) 駛上／駛下型船、滾裝船

A vessel designed to allow road vehicles to drive on and off when embarking and Disembarking.

（指一艘被設計成可以允許陸上汽車直接駛上船或駛下船的船舶。）

435.**Rotary streams** (*n*) 旋轉流

Tidal stream, the direction of which gradually turn either clockwise or anticlockwise through 360° in one tidal cycle.

（指一個潮流在一個潮流週期中，其流向會順時鐘或逆時鐘完成 360°旋轉。）

436.**Roundabout** (*n*) 迴旋分道區

A routeing measure comprising a separation point or circular separation zone and a circular traffic lane within defined limits. Traffic within the roundabout is separated by moving in a counter-clockwise direction around the separation point or zone.

（一個在明確界線內包含分隔點或圓環型分隔區，以及迴轉型分道航行巷道的航路措施；在迴轉區內的船舶必須繞著分道點或分道區循順時鐘或反時鐘方向航行。）

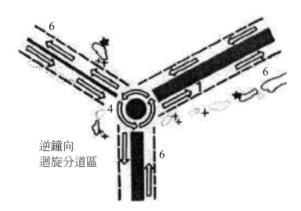

圖2.23 迴旋分道區

437.**Routeing system** (*n*) 航路系統

Any system of one or more routes or routeing measures, or both, aimed at reducing the risk of casualties. It includes TSS...

（任何由一個或多個航路或航路措施，或兩者結合構成的交通系統，旨在降低事故風險，包括分道航行制。）

438. **Rudder** (*n*) 船舵

A swinging flat frame hung to the stern post of a ship, by which the ship is steered.

（一只懸掛於船舶艉柱上可以轉動的板面，操船者可以藉由扳動它以操縱船舶。）

439. **Safe overhead clearance** (*n*) 安全淨空高度

The height above the Datum of Heights at which the highest point of a ship can pass under an overhead power cable without risk of electrical discharge from the cable to the ship.

（高出高度基準面的高度，船舶的最高點可安全自頂頭的電纜下方通過，而不會有從電纜放電到船上之危險。）

440. **Sailing Directions** (*n*) 航行指南

Are books issued by Hydrographic Offices containing matter concerning the waters, coasts, harbours, &c., of value to the navigator to supplement the chart.

（由水文機關所發行包含海水、海岸、港口等相關事項的書本，以補充紙本海圖的不足，對海員極具價值。）

441. **Sand dunes** (*n*) 沙丘

Mounds, ridges, or small hills of drifted sand.

（由流沙所堆積而成的沙丘或隆起的砂堆。）

442. **Sand waves** (*n*) 砂波

Wave-like sediment formations on the sea bottom, often composed of sand, which occur widely in shallow seas where there is relatively fast water movement.

（在海底形成的波浪狀沉積物，通常由沙組成，大多發生在水體快速通過大面積淺水區時。）

443.**SBM (Single Buoy Mooring)** (*n*) 單浮筒繫泊法

A large mooring buoy in open water to which a vessel, such as a tanker, moors to load or unload.

（位於空曠海域供船舶繫泊並裝卸貨物用的大型浮筒，如油輪即是。）

444.**Scale (on a chart)** (*n*) 海圖上的比例尺

A graduated line used to measure or plot distances.

（海圖上用以量度或測定距離的刻度線。）

445.**Scantling** (*n*) 材料構件的尺寸

A term applied to the dimensions of the frames, girders, plating, etc.

（船舶肋材、縱梁與船殼板的尺寸。）

446.**Scend or Send** (*n*) 隨波浪載沉、被海浪抬起、波浪的推（進）力、船的縱搖

A ship is said to scend heavily when her bow or stern pitches with great force into the trough of the sea.

（指船舶的艏部或艉部遭受波浪作用縱搖衝入浪谷的現象。）

447.**Scope** (*n*) 放出錨鏈的長度

The length or sweep of a mooring cable.

（船舶拋錨後，錨鏈放出或延伸的長度。）

448.**Screw driver** (*n*) 螺絲起子

圖2.24　螺絲起子

449.**Scupper** (*n*) 排水口、排水管

Any opening or tube leading from the water way through the ship's side, to carry away water from the deck.

（任何銜接船邊的排水道的開口或管子，用以排洩甲板上的積水。）

450.**Sea** (*n*) 海浪

The waves raised by the wind blowing in the immediate neighbour-hood of the place of observation at the time of observation.

（觀測者在觀測所在地當下所觀察到由鄰近地區的風力吹襲所造成的波浪現象。）

451.**Sea-buoy** (*n*) 標識港口或航道口最外邊的浮標

An object floating in water, moored to the bottom, to mark a point) usually the last seaward aid to navigation see when a vessel is leaving port and proceeding to sea.

（用以指示某一位置並繫固於海底的漂浮物。通常用於船舶自外海進入港口或河道，或離開港口與河道的最外端處的導航標誌。）

452.**Sea room** (*n*) 可供船舶運轉的水域

Space clear of the shore which offers no danger to navigation and affords freedom of manoeuvre.

（遠離岸邊無航行危險物，可供船舶自由運轉的水域空間。）

453.**Seasonal Changes (in Sea Level)** (*n*) 海平面的季節性變化

Variations in the sea level associated with seasonal changes in wind direction, barometric pressure, rainfall, &c.

（隨著風向、氣壓、降雨等季節性變化所造成的海平面差異。）

454.**Sea-way** (*n*) 外海

The open water outside the confines of a harbor.

（港口限制水域外的開闊海域。）

455. **Set (of the stream)** (*n*) 流向

The direction in which a tidal stream or current is flowing.

（潮流或洋流所流動的方向。）

456. **Secondary Port** (*n*) 次要港

A port for which tidal data is given in Tide Tables but for which daily predictions are not given.

（指一個潮汐資料被刊載於潮汐表中，但不包括每日預測值的港口。）

457. **Sector of a light** (*n*) 光弧

The portion of a circle defined by bearings from seaward within which a light shows a specified character or colour, or is obscured.

（從海上觀測某一燈塔，只能在界定的方位弧度內看到該燈塔顯示特定的燈質或顏色，或全滅。）

458. **Seiche** (*n*) 波動

Oscillations in water level which occur in harbours, bays, lakes, &c., having periods of a few minutes or more, the more spectacular ones being caused by abrupt changes in barometric pressure and wind.

（在港口、海灣、湖泊內發生的水平面振動，可持續幾分鐘甚或更久。如果是因氣壓或是風力的劇變產生者則更為明顯。）

459. **Self-sustaining ship** (*n*) 自備起重機的貨櫃船或裝卸設備的散裝船

Referring to a vessel able load and discharge itself.

（可以利用船上自備機具裝、卸貨物或貨櫃的船舶。）

460. **Semi-diurnal (Stream or Tide)** (*n*) 半日潮

Undergoing a complete cycle in half a day.

（在半天內經歷整個潮汐或潮流週期。）

461. **Separation zone or Separation line** (*n*) 分隔區或分隔線

A zone or line separation the traffic lanes in which ships are proceeding in opposite or nearly opposition direction, or separation a traffic lane from the adjacent inshore traffic zone.

（用來分隔相反或近於相反方向船舶航行巷道間，或分隔航行巷道與近岸航行區之間的區或線。）

462.**Shallow** (*n*) 淺灘

A shoal area in a river, or extending across a river, where the depths are less than those upstream or downstream of it.

（位於河流中或橫過河流，深度較其上游或下游水域淺的淺灘或沙洲區。）

463.**Shackle of cable** (*n*) 節；錨鍊的單位長度

The length of a continuous portion of chain cable between two joining shackles.

（在兩個連結卸扣之間，錨鍊連續部分的長度。）

1 Shackle = 15 fathoms or 90 feet

（1 節 = 15 噚或90呎）

464.**Shallow water effects** (*n*) 淺水效應（不同於船舶操縱領域所指的淺水效應）

A general term description of the distortion of the tidal curve from that of a pure cosine curve, most marked in areas where there is a large amount of shallow water.

（用來敘述潮汐曲線自純粹的餘弦曲線產生變形現象的通用名詞，在廣闊的淺水區域最爲明顯。）

465.**Sheer** (*n*) 船舶的突然偏轉 (*n*) 舷弧

A ship takes a sheer if, usually due to some external influence, her bows unexpectedly deviate from her course.

（當船舶突然遭受外力時，常會使船艏無預期地偏離既定航向。）

The upward curve of the upper deck in the fore-and-aft line of a ship.

（船舶主甲板在縱向面上的向上曲度。）

466. Shifting sand (*n*) 流沙

Sand of such fine particles and other conditions that it drifts with the action of the water or wind.

（由於水體或風的作用造成微粒或其它狀態沙子的移動。）

467. Ship's head (*n*) 船艏向

The direction in which a ship is pointing at any moment.

（在任何瞬間船艏所指向的方向。）

468. Shoal (*n*) 淺灘、沙洲

A detached area of any material the depth over which constitutes a danger to surface navigation.

（一片由任何物質形成且其深度對水面航行構成危險的孤立分離區域。）

The term shoal is not generally used for dangers which are composed entirely of rock or corol.

（淺灘一詞通常不指完全由礁石或珊瑚所構成的危險物。）

469. Shore (*n*) 海岸

The meeting of sea and land considered as a boundary of the sea.

（海與陸相會交際處，通常被認定爲大海的分界線。）

470. Silt (*n*) 淤泥

Sediment deposited by water in a channel or harbor or on the shore.

（由航道或港口或岸上的水體所沖積的沉澱物。）

471. Situational awareness (*n*) 情境警覺

Situational awareness means knowing what is going on around the ship at all times, enhancing the ability of the OOW to quickly recognize any ambiguities in the navigational situation and to take action before a hazardous situation develops.

（情境警覺係指隨時認知船舶四周正在發展中的事物，以提升駕駛臺當值駕駛員快速認知航行情境的任何疑惑狀況，並在發展成危險情勢之前採取行動。）

472.**Slack water** (*n*) 憩流

The period of negligible horizontal water movement when a rectilinear tidal stream is changing direction.

（指往復型潮流在改變潮流方向時，會有一段時間幾乎沒有水平向的水體運動。）

473.**Slick** (*n*) 浮油 (*n*) 船體迴轉造成的平靜水面

A local calm streak on the water caused by oil.

（油類漂浮在水面上的局部靜態斑紋或條紋。）

The calm patch left by the quarter of a ship when turning sharply.

（船舶採大舵角迴旋時，船艉橫掃水面後，會在船艉內側部留下一片平靜水面。）

474.**Snap back zones** (*n*) 繩索斷裂反彈區

A snap-back zone is the predicted area swept by sudden recoil of a mooring line as a result of its failure under tension.

（繩索斷裂反彈區是指繩索因張力過大斷裂，導致繩索急速反彈的預測區域。）

475.**Solstices** (*n*) 至點

The two points at which the Sun reaches its greatest declination N or S, or the dates on which this occurs.

（太陽在其運行軌道上運行至南、北赤緯最高時的兩點，即冬至與夏至；或是太陽抵達冬至與夏至的日期。）

476.**Sound** (*n*) 海灣、航道

A passage between two sea areas. A passage having on outlet at either end.

（兩個海域之間的水道；兩端有出口的水道。）

圖2.25　海灣

477.**Spate** (*n*) 大雨、洪水

The greatly increased rate of the current and rise in level in a river due to heavy rain or melted snow in the headwaters) under these conditions the river is said to be "in spate".

（由於暴雨或水源上游的融雪造成流速與河川水位的大幅增加，當河川處於此水位暴漲的狀況時稱為「in spate」。）

478.**Spar buoy** (*n*) 桿狀浮標

A buoy in the form of a pole which is moored to float nearly vertical.

（繫固於海底並幾近垂直的浮動圓桿狀浮標。）

479. **Species of Tide** (*n*) 潮型

The category of tides depending on its approximate period.

（依據潮汐的概略週期將潮汐加以分類。）

480. **Spending beach** (*n*) 破浪沙灘

The beach in a wave basin on which the waves entering the harbor entrance expend themselves, only a small residue penetrating the inner harbour.

（指位處波浪存在水域的沙灘，當波浪自外海通過其上進入港口時會耗盡能量，僅有極小部分的殘餘波浪會灌入港內。此等沙灘的存在有助於港內水面穩靜度的提升。）

481. **Spherical buoy** (*n*) 球型浮標

A buoy, the visible portion of which shows an approximately spherical shape.

（指一個可見部分呈現近乎圓形狀的浮標。）

482. **Spindle buoy** (*n*) 錐形浮標

A buoy, similar in height to a spar buoy, but conical instead of cylindrical.

（高度類似桿狀浮標，但是圓錐型而非圓筒型的浮標。）

483. **Spit** (*n*) 沙嘴、岬、狹長的暗礁

A long narrow shoal (if submerged) or a tongue of land (if above water), extending from the shore and formed of any material.

（由任何物質構成自岸邊向外伸展的狹長型水下淺灘或水面上陸地。）

484. **Spoil ground** (*n*) 廢土傾倒區

An area set aside, clear of the channel and in deep water when possible, for dumping spoil obtained by dredging, sullage. A spoil ground buoy marks the limit of a spoil ground.

（一塊遠離航道，並盡可能設置於深水區，專供拋棄挖濬的廢土或汙泥的區域。廢土傾倒區的界線都以廢土傾倒區浮標標示之。）

485.**Spring line** (*n*) 倒纜

Rope from forward (after) part of a vessel led outside and afterward to a point of attachment outside vessel.

〔自船艏朝後（或自船艉朝前）往船舶外舷送出至某固定點的纜繩。〕

486.**Spring tide** (*n*) 大潮

A tide of relatively large range occurring near the times of New or Full Moon.

（指發生在近新月或滿月時潮差相對較大的潮汐。）

487.**Squall** (*n*) 颮；帶有雨、雪、雹等的暴風

High Wind that arrives suddenly and ceases suddenly. May or may not blow in direction of the prevalent wind.

（指突然吹來的大風而且瞬即停止，吹襲方向不一定與盛行風一致。）

488.**Squat** (*n*) 船艉下沉、船艉下蹲

The difference in the way a ship sits in the water when moving through it compared with when she is stopped.

（船舶在行駛時，船艉部會較停止時產生不同程度的下沉，船速愈快下沉程度愈大。）

489.**Stability** (*n*) 穩定性、穩定度

Tendency of the ship to remain upright.

（船舶保持平正直立狀態的傾向。）

490.**Staith or Staithe** (*n*) 裝卸煤礦的專用碼頭

A berth for ship alongside where the walls or rails project over the ship, enabling the cargo (in most cases coal) to be tripped direct from railway trucks into the vessel's hold.

（一個專供船舶停靠裝運煤礦的碼頭，通常設有壁牆或軌道可延伸至船舶上方，再直接將軌道上車斗運送的煤炭傾倒入船艙。）

491. **Stand by engines** (*n*) 備俥

An order given to prepare the vessel, in all respects, for sea.

（要求船舶備妥出航所需各種相關操作與作業的指令。）

492. **Stand of the Tide** (*n*) 停潮

A prolonged period during which the tide does not rise or fall noticeably. In some cases this is a normal feature of the tidal conditions) in others it is caused by certain unusual meteorological conditions.

（指潮汐沒有明顯上升或下降的一段時間。此大多為潮汐狀況的正常特徵，但亦有因異常氣象條件所造成者。）

【註13】
停潮大都發生在退潮轉為漲潮或漲潮轉為退潮時，其持續的時間一般而言與潮差有關。潮差小時停潮時間較久；潮差大時停潮時間較短。由台灣沿海潮位觀測資料得知，除東北、西南及南端在乾潮時停潮時間最長可達數小時（次數並不多）外，其餘大都在數十分鐘之內。乾潮是指從退潮轉為漲潮時，海水位達相對最低時稱之。

493. **Stand on** (*n*) 保持航向

To continue on the same course.

（保持同一航向航行。）

494. **Standard Port** (*n*) 標準港

A port for which daily predictions of high and low water are gives in Tide Tables.

（在潮汐表上刊載其每日的高、低潮預測值的港口。）

495. **Standard Time** (*n*) 標準時間

The legal time common to a country or area, normally corresponding to that of the Time Zone in which it wholly or mainly lies.

（一個國家或地區共用的法定時間，通常依據該國家或地區全部或部分位於哪一個時區而定。）

496.**Steerage way** (*n*) 舵效速度

The minimum speed required to keep the vessel under control by means of the rudder.

（保持船舶可藉舵的運用而得以控制船舶運動方向所需之最小速度。）

497.**Steering Gear** (*n*) 操舵裝置

A term applied to the steering wheels, leads, steering engine and fittings by which rudder is turned.

（指包含舵輪、管線、舵機與相關設備可以扳動舵板的整套裝置。）

498.**Stem the tide** (*n*) 頂流航行

To proceed against the tidal stream at such a speed that the vessel kept still.

（船舶以某一速率逆著潮流航行，該速度可使船舶對地速度為零，即與陸岸保持相對不動。）

To turn the bows into the tidal stream.

（將船艏轉向頂流。）

499.**Stern line** (*n*) 艉纜

Transporting wire or rope that is run from stern of vessel to a position astern when warping.

（當船舶欲絞靠碼頭或岸邊時，從船艉往後方送出的鋼索或纜繩。）

500.**Stevedores** (*n*) 碼頭工人

The contractors and personnel who perform cargo operations for most ships.

（從事船舶貨物裝卸作業的承包商或人員。）

501. **Storm beach** (*n*) 暴風灘

One covered with coarse sand, pebbles, shingle, or stones, as the result of storm waves above the foreshore.

（當暴風浪沖擊前灘後，形成由粗砂、小卵石、礫石或石頭所覆蓋的海灘；前灘指高潮線和低潮線之間的海灘。）

502. **Storm signals** (*n*) 風暴信號

Visual warnings of bad weather in the form of cones and other shapes, flags, and lights, displayed at certain stations on the coast and in harbours.

（在岸邊或港口內的某些岸台顯示圓錐形或其他形狀的標誌、旗幟或燈光作為惡劣天候的視覺警報。）

503. **Strait** (*n*) 海峽

A comparatively narrow passage connecting two seas or two large bodies of water.

（連結二個海域或二個較大水體的相對狹窄水道。）

504. **Storm surge** (*n*) 風暴潮

A progressive wave of meteorological origin which, if its crest arrives at the time of high water, can cause exceptionally high tides.

（由氣象因素造成的前進波，如果其波峰在高潮時抵達岸邊，將造成異常高潮。）

505. **Strand** (*n*) 河濱、岸灘

Another name for a beach, especially when it is composed of sand.

（沙灘的別名，特指由沙子構成者。）

506. **Stream** (*n*) 水流

A body of water flowing along a bed in the earth, always in one direction.

（沿著地表底床流動的水體，通常會朝固定方向流動。）

507.**Submerged** (*n*) 淹沒

A feature is said to be submerged if it has sunk under water, or has been covered over with water.

（淹沒一詞係指目標物的外形沉至水下，或是全被水淹沒。）

508.**Sullage** (*n*) 流水所沉澱的淤泥

Refuse, silt or other bottom deposit dredged for disposal in a spoil ground, open sea, or some place clear of channel.

（挖濬作業取得欲拋棄於廢土傾倒區、外海或其他遠離航道的廢棄物、淤泥或其他底層沉積物。）

509.**Surf** (*n*) 碎浪、激碎浪

The broken water between the outermost line of breakers and the shore.

（發生在防波堤的最外緣線與岸邊間的激碎浪。）

510.**Surface current** (*n*) 表面流

A current which does not extend more than about 3m below the surface.

（存在於水面下三公尺以內的水流。）

511. **Surge** (*n*) 波浪高漲；波浪上升

The different in height between predicted and observed tides due to abnormal weather conditions.

（由於異常氣象條件，使得觀測與預測之潮汐產生高度上的差異。）

512.**Surging** (*n*) 船舶在碼頭上前後進動

The horizontal movement of a ship alongside due to waves or swell.

（由於波浪與湧浪的影響造成船舶沿著碼頭做水平向前後運動。）

513. **Survival craft** (*n*) 求生筏

A craft capable of sustaining the lives of persons in distress from the time of abandoning the ship.

（可以讓遇難人員自棄船開始後，得以持續維持生命的船艇。）

514. **Swash** (*n*) 激濺

The thin sheet of water sliding up the foreshore after a wave breaks.

（當波浪破碎後會在前灘上產生激飛的微小浪花。）

515. **Swell** (*n*) 湧浪

Waves which have travelled from some distant area, caused by wind but not breaking. Breaking waves may, however, be superimposed on swell due to local wind.

（由風所引起自遠處傳來而未破碎的波浪，但是也有當地風產生的湧浪會破碎，進而重疊在前述來自遠方的湧浪上。）

516. **Syzygy** (*n*) 朔望、對點、會合

An astronomical term denoting that two celestial bodies are in opposition or conjunction.

（用以表示二個天體約略成一直線的天文學名詞，日、月、地球成一直線即是。）

517. **Tank farm** (*n*) 儲油站、油庫

A large group of oil storage tanks, usually near an oil terminal or refinery.

（許多儲油槽構成的油槽群聚處，通常接近油碼頭或煉油廠。）

518. **Tendering** (*n*) 郵輪自外海錨地駁運旅客上岸與返船的作業

When cruise ships anchor, passengers are "tendered" to shore on tender boats.

（當郵輪因景點所在地的碼頭水深不足或水域狹窄致無法胃納巨輪入港時，只能錨泊外海，再利用郵輪船上稱爲「Tender」的接駁船，接送旅客上岸與返船的過程。）

519. **Territory** (*n*) 領土

Extent of land under the jurisdiction of a Sovereign, State, City.

（國家或城市管轄權所及的土地範圍。）

520. **Tidal harbor** (*n*) 潮汐港

A harbor in which the water level rises and falls with the tide as distinct from a harbor in which the water is enclosed at a high level by locks and gates.

（相對於某些藉由船渠與閘門的控制，於高潮時將水體封閉於港內的船渠港，只要港口內的水位會隨著潮汐漲落升降者就稱為潮汐港。）

521. **Tidal stream** (*n*) 潮流

The periodical horizontal oscillations of the sea in response to the tractive forces of the Sun and Moon.

（由於太陽與月球的牽引力，造成海水的週期性的水平向波動。）

522. **Tide pole** (*n*) 潮位水尺、測潮標杆

A graduated vertical staff used for measuring the height of the tide.

（用來量測潮汐高度的垂直刻度標尺。）

523. **Tide-rode** (*n*) 頂流錨泊

An anchored or moored ship is tide-rode when heading into the tidal stream.

（一錨泊或繫固於單一浮筒的船舶，當其船艏朝向潮流來向時稱之。）

524. **Tideway** (*n*) 受潮區、感潮段

Where the full strength of the tidal stream is experienced, as opposed to inshore where only weak tidal streams may be experienced.

（相對於近岸區只有感受較弱的潮流，遠離近岸區則須承受完全的潮流強度的水域稱之。）

525. **Time Zones** (*n*) 時區

Longitudinal zone of the earth's surface, each 15° in extent. Zone

0 straddles the Greenwich meridian from 7.5°E to 7.5°W. Zone 12 straddles the 180°meridian from 172.5°E to 172.5°N, and is subdivided into Zone +12, east of the meridian, and Zone-12 west of it. From Zine 0, zones are numbered in sequence, eastward from-1 to-12 and westward from +1 to +12.

（地表上劃定各含括經度15 的區域；「0時區」跨越格林威治子午線自7.5°E 到 7.5°W；「12時區」則跨越180°子午線自172.5°E 至 172.5°W，子午線之東爲+12時區，子午線之西爲-12時區。從「0時區」起依序向東從-1到-12時區，向西從 +1到 +12時區。）

526. **Tonnage, Gross** (*n*) 總噸位

The entire internal cubic capacity of a vessel expressed in "tons" taken at 100 cubic feet each.

（一艘船舶的內部總容積，以每100立方呎作爲一噸計。）

527. **Tonnage, Net** (*n*) 淨噸位

The internal cubic capacity of a vessel which remains after the capacities of certain specified spaces have been deducted from the gross tonnage.

（一艘船舶自總噸位扣除某些艙間的容積後所剩餘的內部總容積。）

528. **Tonnage Openings** (*n*) 噸位開口

Openings in shelter deck bulkheads for purpose of economy in tonnage rating.

（位於遮蔽甲板艙壁上的開口，可以減少計稅噸位。）

529. **Topmark** (*n*) 頂標

Identification shapes fitted on the tops of beacons and buoys.
（裝置在浮標或浮筒頂部的識別型材。）

530. **Topography** (*n*) 地誌、地形學

Detailed description or representation on a chart or map, of the natural and artificial features of a district.

（在海圖或地圖上對於某一地區的天然或人造的形狀特徵做詳細敘述或以圖像顯示。）

531. **Torrent** (*n*) 洪流、奔流、急流、傾盆大雨

A rushing stream of water.

（湍急的水流。）

532. **Tow** (*n*) 被拖船、被拖物

A group of barges (or ship's) secured together as a unit to be pushed or pulled by a towboat.

（一組繫固在一起被拖船推頂或拖曳，並被視為一個單位的駁船或船艇。）

533. **Track** (*n*) 航線、航跡

Used in ship's routeing to mean the recommended route to be followed when proceeding between predetermined positions.

Stictly speaking that part of a vessel's path which has already been travelled.

（在規劃船舶航路時用以表示船舶在既定位置點之間必須遵循航行的建議航路；嚴謹的說法應是指船舶已行駛過的船舶軌跡的一部分。）

534. **Trade Wind** (*n*) 貿易風

More or less constant winds that "tread" the same path for long periods. They blow from tropical high pressure areas towards the equatorial low pressure area.

（指長期間在相同路徑上固定吹襲的風。貿易風從熱帶高壓區吹向赤道低壓區。）

535. **Traffic separation scheme** (*n*) 分道通航計畫、分道通航制

A routeing measure aimed at the separation of opposing streams of traffic by appropriate means and by the establishment of traffic lanes.

（利用適當的方法與航行巷道的設定來分隔相反方向的交通流的航路措施。）

536. **Traffic lane** (*n*) 航行巷道

An area within defined limit in which one-way traffic is established. Natural obstacles, including those forming separation zones may constitute.

（指僅允許規定單向交通流並有明確界線的區域。可能利用天然障礙物作爲分隔區。）

537. **Training wall** (*n*) 導流堤

A mound often of rubble, frequently submerged, built alongside the channel of on estuary or river to direct the tidal stream or currents through the channel so that they may assist in keeping it clear of silt.

（指沿著河道或港灣岸邊由粗石造成且經常浸入水中的堤防，用來導引河道中的潮流或水流，期以協助改善河道的淤砂。）

538. **Transit** (*n*) 穿越、通過

Two objects in line are said to be "in transit".

（當觀測者觀測到兩目標成一直線時，稱爲「in transit」。）

539. **Transit Port** (*n*) 轉運港

A port where the cargo handled is merely in route to its destination and is forwarded by coasters, river craft, &c. The port itself is not the final destination before distribution.

（一個位於往目的港途中，僅供處理貨載的港口，貨載再由該港利用沿岸航行小船或河船運抵目的港。該港並非最終目的地。）

540.**Transit shed** (*n*) 通棧

A structure or building on a wharf or quay for the temporary storage of cargo and goods between ship and rail or warehouse, and vice versa. There is a legal difference between a transit shed under the shipowner's control and a warehouse which may not be.

（建於碼頭上僅供臨時儲存船舶、鐵路與倉庫間轉運的貨載之結構物或建築。法律上最大的差別是通棧通常是由船東所控制，而倉庫則不一定是。）

541.**Tributary** (*n*) 支流

A brook, stream, or river running into and serving to swell the volume of a larger river.

（流入河川的小溪或小河，並藉由其流入河川以增加河川的水量。）

542.**Trim** (*n*) 俯仰差 (*vt*) 平艙

The difference between the draft at the bow and at the stern.

（船舶艏、艉部的吃水差。）

To balance (a ship) by shifting its cargo or contents.

（藉由移動貨物或其他重物以平衡船體的平正。）

543.**Trough** (*n*) 波谷

The hollow between two waves.

（兩個波浪之間的凹槽部。）

544.**Tropical Spring tide** (*n*) 回歸大潮

The diurnal tide of maximum range associated with the Moon's maximum declination.

（當月球赤緯達到最大時所產生最大潮差時的全日潮。）

545.**Tropical Storm** (*n*) 熱帶風暴

Big storms which originating in tropical and law latitudes.

（源自熱帶與低緯度的大型風暴。）

546. **Tsunami** (*n*) 海嘯

A series of waves caused by a submarine earthquake, often travelling thousands of miles and building up to disastrous proportions on certain shelving beaches.

（由海底地震所造成的一系列波浪，經常可傳送到數千浬之外，並在緩斜坡海濱達到災難性的規模。）

547. **Turn-round** (*n*) 船舶滯港周轉時間

The turn-round of a vessel in a port is the complete operation comprising arrival, discharge and loading of cargo, and departure.

（船舶滯港周轉過程是一個完整的作業，包括抵港、卸貨、裝貨與離港。）

548. **Twilight** (*n*) 曙光／暮光

The light reflected and scattered by the upper atmosphere when the sun is below the horizon. The period when this light prevails.

（指在日出之前或日落之後，散射至地球大氣層的上層，照亮了低層的大氣與地球表面的陽光。這一太陽餘光的持續的時間間隔稱為曙光／暮光。）

549. **Two-way route** (*n*) 雙向航路

A route within defined limit inside which two-way traffic is established, aimed at providing safe passage of ships through waters where navigation is difficult or dangerous.

（位於一個具有明確界線的區域內的既定雙向交通航路，主在提供船舶在具航行難度或危險水域內的安全航路。）

550. **Typhoon** (*n*) 颱風

Violent cyclonic storm prevalent in seas around China, Japan and Philippines.

（盛行於中國、日本與菲律賓的猛烈氣旋風暴。）

551. **Under current** (*n*) 暗流

A sub-surface current. There is an implication that the under current is different either in rate or direction from the surface current.

（指水面下層的水流。其隱含暗流的流速與流向不同於表層流。）

552. **Under way** (*n*) 航行中

Means a vessel is not at anchor, or made fast to the shore, or aground.

（意指船舶處於未錨泊、未繫岸、未擱淺的狀態。）

553. **Unwatched light** (*n*) 無人看守的燈塔

A light without any personnel permanently stationed to superintend it.

（一個長期未派人駐守監管的燈塔。）

554. **Upstream** (*n*) 上游 (*adj*) 溯流而上的

The opposite direction to downstream.

（下游的相反方向；順流的反義字。）

555. **Variation** (*n*) 磁偏差、磁偏角

The Magnetic Declination, i.e. the angle which the magnetic meridian makes with the true meridian.

（磁偏角係指真子午線與磁子午線之間的夾角。）

556. **Veering** (*n*) 風向順轉

It means that wind altering direction clockwise.

（意指風向以順時鐘方向轉變。）

557. **Vertical clearance** (*n*) 垂直間隙

The height about the Datum for Heights of the highest part of the underside of the span of a bridge, or the lowest part of an overhead coble.

（從海圖高度基準面量至橋梁橋墩跨距橋體底部最高處或高架電纜線的最低部之間的高度。）

558. **Vessel Inward** (*n*) 進港船

A vessel which is proceeding from sea to harbor or dock.

（一艘自外海駛入港口或船渠的船舶。）

559. **Vessel Outward** (*n*) 出港船

A vessel which is proceeding from harbour or anchorage to sea-wards.

（一艘自港口或錨地駛往外海的船舶。）

560. **Vessel Turning** (*n*) 正在迴轉中的船舶

A vessel making large alteration in course such as to stem the tide when anchoring, or to enter, or proceed, after leaving a berth or dock.

（指一艘正在進行大角度轉向的船舶，諸如拋錨時需轉向頂流，或離開碼頭後的調頭運轉。）

561. **Vigia** (*n*) 位置可疑的礁石、海上不明事物或現象

A reported danger, usually in deep water, whose position is uncertain or whose existence is doubtful.

（經通報的危險物，通常指位於深水區，其位置不確定或其存在是可疑的。）

562. **Visible horizon** (*n*) 可見水平

The line where, to on observer, sea and sky appear to meet.

（觀測者可以見到海與天空交際的一條線。）

563. **Volcano** (*n*) 火山

A more or less conical hill or mountain from which, when active, steam, gases, molten rock, are ejected.

（近似圓錐形的丘陵或山丘，當其爆發時會噴出熱氣、瓦斯與熔漿。）

564.**Voluntary stranding** (*n*) 搶灘

The beaching or running a vessel purposely aground to escape great-er danger

（船隻有沉沒危險時，設法刻意使船隻擱淺在淺灘上，防止沉沒或遭遇更大的危險。亦有人將此作爲稱爲「Forced Landing」。）

565.**Voyage** (*n*) 航程

A sea journey between terminal points.

（兩端點碼頭之間的海上行程。）

566.**Wake** (*n*) 跡流

The disturbed water astern of a vessel, or the water through which she has passed.

（船舶尾部排出的亂流；船舶前進時沿著兩舷流向船艉的水流。）

567.**Warehouse** (*n*) 倉庫

A building situated on or near a wharf, quay, &c., in which cargoes are stored for distribution or shipment.

（位於或接近碼頭專供儲存與集散貨物的建築物。）

568.**Warm front** (*n*) 暖鋒

An indeterminate line on which a mass of warm air meets and rise over a mass of cold air. Its approach is usually accompanied by rain.

（指一暖氣團上升至冷氣團上方的不規則線。暖鋒接近通常伴隨著降雨。）

569.**Warp** (*vt*) 利用纜繩牽曳

To warp: To move a ship from one place to another by means of a rope used as a warp.

（利用絞進纜繩將船舶自某處移動至他處。）

570.**Wash** (*n*) 船舶航行過後排出的水流、沖積層

The visible and audible motion of agitated water. Especially that caused by the passage of a vessel.

（可以被聽得見也看得見的擾動水流。特別是由船舶通過後所造成者。）

The accumulation of silt and alluvium in an estuary.

（淤泥或沖積土在海灣處的堆積。）

571. **Waterfall** (*n*) 瀑布

The waters of a river or stream falling over a precipice.

（泛指自斷崖或絕壁流落的河川流水。）

572. **Waterline** (*n*) 水線、船舶吃水線

The line along which the surface of the water touches a vessels hull.

（海水平面與船殼相交處形成的一條線。）

573. **Watershed** (*n*) 分水嶺

The line of separation between the water flowing to different rivers, lakes, or seas.

（水流分別流向不同河川、湖泊或大海的分隔線。）

574. **Waterspout** (*n*) 水龍捲

Phenomenon in which a cloud forms a funnel-shaped pendant which descends towards the sea and draws up a corresponding hollow column of whirling spray which may form a pillar of water from cloud to sea, the whole travelling across the surface of the sea.

（由雲層所形成的倒懸煙囪狀，並往海面下降，同時吸取相對的中空圓柱形漩渦水花，常會形成自雲層至海面的水柱，並且產生在海面上移動的現象。）

575. **Watertight Compartment** (*n*) 水密隔間、水密艙間

A space or compartment within a ship having its top, bottom, and sides constructed in such a manner as to prevent the leakage of water into or from the space.

（船上某一經過加強其頂部、底部與四周的強度結構以防止水體從外進入或自內流出的空間或艙間。）

576. **Waterway** (*n*) 水路、航道

Navigable channel.

（可供航行的水道。）

577. **Wave** (*n*) 波浪

An undulation of the sea surface usually caused by wind.

（通常由風造成的海面波動。）

578. **Wave basin** (*n*) 破浪池

A device to reduce the size of waves which enter a harbor, consisting of a basin close to the inner entrance to the harbor in which the waves from the outer entrance are absorbed.

（用以降低進入港內波浪大小或規模的設計。通常由位於接近內港港口處的水池所構成，主在吸收自外港港口湧進的海浪。）

579. **Wave trap** (*n*) 鎮波浪設計

A device used to reduce the size of waves which enter a harbor before they penetrate as far as the quayage.

（用來減低進入港內波浪到達碼頭時的範圍與大小的設計。）

580. **Wave-cut shore** (*n*) 浪蝕海岸

A shore which is not a beach is wave-cut.

（海灘以外的海岸皆屬之。）

581. **Way** (*n*) 進程

The motion of a vessel through the water.

（船舶在水中的移動。）

582. **Weather** (*n*) 天氣

Phenomena of the atmosphere that affect mankind. These include wind, visibility, temperature, air pressure and precipitations.

（影響人類作息的大氣現象，包括風、能見度、氣溫、氣壓與降水等現象。）

583. **Weather side** (*n*) 上風舷

The side of a vessel towards which, or on the side of a channel from which, the wind is blowing.

（指船舶受風之一舷，或是航道、海峽中風吹出的一側。）

584. **Weather shore** (*n*) 上風岸

That from which the wind is blowing.

（風所吹出一側的岸邊。）

585. **Wharf** (*n*) 碼頭

A structure similar to a quay alongside which vessels can lie to discharge cargo, usually constructed of wood, and/or of concrete supported on piles.

（可供船舶泊靠卸貨的結構物，多為木頭材質建造，再由混擬土椿支撐。現今除少數內河或較小碼頭外，已少見木頭建造的碼頭。）

586. **Wharfage** (*n*) 碼頭費

In a general way, a charge made against cargo passed onto or over a wharf, quay or jetty.

（廣以言之，指船舶靠泊碼頭的貨物裝卸或進出倉庫所衍生的費用。）

587. **Wind drift current** (*n*) 風吹流

A horizontal movement in the upper layers of the sea, caused by wind.

（海面上層水流因風吹襲造成的水平向運動。）

588. **Wind-rode** (*n*) 船艏頂風

An anchored or moored vessel is wind-rode when heading or riding, into the wind.

（一艘錨泊或繫泊在浮筒上的船，當其船艏頂風時稱之。）

589. Wreck (*n*) 殘骸

Means a disabled vessel, either submerged or visible, which is attached to, or foul of, the bottom or cast up on the shore.

（意指無論已沉沒或可見，因觸底、陷入海底，或衝撞岸邊的失能船舶。）

590. Yaw (*n*) 水平左右搖轉

Unavoidable oscillation of the ship's head either side of the course being steered or when at anchor, due to wind and waves.

（船舶在錨泊中或航行中，受風與浪的作用，船艏無可避免地會向所欲操縱的航向的左右兩側擺動。）

591. Zone Time (*n*) 區時

The system of time-keeping used by a vessel at sea in which the time kept is that of the Time Zone appropriate to her position.

（船舶在海上所使用的記時系統，該時間為船舶位置所在的時區內的標準時間。）

第三章　航行聯絡用語

第一節　對外聯絡（Communication external）

　　幾乎所有船舶在進、出港，離、靠碼頭或在內河航行時，均須向港口的交通服務中心（Vessel Traffic Service, VTS）報到或報告，而且需要僱請引水人協助引航，因此船長與VTS、引水人與引水站（Pilot Station）之間會因為建立聯絡而產生許多對話，本章旨在介紹處此情境下海員應如何使用國際海事組織建議的常用標準航行聯絡用語。

- Given the global nature of the shipping business, language is always an issue in international shipping operations. English is the standard language of shipping and the IMO has developed a navigational code of basic commons in English.

  （由於海運業的全球性質，語言一直是國際海運運作的一個話題。英文爲海運社會的標準語言，而且國際海事組織亦已發展一套基本航海英文。）

- However, the pilot, captain, crew and VTS can communicate in whatever language everyone is most familiar with, if different from English.

  （無論如何，引水人、船長、船員及VTS在當前環境下，亦能使用除英文以外每個人都最熟悉的語言溝通。）

- Language barriers on foreign ships continue to be a serious obstacle to the safe navigation of other vessels in pilotage waters.

（外國船舶的語言障礙，仍然是影響引水區內其他船舶航行安全的最嚴重的障礙。）

- There is no doubt that email has revolutionized communication. But part of that revolution has been to multiply the to and fro communications to infinity.

（毫無疑問的，電子郵件已對聯絡造成革命性影響，但是此一革命的一部分已使往返的聯絡被增多至無限大。）

一、Vessel Traffic Services, VTS 船舶交通服務中心

在介紹常用標準航行聯絡用語之前，特介紹各國際商港配置的船舶交通服務中心。

- VTS is an essential service provided by a shore authority to help manage ship'straffic.

（VTS為岸際管理機關所提供，用以協助管理船舶交通不可或缺的服務。）

- A Vessel Traffic Service is a service implemented by a Competent Authority, designed to improve safety and efficiency of vessel traffic and to protect the environment. The service should have the capability to interact with traffic and respond to traffic situations developing in the VTS area.

（VTS為一由主管機關執行的船舶交通服務，設計用來改善船舶交通的安全與效率，以及保護環境。此一服務必須具備與VTS轄區內船舶互動，以及回應發展中交通情勢的能力。）(Re: IMO Guideline for Vessel Traffic Service Resolution A.857(20))

- VTS advice never <u>overrides</u> the primary function of the onboard navigation team, which is to maintain safety at all times.

  （VTS所提出勸告的執行位階不得<u>凌駕</u>於船上航行團隊為隨時保持船舶安全的主要功能。）

- It <u>aims to</u> improve safety and security, protect the environment and improve commercial efficiency, particularly in congested areas.

  （VTS的目的在於改善安全與保全、保護環境，以及改善商業效率，特別是對於海上交通擁擠區域。）

- Not all ports have a VTS；it is up to the country's government to arrange for this service where, in their opinion, the volume of traffic or the degree of risk requires it under their responsibilities stated in SOLAS.

  （並不是所有港口都設有VTS；沿海國政府根據其轄管水域的交通量，或是依據國際海上人命安全公約規定所賦予的責任下對於風險承擔程度的需要，決定是否設置VTS。）

- It is vitally important that VTS provision is harmonized on a global basis so that all ports are consistent and that mariners can feel comfortable using these services wherever they are in the world.

  （最重要的是，VTS的設置是以全球性運作為協調基礎，也因此所有港口的運作都是一致的，故而海員在全世界的任何地方使用此等服務時都能感到非常自在。）

- This crucial work is carried out by the International Association of Marine Aids to Navigation and Lighthouse Authorities (IALA).

  （此一艱難的協調作業由國際海上助導航與燈塔協會執行。）

- VTS is shore-based and the support it provides can range from providing simple information messages, such as the position of other traffic or meteorological hazard warnings, to extensive traffic organization within a port or waterway.

（VTS是以岸上爲基地，其所提供的幫助，從提供簡單的資料訊息，諸如其他船舶的位置或氣象（學）的危險警報，到港區或水道內的大量的交通安排。）

- The VTS can provide positioning or navigation assistance on request, in times of uncertainty or if a vessel's navigation equipment is malfunctioning. Such assistance can also be given if the VTS deems it necessary.

（VTS可以在不確定狀況或船舶航儀失常時候，應船方請求提供定位與航行協助。該等協助亦可在VTS認爲有需要時主動提供。）

- IMO Resolution A.857(20) stressing that, "when the VTS is authorized to issue instructions to vessels, these instructions should be result-oriented only, leavingthe details of execution, such as course to be steered or engine manoeuvres to beexecuted, to the master or pilot on board the vessel."

（IMO第A.857（20）決議案強調：「當VTS被授權可以對船舶發出指令，此等指令只能具有結果導向，而且須要將執行細節，諸如船舶操縱船的航向，主機的操作等留給船上的船長或引水人定奪。」例如，VTS不能指示船舶必須走什麼航向，以及多快的速度。）

- VTS tells you what the outcome of your actions should be, but not what to get the outcome. For example, the VTS may tell you to make good a course, but not what to steer to make that course good.

（VTS只告訴你「貴輪所採取行動的結果必須爲何」，但不會告訴你

124

「必須如何」達到其指示的結果。例如，VTS可能告訴你應行駛哪一航向，但不會告訴你「應如何」操船才能達致其所指示的航向。）

- The master of a vessel is not relieved from responsibility for the conduct and navigation of the vessel merely because the vessel is subject to vessel traffic service arrangements.

  （船長不能僅因為遵從VTS的安排，解除其對船舶操縱與航行的責任。）

- The authority of the Master is never compromise by participation in a VTS.

  〔船長的權力絕不因參與VTS（的系統運作）而被妥協掉。〕

- Care should be taken that VTS operations do not encroach upon the master's responsibility for safe navigation, or disturb the traditional relationship between master and pilot.

  （VTS的運作必須注意，不得侵犯船長關於安全航行的責任，或干擾船長與引水人之間的傳統關係。）

- Authorities that provide VTS should train their VTS personnel to high international standards, in line with the types of services being provided.

  （提供VTS服務的機關必須訓練其VTS人員達到符合其所提供的服務類型之高階國際標準。）

- Port authority should appoint dedicated VTS radar operator/traffic controllers with knowledge of collision avoidance, to watch and control precautionary areas.

  （港口主管機關應指派具備避免船舶碰撞知識的專職VTS雷達觀測操

作員或交通管制員以利監督並管控警戒區域。）

- Most VTS use radar and the Automatic Identification System (AIS) in order to detect, identify and monitor vessel movements.

  （大部分的VTS為了偵測、識別與監視船舶的運動，而使用雷達與自動識別系統。）

- Co-operation and understanding between the ship and the shore are essential to the safe operation of vessels in a VTS area.

  （船、岸之間的合作與了解對於VTS轄區內船舶的安全運作是非常重要的。）

- Most VTS operating procedures have been designed to meet international standards. For example, mariners can expect that VTS personnel are familiar with and, capable of, communication using the IMO Standard Maritime Communication Phrases (SMCP).

  （大部分的VTS操作程序都被設計成符合國際標準，例如，海員都期望VTS人員熟悉而且能夠以國際海事組織制訂的「標準海事通訊用語」進行聯絡。）

- What shipmasters can expect from VTS.

  （船長希望從VTS得到什麼。）

- Masters are expected to make best use of VTS in navigational decision making.

  （吾人期望船長在做航行決策時應善用VTS。）

- Mariners can expect that VTS has complete and reliable communications coverage of its area of responsibility.

（海員期待在VTS的責任區內能夠有完整且可靠的通訊（服務覆蓋）範圍。）

• Vessels operating in a VTS area should acknowledge information from the VTS when asked and respond promptly to inquire.

（在VTS區域內運航的船舶，請求VTS提供訊息時，必須確認所收到來自VTS的資訊，並迅速回應VTS的詢問。）

• Shipmasters are expected to adhere to VTS operating procedures and react to all warnings, advice and instructions.

（船長必須謹守VTS的操作程序，並對所有警告、勸告與指示做出反應。）

• As in any navigation situation, navigators are expected to exercise good seamanship and comply with the Collision Regulations.

（在任何航行情境下，航海員都被期待應施展優良船藝，並遵守避碰規則。）

第二節　專業海事通訊用語（Professional Words and Phrases）

一、IMO 字彙中動詞的用法

(一) 命令式 Imperatives

當執法（公務）單位或港埠管理機關有命令下達時，必須遵循清楚的規則，即每句用語必須以下列之句型起始：

- You <u>must</u> heave up anchor.（貴輪必須起錨。）
- You <u>must</u> increase speed.（貴輪必須增加船速。）

(二) 建議性字彙 Advisory words

不需用直接命令時，則不用命令式，句子可如下開始：

- (I) <u>advise</u> (you) ...（我建議您要……）
- (I) <u>advise</u> (you) not (to do ...)（我建議您不要……）
- (What ...) do you advise?（您的建議為何？）
- Advise you keep your present course.（建議貴輪保持目前的航向。）

(三) 標準動詞 Standard Verbs

1. 肯定式 Affirmative

You may ... 貴輪可以……

- You may enter.（貴輪可以進港。）

Advise ... 建議……

- Advise you slow down.（建議貴輪減速。）

There is ... 有……

- There is a vessel turning.（有一艘船舶在迴轉中。）

2. 否定式 Negative

I do not require ... 本輪不需要……

- I do not require a pilot.（本輪不需要引水人。）

I am not ... 本輪未……

- I am not passing ...（本輪未通過……）

3. 疑問式 Interrogative

Are you ... ? 貴輪是否……？

- Are you obstructing fairway?（貴輪是否阻礙航道？）

Do you have ... ? 貴輪是否具有……？

- Do you have steerage way?（貴輪是否仍保有操舵有效速度？）

4. 回答 Reply

(1) 當回答問題是肯定時即說「Yes」。

(2) 當回答問題為否定時說「No」。

(3) 當所需情報無法立即獲得，但將馬上獲得時即說「Stand by」。

(4) 當所需之情報不能獲得，即說「No information」。

(5) 當訊息並未聽清楚，請求重發時應說「Say again」。

(6) 當訊息不了解時，應說「Message not understood」。

實務上，不正確的術語常被使用。茲將職場上常聽聞的錯誤術語列舉如下：

(1) 「Affirmative」、「Roger」、「Willdo」（照辦）、「Right」等代替「Yes」。

(2) 「Negative」、「No way」代替「No」。

(3) 「Wait」（「Wait on」即「Wait one minute」），或「Hang on」代替「Stand by」。

(4) 「Don't know」代替「No information」。

(5) 「Repeat」代替「Say again」。

(6) 「Who is calling」代替「Station calling」。

(四) 緊急通訊 Emergency message

依據狀況緊急的程度，緊急通訊分成下列四類：

1. 「Mayday」用於遇難信號之前。

2. 「Pan」用於緊急信號之前。

3. 「Securite」用於安全信號之前。

4. 「Attention」用於重要通訊開始時。

• Mayday! Mayday! This is Ocean. I need help, I am sinking.

（Mayday！Mayday！這裡是「海洋」輪，本輪需要援助，本輪正在沉沒中。）

- Pan! Pan! This is Sky. I require medical assistance.

　（Pan！Pan！這裡是「天空」輪，本輪需要醫藥援助。）

- Vega: Pan-Pan! Pan-Pan! Tulip. This is Vega. You are running into danger. Shallow water ahead of you. Over.

　（「織女星」：Pan-Pan！Pan-Pan！「鬱金香」。這裡是「織女星」，貴輪正駛向危險，淺水區位於貴輪前方，完畢。）

- Securite! Securite! Floating ice in position...

　（Securite！Securite！有浮冰位於……）

- Attention! Attention! all ships, A warning of storms was issued at 2000 hours starting ...

　（Attention！Attention！所有船舶！暴風雨警報已在2000時發布，自……開始。）

(五) 通訊品質、強度 Communication quality

　　通訊品質係指通訊各方所收到對手方的語音強度與清晰度，分成下列五級：

I read you
- bad/I with signal strength 1 / barely perceptible（僅可收到）
- poor/2 with signal strength 2 / weak（微弱）
- fair/3 with signal strength 3 / fairly good（普通）
- good/4 with signal strength 4 / good（良好）
- excellent/5 with signal strength 5 / very good（非常很好）

- I read you with signal strength 4 (or good)

　〔本輪收到（聽到）你的信號強度良好。〕

- Stand by on channel...〔請在……頻道稍候（守聽）。〕

- Change to channel ...（請轉至……頻道。）

- I cannot read you. (Pass your message through vessel...) / (Advise try channel ...)

（我無法收到您的信號。）（請經由……船轉傳。）／（建議試試……頻道。）

- I cannot understand you. Please use the Standard Marine Vocabulary / International Code of Signals.

（我無法了解你的意思，請使用IMO標準海事用語。）

- Pilot is coming to you. Stand by on channel 12.

（引水人正在前往貴輪途中，請守聽第12頻道。）

二、常用專業詞彙

1. Position 位置

位置可用兩種方法來表示：

- 以緯度及經度表示之。

Your position is 15 degrees 20 minutes North, 30 degrees 10 minutes West.（你的位置在北緯15°20'、西經30°10'。）

- 以岸上一個定點或固定目標物的方位及距離標示之。

Your position is 330 degrees 4 miles from Yeliou Cape.（你的位置在野柳岬方位330°、距離4浬處。）

2. Course 航向

航向皆自正北起算，順時鐘方向360°表示之（除非另有說明，否則皆以真北為準）。為了要到達某一目的港，或是由某一地點起航，都必須要有正確的航向。

例：某船到達目的港，港口VTS利用VHF給予該船指令，指示該船的航向以便到達航道浮標。

- YM Happy this is Keelung VTS.

（Y輪！這是基隆船舶交通服務中心。）

- You are on port side of fairway.

（貴輪船位位於航道的左側。）

- Advise you make course 220 degrees to reach fairway buoy.
  （建議您航向220°，始可抵達航道浮標。）
- Your position is 045 degrees 6 miles from fairway buoy.
  （你的位置在航道浮標方位045°、距離6浬處。）

3. Bearing 方位

真方位乃以360°表示之，與相對方位不同，因相對方位是由船艏向左或向右算起。真方位乃是以真北為準，順時鐘起算360°。方位亦可以目標為準，量向本船；或以本船為準，量向目標。

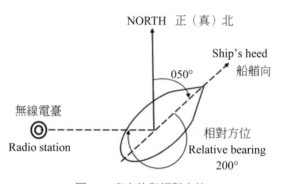

NORTH 正（真）北

Ship's heed 船艏向

050°

無線電臺
Radio station

相對方位
Relative bearing
200°

圖3.1　真方位與相對方位

4. Distance 距離

在航海領域，距離應以海浬（mile）或鏈（cable）表示之。

- Your position is 230 degrees 10 miles from Keelung Pilot Station.
  （你的位置位於基隆引水站方位230°、距離10浬處。）

5. Height 高度

幾乎全世界所有的國家皆以公尺來表示高度。因此高度需以公尺（meter）為單位來標示。單位標示必須清楚，否則極易造成嚴重的錯誤及影響。

例：

- My height is 25 meters. （我的高度是25公尺。）可改為：My

height is 82 feet. （我的高度是82呎。）

- My height is 25 meters, repeat 25 meters. （我的高度是25公尺、重複！是25公尺。）可改為：My height is 82 feet, repeat 82 feet. （我的高度是82呎、重複！是82呎。）

【註1】
如在習慣以「呎」為單位的國家（如美國），若單位誤用成「公尺」或未註明所使用的單位，極可能因誤導而造成船舶撞擊碼頭的危險。

6. Depth 深度

大部分的國家，皆用公尺表示海圖圖示水深的深度及船舶的吃水。不過，仍有許多海圖沿用「噚」（Fathom）為單位（1噚 = 6呎），或是以「呎」（Feet）為單位（如美國）。基本上，每張海圖上面皆須註明所使用的深度單位，否則極易導致嚴重的意外。

例：

- Minimum depth of water in fairway is 10 meters.

  （航道的最小水深為10公尺。）

7. Speed 速度

速度以「節」（Knot；一浬／時）來表示，可表示水面（對水）速度或實際（對地）速度。

例：

- 表示水面速度

  My present speed is 14 knots.

  （我目前的速度為14節。）

- 表示實際速度

  Advise speed over the ground 13 point 5 knots.

  （建議貴輪對地速度13.5節。）

8. Numeral 數字

數字須以英文逐字且清楚地唸出，如270應唸成「Two-Seven-Ze-ro」，而7.5應唸成「Seven Point Five」。又大部分以英語為母語的地區，都會將「Zero」，即「O」唸成「Oh」。須注意在IMO標準海事英語詞彙中「Zero」的唸法才是對的，而「Oh」是錯誤的。

9. Time 時間

時間以24小時制表示之，無論是格林威治時（GMT）、區時（ZT）或當地平均時（LMT）皆是如此。

10. Underway 航行中

- I am underway.
  （本輪在航行中。）

【註2】

「Underway」一詞在1972年國際海上避碰規則第3(1)條的解釋為：「指船舶未錨泊、未繫岸或未擱淺者（means that a vessel is not at anchor, or made fast to the shore, or aground.）。」

11. Destination 目的港

- My destination is Keelung port. （本輪的目的港是基隆港。）

某些大港口有好幾個航道入口處，那就必須明示出本船欲前往之引水站名稱，例如：「Keelung port, North Pilot Station.」（基隆港北引水站。）

12. ETA (Estimated Time of Arrival) 預計到達時間

- My ETA is 2200 hours local time.
  （本輪預計於當地時間22:00到達。）

【註3】

所謂「預計到達時間」，實務上通常就是抵達目的港引水站的時間。

時間必須以24小時制來標示。有時為了要確定目的港時區之時間，抵港前可先查詢當地分公司或船務代理業者。在某些施行「夏令時間」國家，時間並未依常例向前撥快，所以最好同時申報當地及格林威治兩種時間。

13.ETD (Estimated Time of Departure) 預計離港時間

14.Draught 吃水

• My draught forward is 6.5 meters, and my draught aft is 7.2 meters.

（本船船艏吃水為6.5公尺，船艉吃水為7.2公尺。）

【註4】
「吃水」係指由水線量到船底之深度。船舶之「吃水」會因載重不同而有變化，考量安全餘裕，「吃水」一般均採用最深者，即船舶艏艉之最深「吃水」值。

135

15.List 傾斜

• I have a list to port of one degree.

（本船向左舷傾斜一度。）

【註5】
「List」一詞為船舶向左舷或右舷傾斜之意。由於裝貨時未將貨物左右平均分配於船中線兩側，而導致船體傾斜。在淺水區如船體傾斜會增加船舶吃水，而減低龍骨下之水深，尤其對於船寬較大的船舶，此一影響因素更加重要。而且操船時亦難保持艏向穩定。

16.Visibility 能見度

• Visibility is reduced by fog.

（能見度因降霧而減低。）

能見度增加（to increase／become greater）或減少（to decrease／become less）或減低（be reduced／make less）。

17.Fog 霧

當大氣中之小水滴減低能見度至1,000公尺以下時，即發布有霧。

又當大氣中之小水滴減低能見度至1,000公尺與2,000公尺之間時稱之為靄（Mist）。

18.Salvage operation 海難救助作業

- There are salvage operation on South side of fairway...

（在航道南邊有救難作業。）

【註6】
一般救助遇難船舶或貨物的行動，不會僅是單純的拖救作業而已，常包括拖救擱淺後的危險船舶，使擱淺船舶再浮起（Refloating），或清除沉船，故而遇到此種作業時，均應遠離，並以慢速前進。

19.With caution 小心、謹慎，即Carefully之意

- Vessels must navigate with caution.

（船舶必須小心航行。）

20.Turn 轉向

- Vessel YM Happy will turn at Refinery Quay.

（YM Happy將在煉油廠碼頭水域迴轉調頭。）

【註7】
IMO對船舶轉向（Turn）之定義為「船舶之航向有大角度的改變，譬如利用拋錨以讓船艏頂流，或進港時，或於離開船席、碼頭準備航行時。」在此種狀況下即可確知「YM Happy」將由拖船協助轉向，而且會阻礙航道一段時間。

21.Vessel turning 船隻調頭中

- The vessel ahead of you is turning.

（位於貴船前方的船舶正在調頭中。）

表示位於您前方的船舶正在進行近180°的轉向，例如下錨頂潮流而行，或進入港、河或離開碼頭泊地。船舶能自行或招請拖船協助調頭。

22.Fairway 航道

- I will wait...before entering the fairway.

（在進入航道前，本船將等候……。）

23.Reduced speed 較慢的速度

- I am proceeding at reduced speed.

（本船正減速航行。即以慢於平常的速度航行。）

24.Clear 無障礙

- I will wait for YM Happy to clear.

（我將等待Y輪至無障礙爲止。即等到「YM Happy」完成轉向，而航道不再受阻之時。）

25.Last port of call 上次靠泊之港口

- Where you have come from?

（你從何處來？）

- My last port of call is Keelung.

（本船上一個灣靠港口爲基隆。）

26.Angle of loll 傾覆角度

【註8】

「list」為傾斜角度，乃因裝貨不當所引起者，雖然有傾斜之角度，但並非意味船舶處於不穩定狀態或疑似將翻覆。但「Angle of loll」則為傾覆角度。

27.Aground 擱淺

- Keelung Port VTS! This is Giant. I am aground.

（基隆港VTS！這裡是Giant輪，我已擱淺。）

【註9】

當船舶的吃水大於當時的水深，而在海底上停住時稱之為「擱淺」，此種情形可因意外，或故意（Intentional）造成。如係故意擱淺，也許是為了裝貨之目的，須加強其穩定性而搶灘，一般大船很少這麼做。基本上，實務上的故意擱淺，大多是為避免造成更大損害發生的停損措施。船舶僅在其不能移動時，始稱之為擱淺，若船舶在泥濘的海底上，還能夠移動的狀況下，則不能稱為擱淺。

28.Cable 鏈（1鏈為1/10浬）

- 180° one cable from Keelung.

  （位於基隆港方位180°、距離1鏈之處。）

29.Navigation is closed 航行（區域已）被關閉

- Navigation is closed in area one mile upstream...

  （在⋯⋯上游1浬處之航行區域已被關閉。）

30.Upstream、Downstream 上游、下游

- ...in area one mile upstream, one mile downstream Taipei.

  （在台北上游/下游1海浬之區域。）

【註10】

「Upstream」為上游，即朝內陸的方向，亦即遠離河口的方向。「Downstream」為下游，即朝向大海的方向，亦即朝河口接近的方向。

31.Casualty 海難

- ...unless you have message about the casualty.

  （除非你有關於此次意外海難的消息。）

  此指涉及該次意外海難之所有船舶而言。

32.Allocate 指派、指泊

- Anchor position...has been allocated to you.

  （已指派錨位給貴輪。）

  此句表示基隆VTS指定了拋錨的錨位給該抵港船舶。

33.Obstruct 阻礙

- You are obstructing other traffic.

  （你正阻礙到其他船舶的航道。）

34.Assistance 援助

- Assistance is no longer required.

  〔（本船）不再需要援助。〕

因為緊急狀況已經結束；若是拒絕他船或陸上單位之協助，則應說成「Assistance is not required.」。

35.Sufficient depth of water 足夠之水深

* Is there sufficient depth of water?

（有足夠水深嗎？）

即水深是否足夠？對擱淺船而言，要由擱淺的地方脫離，必須等待水深增加，如等待漲潮或高潮。

VTS確定地回答：「Yes, there is sufficient depth of water.」（是，水深足夠。）

36.Tides 潮汐

吾人應注意到在港口作業實務領域中，相關作業人員關於潮汐現象所使用的相關名稱，並非如IMO標準船用航行用語所述一樣。以下特列舉差異比較：

IMO Term	Common Equivalents
The tide is rising.	The tide is flooding. Flood tide.
The tide is falling.	The tide is ebbing. Ebb tide.
The tide is slack.	Slack water. Top of the flood. Bottom of the ebb. High water. Low water.

【註11】

由於各種原因，當海水之深度到達最大值或最小值時，不一定會發生憩潮（Slack water）現象。

1. 漲潮時，隨而產生之海水的移動稱之為漲潮流。

2. 落潮時，隨而產生之海水的移動稱之為落潮流。

3. 假如因風之狀況，導致圖示水深增加或減少，吾人稱之為不正常潮水。

37.Assistance 援助

船舶一定是因本身技術與動力無法行動，而真正需要幫助之時，才請求援助。例如：

(1) 船舶在航道中擱淺，需由拖船之協助，使其再浮起。

(2) 船上有受傷之海員，需要醫藥援助。

(3) 船舶失火時，需要滅火之援助。

38.Heave up anchor 起錨

• I am heaving up anchor.

（本船正在起錨。）

IMO航行用語所述的「起錨」一詞為將錨自錨地絞起，一直到將錨收回錨鏈筒內之整個過程。

39.Traffic 航行船舶及交通狀況

• Is there any other traffic?

（在航道上是否有任何其他船舶移動？）

【註12】

實務上，「Traffic」一詞係指船舶與由其航行運動構成之整體交通狀況。IMO用語中「Traffic」一詞則指包括所有水上航行的船艇，由大船到小船，凡能影響或干擾其他船舶之航行者均屬之。

40.Fairway speed 航道速度

• Fairway speed is eight knots.

（航道速度是8節。）

【註13】

在IMO之定義中，此為船舶行駛航道中之規定速度，但有時因潮流影響，會產生不同的對地速度（Speed Over Ground），也許會增加或減少。

41.Rig 裝置或架設船上某種設備或屬具

- You must rig pilot ladder on port side.

  （你必須在貴船左舷裝置引水梯。）

42.Mayday relay 轉播遇難信號

意指某船所發出的遇難信號，將經由他船或海岸電臺予以轉播者。

【註14】

當某船或某海岸電臺收到一遇難船發出之「Mayday」遇難信號時，該船或海岸電臺可將信號重新再轉播出去，即稱之為「Mayday relay」。此可能因為發送台所發射之信號太微弱，或是其無線電頻率不適用於遇難信號之發送，故有此必要之轉播機制。

43.Say again 再說一遍

- What is position of vessel ...? Say again.

  （某船之船位為……？再說一遍。）

即訊息未明確收到，請求再複述一遍。

【註15】

儘管IMO倡議「Say again」多年，但實務上無論船台或岸台仍常用「Repeat」一詞，有識者應避免使用。

44.Following received 下述之信文已被收到

- Following (message) received from yacht Yusho.

  （以下信文是收自遊艇Yusho。）

即「the following message has been received.」

（下述之信文已被收到。）

45.Correction 更正

- ... 160° six miles from Taipei Pier. Correction: 160° four miles from Taipei Pier.

（由Taipei Pier量起，方位160°、距離6浬處。更正，由Taipei Pier量起，方位160°、距離4浬處。）

即因先前無線電臺將遇難船舶之船位報錯，故使用更正程序將錯誤改正。

46.Standard Marine Vocabulary (IMO) 標準海事通訊字彙與用語

- I cannot understand you. Please use Standard Marine Vocabulary.

（我不了解你的意思，請用標準海事通訊用語。）

47.Search and Rescue (S.A.R) 搜索與救助行動

- Please take command of search and rescue.

（請接手指揮搜索與救助行動。）

【註16】
船舶遇難情境如發生在交通頻繁或擁擠的水域，常會有多艘船舶先後抵達遇難位置，此時應由其中一艘船舶擔任現場指揮船，統籌運用救難資源，以爭取時效。

48.Rocket 火箭

- Is it safe to fire a rocket?

（施放火箭安全嗎？）

此種火箭為降落傘式火箭，若該船有可燃性液體或瓦斯存在時，就會很危險。

49.Make a lee 營造下風（環境）

- I will make a lee for you.

（我將使你處於下風位置。）

即救援船可在遇難船正橫上風位置處，為其擋風，使遇難船位在下風位置，可免被風和水流之侵襲，以便進行救援工作。大船接送引水人時亦應營造下風，以確保引水人安全。

50.Weighing anchor 起錨

起錨是將錨自海底絞起，直到錨具完全離開海底為止。

51.Let go 下錨

- Let go starboard anchor.

  （拋下右錨。）

當船舶到達錨位而必須拋錨時，即下達此命令。如船舶進港靠泊碼頭，趨近岸壁速度太快時，引水人也會下達緊急之拋錨指令，此時下錨之行動必須快速，以免導致危險。

52.Shorten cable 將錨鏈絞短

- You must shorten your cable to three shackles.

  （你必須將錨鏈絞回至3節。）

亦即必須起錨直到只有三節錨鏈留在水中，此指令通常是引水人欲將船舶由錨地帶領進入港口時，為縮短起錨作業時間，於登船前由引水站所下達的。

53.Slip anchor 錨滑脫

- I have slipped my anchor in position ...

  （本船的錨具已滑脫掉在……。）

在緊急狀況時，可能考慮將某一卸扣（shackle）拆掉，以切斷錨鏈，使錨或整個錨鏈滑脫掉入水中。

54.Dredging anchor （故意）拖錨

如謂某船「拖錨」行駛，乃指其將錨放至海底，並鬆出短鏈拖著錨航行。大多是操船者為方便操控船舶所採取的技術性運用。

55.Dragging anchor 流錨、走錨

如謂某船「流錨、走錨」，乃表示其所拋之錨在不可抗力因素影響下已無法防止船舶之移動，而導致錨在海底移位。大多是外力影響所造成的。

56. Anchor position 錨位

錨位乃指船舶已下錨或欲下錨的位置。

57. Foul anchor 錨障

錨與本身的錨鏈互相絞纏，或是纏住他船錨鏈或障礙物。

三、分道航行制 Traffic Separation Scheme

此種海上交通制度是將航行方向相反或近似相反的航道利用分道區（Separation zone）、分道線（Separation line）、分道巷道（Traffic lane）或其他的方式做分隔。

1. Traffic lane 航行巷道

- Is it clear for me to enter traffic lane?

（此時本船進入航行巷道是否可以避開他船或障礙物？）

2. Alter course for identification 轉變航向做識別

- You must alter course for identification.

（貴輪必須做大角度轉向以供識別。）

【註17】

當岸上的航行管制台在它的雷達幕上發現許多船舶時，很不容易知道哪一艘船發出無線電訊號要求指引。一旦要求指引的船舶做出大角度的改變航向，將有助於岸上航行管制台由雷達幕上辨認出來。

3. Crossing traffic 橫越航行巷道或航路的船舶

- You will meet crossing traffic at position off Fuguei Cape.

（貴輪將在富貴角外海遭遇橫越貴船航路的船舶。）

4. Separation zone or line 分隔區或分隔線

為利用一區塊或線段將某一方向航行的船舶與另一方向航行的船舶分開，分隔區也可以用來分隔航行巷道與附近的「近岸航行區」。

5. **Traffic lane** 航行巷道

在指定範圍內的航行區域，通常將該範圍設為單向航行區域，並規定航行方向。

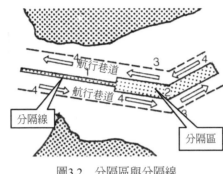

圖3.2　分隔區與分隔線

6. **Fairway** 航道

可供船舶航行的水域。

7. **Roundabout** 圓環、圓形迴轉區

係指一限定範圍之圓形區，在該區域內各船均以一特定點或區域為中心，逆時鐘方向環繞航行。

8. **Inshore traffic zone** 近岸航行區

係分道航行區的陸岸側界線與陸地海岸線之間某指定範圍之區域，此區域專供沿岸航行之船舶使用。

9. **Two-way route** 雙向航道

為指定界限的範圍內，供船舶做雙向航行之區域。

10. **Track** 航跡

為兩預定地點之間，最易被船上接受之建議航路。

11. **Vessel crossing** 橫越船

指以90°或近似90°的角度橫越航行巷道或航路之船舶。

12.Hampered vessel 運轉能力受限之船舶

指某些因工作關係致使船舶運轉能力受限制之船舶。

13.Navigational hazard/risks 航行危險

- The vessel failed to monitor its passage after altering course due to current, and was at risk of grounding on Stagg Patches.

（該船在轉向後疏於檢視其受流水影響的航跡，因而陷入即將擱淺於SP淺礁的風險。）

- Keelung VTS contacted the vessel to alert them to the danger. The vessel changed course and the grounding was averted.

（基隆VTS與該船聯絡並警告其危險，該船於轉向後避免擱淺。）

四、航行警告 Navigational warnings

1. Situation report 情境報告

情境報告可分為三大部分：

(1) 航行報告：

此報告包含通報某些具特殊航行要求或限制的船舶，例如被拖帶的巨大物體，諸如鑽油井（Oil rig）或浮塢（Floating dock）等都視為運轉能力受限的拖航行為。同時也包括航行在錯誤航行巷道中的船舶。

(2) 天氣及能見度報告：

包含可能預期到的任何不正常天氣狀況。

(3) 助航設備報告：

如浮標移位或不亮，造成航行障礙的新沉船，或一些移動中的危險障礙，以及第一項所述造成操作困難的拖航作業等。

2. Not complying with 未遵守

- There is a vessel ... which is not complying with traffic regulations.

〔有一艘船舶（船名）目前未遵守交通守則。〕

3. **Wreck buoy** 沉船浮標、做沉船記號之浮標

- There is a wreck buoy in position ...

  （有一沉船浮標位於……。）

4. **Unlit** 不亮

- ... a wreck，buoy ... unlit. （標示沉船、殘骸；浮標的燈光熄滅。）

5. **A difficult tow** 讓船舶運轉困難的拖航作業

- There is a vessel with difficult tow ...

  （有艘船舶正拖帶著影響其運轉的被拖船或物。）

6. **Squall** 暴風

- Winds North-West force 6, gusting to force 10 in squalls.

  （西北風六級，陣風增至10級暴風。）

暴風有時還伴隨著下雨、雪。Gusting指瞬間風速高於當下一段時間內平均風速的較強陣風。

7. **Running into danger** 將進入或陷入危險狀況

- Unknown ship ... You are running into danger.

  〔不知名船舶！（貴輪若持續目前運動狀態）貴輪將陷入危險狀況。〕

8. **Flammable / inflammable** 可燃性（貨載）

- I am leaking flammable cargo.

  （本船裝載的可燃性貨載正在洩漏中。）

9. **Noxious** 有害的、有毒的

「有害的」物質具有「毒性（Toxic）」，但其所具危險性低於「Poisonous」。

10.Poisonous（toxic）毒性的

如果吞入、吸入或接觸到有毒性物質，恐會嚴重損傷身體健康，甚至死亡。

11.Jettison 拋棄貨物入海

- I am jettisoning dangerous cargo.

（本船正拋棄危險貨物入海。）

【註17】

傳統航海實務上，拋棄貨物入海的目的是為避免船舶遭受更嚴重的損壞，如船舶擱淺後，藉由減輕船舶重量以便順利浮起，或改善船舶穩定性不良拋棄甲板貨的情形。但貨物意外落入海中並不能解釋成「Jettison」，如天候惡劣。

必須強調的是，上述例句中拋棄「危險貨物」入海的做法，除非有急迫危險，在當前環保法規嚴謹的約束下，絕對不是明智合法之舉。採行之前務必要先諮詢公司風險管控與危險貨物主管部門。

12.Stand by 備便、稍待、隨時候召

- 依據IMO航行字彙：「Where information is not available, but soon will be, say stand by.」。

（所謂「稍待」，係指目前沒有消息，但很快就會答覆。）

- Stand by to give assistance.

在海難救助的情況下，針對提供救援的船：「貴船在安全可能範圍內，盡量接近遇難船舶，並在該處等待，一直到對方要求援助」的意思。

13.Wind force / speed 風力 / 風速

- Wind North-West force 4.（西北風風力4級）

風力利用蒲氏風級表（Beaufort scale）表示。風速的單位為「節」（Knots）或「公里」（Kilometers）/ 小時。表示風速時，必須附加上所使用的「單位」名稱。

- Wind direction and force at Keelung Port is South-West force 9.

（基隆港的風向與風力為西南風，風力9級。）

14.Sea *海浪狀況*

• There is a sea of height 5 meters.（目前浪高5公尺。）

例句中的「Sea」做「Sea waves」解釋。而此處所謂海浪係指該地區內受風力影響所形成的海浪而言。

15.Swell *湧浪*

• Swell is expected to increase ...

（預計湧浪會繼續增強……。）

【註18】

湧浪係指一系列遠離「起浪區」的海浪。湧浪常能擴散達數千浬外才慢慢減小，湧浪與一般海浪的差異在於湧浪有光滑且不鬆散（沒有水花）的表面。

16.Hampered vessel *行動受限的船舶*

• There is a hampered vessel in fairway.

（有一艘行動受限的船舶在航道中。）

【註19】

Hampered vessel依照IMO的標準用語定義為：「一船舶之運轉能力受其工作性質所限制者，是為行動受限船舶。」又依據國際海上避碰規則第9條規定，帆船與小船對僅能在狹窄水道或適航水道中安全航行之船舶，不得妨礙其通行，但後者（如深吃水的重載油輪）依照IMO的解釋，並不能視為「Hampered vessel」。

五、港口管制 Port Control

在交通繁忙或能見度不佳的情形下，許多港口對該港區內各船舶的移動均由港口管制站（Port control）管控，船舶的航行運動均須依照港口管制站的指示進行。這些指示可能在引水人上船前即已發布，並隨時在船舶航行進入港口途中提供協助。

1. Shore-based radar assistance 岸基雷達協助

- Is shore-based radar assistance available?

  （請問是否有岸基雷達協助的服務？）

【註20】

在港口管制站雷達有效範圍內，管制站一定會監測所有船舶的運動狀態，如航向及船速、船位等。基於安全考量，只要船舶需要管制站提供相關的雷達資訊，管制站通常都會配合。但眼前船舶航儀與通訊設備精進發達，類似船舶請求管制站提供雷達資訊的機會甚少。

2. Berthing instruction 靠泊指示、靠泊計畫

- What are my berthing instructions?

  （請問本船的靠泊指示為何？）

【註21】

Berthing instruction為港口管理機關（Harbour Authority）所下達的指示，確實指明該船舶將靠泊的時間與位置。船舶應於進入引水區（Pilotage area）前再度確認靠泊指示，以便及早因應。因為靠泊指示常會因港口作業的延遲產生變化。例如：「No information berthing instructions.」，表示船舶預定靠泊的時間及位置尚不知道。

3. Way point 報告點

- A mark or place at which a vessel is required to report to establish its position.

  （船舶依規定必須提出其位置報告的某一標誌或地點。）

【註22】

「Way point」亦稱「Reporting point」或「Calling-in-point」。該報告點為船舶航向港口途中或離港駛向外海途中的某一地點。船舶常被要求在該點與港口管理單位或引水站聯絡，說明該船當時位置，以便港口方預為準備船舶進、出港口的所有安排與服務。

4. Radar contact 雷達顯示

- I have lost radar contact.

〔本船已看不到（某目標或他船的）雷達回跡顯示。〕

5. Available 可行的、可利用的、可得到的

- At what time will the pilot be available?

（引水人何時可以上船？）

因為港口作業延遲、天氣狀況、潮汐狀況都可能使引水人登船時間改變。

6. Compulsory 強制的、強制性

- Is pilotage compulsory?

（請問貴港或本水域是否採用強制引水制度？）

【註23】

基於安全考量，大多數國家實施強制引水制度（Compulsory pilotage system），此表示船舶進、出港前必須有引水人登船引領。但仍有極少數港口採行非強制引水制，亦即在此等港口僱請引水人與否，全由船長自行決定。但海軍軍艦各國有不同的規定，一般沿海國政府皆會堅持來訪的外籍軍艦一律要僱請引水人。

7. Suspended 暫停

- Pilotage suspended for all vessels.

（對所有船舶暫停引航服務。）

【註24】

表示引航作業已暫停（Pilotage suspended），抵港船隻須在離港口稍遠處等候引水站通知，直至引水作業恢復正常後，再行趨近招請引水人上船。引航作業暫停的原因或為港內船舶交通繁雜、浪大風強或其他原因。「Pilotage suspended」與「Harbour closed」不同，前者僅是暫時停止引航作業，後者則是所有港口作業全部停止，例如颱風來襲，不僅所有船舶禁止進出港，連帶的亦迫使泊岸船舶停止裝卸作業。

六、接近港口 Approaching harbor

1. Deep vessel 深吃水船

- Deep vessel has entered fairway inwards.

（某深吃水船已進入進港航道。）

【註25】
深吃水船因為吃水較深，基於安全考量必須航行於航道、或航路中最深的部分，以降低擱淺或觸底的風險。

2. Large vessel 巨型船

- Wait for large vessel to clear Devil Shoal.

（等候巨型船通過魔鬼淺灘。）

【註26】
(1)巨型船的「巨型」是指船舶大小相對於港口幅員大小的比例而言，例如十萬總噸的貨櫃船在高雄港不算巨型船，但在基隆港就屬巨型船。故而巨型船專指能夠使用該港口或港道的最大型船舶。
(2)深吃水船舶的大小沒有絕對的標準，全依照當地水深的情形而定。深吃水船舶通常指船底及海底之間僅有極小的間隙。這種深吃水船須掛出特別的信號，以顯示該船為「深吃水船」，而其他船舶，尤其是小型船艇必須避讓，以免阻礙該船航行。此外，某船雖顯示深吃水船舶的信號，並不表示可以免除該船之避讓義務，因為國際海上避碰規則中並未將深吃水船視為「行動受限制船舶」。一艘船舶可能同時是巨型船也是深吃水船，因為巨型的深吃水船卸完貨物後即為巨型船。巨型船與其吃水深度無關，但與其船殼受風面（Sail area）有關，這種船舶常因受風面積較大的影響致操船困難。

3. Deep-water route 深水航道

【註27】
依照IMO標準用語，深水航道為一指定航道，且該航道區域內已清除海底障礙，經精確測量並指出其最淺的水深。此深水航道通常為深吃水船所遵行的航道。

4. **Where do you come from?** 請問貴輪從何處來？

【註28】
本句對於船舶之健康、檢疫方面特別重要。港務機關與檢疫單位（Quarantine Authority）為保障本國人民免受動、植物傳染病、流行病毒的影響，例如新冠病毒，所以要了解抵港船隻是否來自疫區。有些國家對某些原產地國實施經濟抵制（禁運）時，也須詳加確認。

5. **From what direction are you approaching?** 請問貴船從那個方向趨近本港？

- I am approaching from the South.
  （本輪從貴港南方趨近。）
- I am approaching from Yehliu peninsula.
  （本輪從野柳半島方向趨近貴港。）

6. **Slick of oil** 浮油、油跡

- There is a slick of oil in position 25°40' North 121°40' East, extending 100 miles eastwards.
  （在北緯25°40'、東經121°40'處有一片向東延伸達100浬的浮油。）

7. **Oil clearance operations** 清除油汙作業

- There are oil clearance operations in position 25°40' North 121°40' East.
  （在北緯25°40'、東經121°40'處正在清除油汙作業。）

8. **Gear** 敢用於船上工具、設備、裝置用具、索具的名稱

9. **Fishing gear** 捕魚用具

- Is there fishing gear ahead of you?
  （請問有無漁具在貴船前方？）

【註29】

捕魚用具包括各種魚網，如拖網（Trawls）、流刺網（Drift nets）及圍網（Purse seine nets）。雖某些捕魚用具不影響海面航行，但船隻航行時仍應與網具保持較遠的距離。

10.Fishing gear has fouled my propeller 漁具已纏住本船之推進器

【註30】

此句用於船舶航行時，不慎從漁具上方駛過，或太過接近漁網與網具，致使網具或其拖曳鋼索纏住推進器（螺旋槳）。而該漁具的網、索強度又足以使大船停止或降低螺旋槳轉速，通常發生在近岸航行時。遇有此等情況，商船或漁船勢必須要雇請潛水伕潛入水中清理，才能清除被絞絆的網具、繩索或鋼索。

11.You have caught my fishing gear 貴船已纏住本船的漁具

本句用於漁船從事捕魚時，網具被其他接近之船舶所絞絆或損壞的時候。

12.Advise you recover your fishing gear 建議貴輪收回貴輪的網具

本句為公務執法單位對於妨礙航行或對航行有危險的漁船，（如在航道或航行巷道內捕魚之漁船）所下的指令。

13.Fishing in this area is prohibited 本水域禁止捕魚

本句為公務執法單位所下達的堅定命令。如果漁船不服從勸導可能被逮捕或扣留，也可能被割斷網具。

七、航安相關用語 Sentences regarding the Navigation safety

1. Warnings 警告

(1) You are running into danger. 貴輪正航向危險（區）。

（Shallow water ahead of you）（淺水區位於貴輪前方。）

（Submerged wreck ahead of you）（水下殘骸位於貴輪前方。）

（Risk of collision imminent）（即將出現碰撞風險。）

（Fog bank ahead of you）（貴輪前方有霧團。）

• Dangerous obstruction or wreck reported at...

（危險障礙物或殘骸據報位於……。）

• Navigation is closed（prohibited）in area...

〔……水域已禁止（暫停）航行。〕

• There has been a collision in position...

（在……位置有船舶碰撞。）

（keep clear）（請保持遠離。）

（stand by to give assistance）（請留候原地等待提供協助。）

(2) It is dangerous to...〔……是危險的（加入下列適用例句）。〕

（stop）（停俥是危險的。）

（remain in present position）（停留在目前的位置是危險的。）

（alter course to starboard）（向右轉向是危險的。）

（alter course to port）（向左轉向是危險的。）

• Vessel is aground in position...（某船正擱淺於……位置。）

• Vessel...is on fire in position...〔某船（船名）於……位置發生火災。〕

• Large vessel leaving. Keep clear of approach channel.

（巨型船舶離開中，請離開趨近航道。）

• Your navigation lights are not visible.

（貴輪的航行燈未點亮。）

• You are going to run aground.

（貴輪即將擱淺。）

• Keep clear...（vessel is leaking、inflammable cargo in position...）

（請保持遠離……。）（某船的可燃貨載正洩漏於……。）

155

2. Assistance 協助

- I need help...〔本輪需要協助……（加入下列適用例句位置）〕

  （I am sinking）（本輪正在沉沒中。）

  （I am on fire）（本輪目前陷於火災中。）

  （I have been in collision）（本輪已與……碰撞。）

  （I am aground）（本輪已擱淺。）

- I am on fire and have dangerous cargo on board.

  （本輪失火而且有危險貨物在船。）

- I am on fire...〔本輪失火……（加入下列適用例句）〕

  （in the engine room）（位在機艙。）

  （in the hold）（位在貨艙。）

- I have lost a man overboard (at...). Please help with search and rescue.

  （本輪在……有一位人員落海，請協助搜索與救助。）

- What is your position?

  （貴輪位置在哪？）

- What is the position of the vessel in distress?

  （遇難船舶的位置爲何？）

- What assistance is required?

  （貴輪需要什麼服務？）

- I require...（本輪需要……。）

  （medical assistance）（醫藥協助。）

  （fire-fighting assistance）（滅火協助。）

- I am coming to your assistance.

  （本輪正趕來協助貴輪。）

- I expect to reach you at...hrs.

  （本輪預計在……時抵達貴輪所在。）

- Please take command of search and rescue.

  （請貴輪接掌搜索與救助指揮官職務。）

156

- I am in command of search and rescue.

  （本輪已接掌搜索與救助指揮官職務。）

- Vessel... is in command of search and rescue.

  （……輪已接掌搜索與救助指揮官職務。）

- Assistance is not required. You may proceed.

  （本輪不需協助了。貴輪可以駛離了。）

- Assistance is no longer required. You may proceed.

  （本輪已經不需再協助了。貴輪可以駛離了。）

- You must keep radio silence in this area unless You have messages about the casualty.

  （除非貴輪要發布有關事故的訊息，否則在本水域請保持無線電靜默。）

3. Anchoring 錨泊

- I am anchored (at...).

  （本輪已在……錨泊了。）

- I am heaving up anchor.

  〔本輪正在絞（起）錨中。〕

- You can/must anchor...

  （貴輪可以／必須拋錨在……。）

  （at...hours）〔在……（時間）。〕

  （in...position）〔在……（位置）。〕

  （until pilot arrives）（直至引水人抵達。）

- Do not anchor (in position...)〔請勿在……（位置）錨泊。〕

- Anchoring is prohibited.

  （禁止錨泊。）

- My/Your anchor is dragging.

  （本輪／貴輪正在流錨中。）

- You must heave up anchor.

（貴輪必須絞起貴輪的錨具。）

- My anchor is foul.

（本輪的錨具已糾纏到異物。）

- You are obstructing...

〔貴輪正阻礙到……（加入下列適用例句）〕

（the fairway）（航道）

（other traffic）（其他船舶）

- You must anchor clear of the fairway.

（貴輪必須在遠離航道處錨泊。）

- You have anchored in the wrong position.

（貴輪已錨泊在錯誤的錨位上。）

4. Arrival, Berthing and Departure 抵港、靠離碼頭、離港

- Where do you come from?

（請問貴輪來自何處？）

- What was your last port of call?

（請問貴輪上一港口為何？）

- From what direction are you approaching?

（請問貴輪從哪個方向趨近本港？）

- What is your ETA (at...)?

〔貴輪抵達……（地點）的預定時間為何？〕

- What is your ETD (from...)?

〔貴輪離開……（地點）的預定時間為何？〕

- My ETA (at...) is ... hours.

〔本輪抵達……（地點）的預定時間為……〕

- My ETD (from...) is ... hours.

〔本輪離開……（地點）的預定時間為……〕

- What is your destination?

（請問貴輪的目的地為何？）

- My destination is...

  （本輪的目的爲⋯⋯）

- What are my berthing instruction?

  〔請問本輪的靠泊指示（計畫）爲何？〕

- What are my docking instruction?

  〔請問本輪的進塢指示（計畫）爲何？〕

- Your berth is clear (at...hours).

  〔貴輪的泊位已在⋯⋯（時間）空出。〕

- Your berth will be clear (at...hours).

  〔貴輪的泊位將在⋯⋯（時間）空出。〕

- May I enter?

  （本輪可以進港了嗎？）

- You may enter (at...hours).

  〔貴輪可以在⋯⋯（時間）進港。〕

- May I proceed?

  （本輪可以動俥趨近嗎？）

- You may proceed (at...hours).

  〔貴輪可以在⋯⋯（時間）動俥趨近。〕

- Is there any other traffic?

  〔請問有無其他船舶（同時抵達）？〕

- There is a vessel turning at...

  〔有一艘船舶在⋯⋯（位置）迴轉。〕

- Vessel ... inward in position...

  〔進港船⋯⋯（船名）位於⋯⋯（位置）。〕

- Vessel... outward in position...

  〔出港船⋯⋯（船名）位於⋯⋯（位置）。〕

- Are you underway?

  （請問貴輪目前在航行中嗎？）

- I am underway.

（本輪在航行中。）

5. Course 航向

- What is your course?

（貴輪航向爲何？）

- My course is...

（本輪航向爲……）

- Advise you make course...

〔建議貴輪行駛航向……（羅經度數）。〕

- Advise you keep your present course.

〔建議貴輪保持目前航向……（羅經度數）。〕

- You are steering a dangerous course...

〔貴輪目前行駛的航向……（羅經度數）是危險的。〕

6. Draught and Height 吃水與高度

- What is your draught?

（請問貴輪吃水爲何？）

- My draught is...

（本輪吃水爲……）

- What is your draught forward/aft?

（請問貴輪前、後吃水各爲何？）

- Vessel... is of deep draught.

（……船爲深吃水船。）

- Maximum permitted draught is...

（最大允許吃水爲……）

7. Fairway Navigation 水道／航道航行

- Proceed by...fairway.

（請航行於……航道。）

- Proceed by...route.

（請航行於……航路。）

- I am stopped (at...).

  〔本船停止在……（位置）。〕

- The vessel ahead of you is stopping/turning...

  （位於貴輪前方的船舶正停俥中／迴轉中。）

- The vessel astern of you is stopping/turning...

  （位於貴輪後方的船舶正停俥中／迴轉中。）

- The vessel to port of you is stopping/turning...

  （位於貴輪左舷的船舶正停俥中／迴轉中。）

- The vessel to starboard of you is stopping/turning...

  （位於貴輪右舷的船舶正停俥中／迴轉中。）

- Fairway speed is... knots.

  （航道速度／速限為……節。）

- You must stay clear of the fairway.

  （貴輪必須遠離航道。）

- Do not overtake.

  （請勿追越。）

- Do not cross the fairway.

  （請勿橫越航道。）

8. Manoeuvring 船舶操縱

- What are your intentions?

  （貴輪的運轉企圖為何？）

- Do not overtake ... 〔請勿追越……（船名）。〕

- You may overtake ... 〔貴輪可以追越……（船名）。〕

- I am not under command.

  （本輪操縱失靈。）

- I am a hampered vessel because...

  （本船因為……致運轉能力受限。）

- Advise you stop engines.

（建議貴輪停俥。）

- I will stop engines.

（本輪將停俥。）

- Do not pass ahead / astern of me.

（不要從本船船頭／船艉通過。）

【註31】

實務上，在引水區的對話過程中常發現部分駕駛員每每將「Stop your ship」一詞錯誤認知為「Stop your engine」。「Stop ship」係指操船者積極地運用倒俥或拋錨將船停住。反之，「Stop engine」則只是消極地讓船舶的主機停止運轉而已，結果仍因慣性或外力作用，根本無法「停住」船舶。

---

9. **Pilotage** 引水作業

- I require a pilot.

（本輪需要引水人。）

- Where can I take pilot?

（本輪可在何處接領引水人？）

- You can take pilot at point.../near... (at...hrs.)

〔貴輪可於……（時間）在……（地點）／接近……（地點）接領引水人？〕

- At what time will the pilot be available?

（請問引水人何時可以上船？）

- Is pilotage compulsory?

（請問本港／本水道是否為強制引水區？）

- You may navigate by yourself or wait for pilot at...

〔貴輪可以不僱用引水人自主航行，或在……（地點）等候引水人。〕

- Pilot is coming to you.（引水人正前往貴輪途中。）

- Pilotage suspended for all/small vessels.

（暫停所有／小型船舶的引航作業。）

- Pilotage resumed for all/small vessels.

（恢復所有／小型船舶的引航作業。）

10. **Position** 位置

- What is your position?（貴輪位置為何？）
- What is your present position, course and speed?

（貴輪目前的位置、航向、船速為何？）

- My present position, course and speed is...

（本輪目前的位置、航向、船速為……）

- Do not arrive at...before...hrs.

〔請勿在……（時間）前抵達（地點）。〕

- Do not arrive at...after...hrs.

〔請勿在……（時間）後抵達（地點）。〕

- Say again your position to assist identification.

（請重複貴輪位置以協助識別。）

11. **Radar-Ship-to-Ship/Shore-to-Ship/Ship-to-Shore** 船／岸、船／船、岸／船間雷達

- Is your radar working?

（請問貴輪雷達正常運轉嗎？）

- My radar is working/not working.

（本輪雷達正常運轉／不能正常運轉。）

- I have located you on my radar.

〔我已經在本輪雷達上探測出貴輪所在（回跡）。〕

- I cannot locate you on my radar.

〔我無法在本輪雷達上探測出貴輪所在（回跡）。〕

- You must alter course/speed for identification.

（你必須轉向或改變速度以供識別。）

- Report your position to assist identification.

（報告貴輪位置以便協助識別。）

- I require shore based radar assistance.

（本船需要岸基雷達協助。）

- Shore based radar assistance is / is not available.

（岸基雷達可以提供協助 / 岸基雷達無法提供協助。）

12.Navigational warnings航行警告

- There is a dangerous wreck/rock/shoal in position (marked by...showing...)

（有一危險沈船 / 礁石 / 淺灘位於……）（藉由……顯示……）

- There is a vessel with a difficult tow on passage from...to...

（有一艘船舶在航道上自……往……拖曳著影響運轉能力的被拖物。）

- Vessels must keep clear of this area.

（船舶必須遠離此水域。）

- Vessels are advised to keep clear of this area.

（建議船舶遠離此水域。）

- Vessels are advised to avoid this area.

（建議船舶避開此水域。）

- Vessels must navigate with caution.

（船舶必須小心航行。）

- There is a vessel not under command in position/area...

〔有一艘操縱失靈船舶位於……（經緯度）/ ……（地名）水域。〕

13.Routing 航路

- Is it clear for me to enter traffic lane/route?

（請問本船此時進入交通巷道 / 航路是否安全無礙？）

- It is clear for you to enter traffic lane/route.

（貴輪此時進入交通巷道 / 航路是安全無礙的。）

- It is not clear for you to enter traffic lane/route.

  （貴輪此時進入交通巷道／航路是不安全的。）

- You are not complying with traffic regulations.

  （貴輪現在未遵守交通規則。）

- There are many fishing vessels at...

  〔有許多漁船位於……（位置）。〕

14.Speed 速度

- What is your present speed?

  （貴輪目前速度爲何？）

- What is your full speed?

  （貴輪的全速可達幾節？）

- You must reduce speed.

  （貴輪必須減速。）

- You must increase speed.

  （貴輪必須加速。）

- You must keep your present speed.

  （貴輪必須保持目前速度。）

15.Tide and Depth 潮汐與深度

- Is there sufficient depth of water?

  （請問水深是否足夠？）

- There is sufficient depth of water.

  （水深是足夠的。）

- There is not sufficient depth of water.

  （水深是不足夠的。）

16.Tropical Storms 熱帶風暴

- What is your latest tropical storm warning information?

  〔請問貴（站）台最新的熱帶風暴警報資訊爲何？〕

- The tropical storm centre (name) was (at...hrs.) in position ...

165

moving ... at ... knots.

〔熱帶風暴（名稱）中心……（時間）位於……（位置）以……節速度移向……〕

17.Tugs 拖輪

- I require a tug.

（我需要一艘拖輪。）

- I require...tugs.

（我需要……艘拖輪。）

- Tug(s) will meet you at (position...) / (near...) (at...hrs.).

〔拖輪將於……（時間）在接近……（位置）處與貴輪會合。〕

18.Weather 天氣、氣候

- What is the weather forecast (for area...)?

（請問……水域的天氣預測為何？）

- Wind direction and force/speed at...is...

〔……（時間）在……（位置）的風向與風力（或風速）為……〕

- What is the visibility at...?

（請問……水域的能見度為何？）

- Visibility at ... is ... meters / miles.

（……水域的能見度為……公尺／浬。）

- Visibility is reduced by fog / rain / snow / dust.

（因霧／降雨／降雪／落塵致能見度降低。）

- Are sea conditions expected to change within the next... hours?

（請問海面狀況在未來……小時內是否會發生改變？）

19.Fishing 捕魚

- Navigate with caution small fishing boats are within...miles of me.

（因為有小漁船在本船……浬內，請小心航行。）

- You are heading towards fishing gear.

〔貴輪正航向（海上或水中）漁具中。〕

- There are nets with buoys in this area.
  （此水域有以浮標顯示的漁網存在。）
- Fishing gear has fouled my propeller.
  （本船螺旋槳已絞纏到漁具。）
- Advise you recover your fishing gear.
  （建議貴船收回漁網或漁具。）
- Fishing in this area is prohibited.
  （此水域禁止捕魚。）
- You are approaching a prohibited fishing area.
  （貴輪正駛向禁止捕魚區。）

167

第四章　航行與安全

第一節　人因影響（Effect of Human factors）

1. Safety is paramount!

　　（安全是最高選項。）

2. A ship's owner (charterer) will almost certainly require a 100 per cent score on safety but be more flexible on others.

　　〔船東（租船人）對於其他船務運作或有彈性，但安全絕對是百分百的要求。〕

3. Ship's owners and operators have an obligation to provide a trained and competent crew.

　　（船東與運航人有責任提供經過訓練而且適任的船員。）

4. It must be emphasized that it is the shipmaster who is responsible for the safe navigation of the ship at sea.

　　（必須強調的是，船舶在海上的航行安全由船長負全責。）

5. Professional seafarers quickly develop a respect for the marine environment and an awareness of the power of the elements. In comparison to these elements we know that we are insignificant and that even the best designed and powered vessel may be overcome by them.

　　（專業的海員終將學會尊重海洋環境與大自然的力量；吾人知道相

較於此等自然因素，我們是多麼微不足道，而設計再好，裝備再精良的船隻都無法與其相抗衡。）

6. We must accept that those working onboard are human beings who are not perfect.

（我們必須接受的是，在船上工作的是人，只要是人就不可能是完美的。）

7. Various factors around human error, including complacency, commercial pressure, fatigue and even an overload of information.

（造成事故的各種原因多指向人為疏失，包括自滿、商業壓力、疲憊，甚至是資訊氾濫。）

8. A reasonable seaman would not ignore a risk and would not rely on luck. It is irrational to do nothing and expect that a problematic situation will end well.

（一個合理的海員不會忽視危機，也不會依賴幸運。不採取任何作為只寄望情勢會完美結束，是極不合理的。）

9. It is widely agreed that competence requires a combination of understanding, skill and attitude.

〔眾所周知，適任性需要判斷力（理解）、技術與態度的結合。〕

10. Despite advance in shipboard navigation technology, the basic principle of keeping a safe navigational watch, as set out in SOLAS and STCW regulations, remain as important as ever.

（無論船上配置的航行科技如何發達，遵守SOLAS與STCW規定保持安全航行當值的基本原則仍是最重要的。）

11. <u>Situational awareness</u> means knowing what is going on around the ship at all times, enhancing the ability of the OOW to quickly recognize any ambiguities in the navigational situation and to take action before a hazardous situation developed.

〔情境警覺係指隨時認知船舶四周正在發展中的事物，提升駕駛臺當值駕駛員快速認知航行情境的任何不明確（模擬兩可）事物的能力，並在發展成危險情勢之前採取行動。〕

12. Professional <u>navigators</u> need constant <u>situational awareness</u> to ensure the safety of lives, the vessel, her cargo, the environment and to ensure commercial effectiveness.

（專業的<u>河海航行員</u>需要持續的<u>情境警覺</u>，以確保生命、船舶、貨載與環境的安全，以及商業效用。）

13. As the primary role of the bridge team is to execute the passage plan safely, while keeping the vessel out of collision with other vessels or objects and in safe water, it is useful and necessary that the bridge team have a good understanding as to what constitutes a safe distance from moving or fixed hazards and what is the latest time at which action should be taken to avoid collision.

（由於駕駛臺團隊的主要任務係安全的執行航行計畫，同時確保船舶不會與他船或物體碰撞，而且在安全水域時，駕駛臺團隊必須要充分了解是什麼構成了移動與固定危險物的安全距離，以及採取避碰時機的底限時間。）

14. The question is not whether everything that could be done was done as soon as the danger of collision arose, but whether sufficient precautions had been taken much earlier.

（問題不在於碰撞危機發生時該做的都已做了，而是在於是否及早

採取充分的預防措施。）

15. In the case of collision avoidance, since we cannot know what situational awareness exists on other vessels then "defensive driving" is required.

（在避碰的情況下，因為我們無法得知他船的情境警覺程度，所以需要採取「防衛性的駕駛」。）

16. If you have any doubt whatsoever regarding any situation developing, you must call the Master.

（如果您對於任何發展中的情勢有任何疑慮時，您必須籲請船長至駕駛臺。）

17. Sometimes, the presence of the Master on the bridge has resulted in confusion as to who has responsibility for safety navigation of the vessel.

〔有時候船長現身於駕駛臺會造成（當值駕駛員產生）當下究竟是誰負責船舶安全航行的疑惑。〕

18. The guiding principle is that OOWs must continue to execute their duties normally until the Master positively declares that they have the con（＝conn船舶操控權）.

（指導守則是當值駕駛員必須繼續正常執行其職務，直至船長明確表示其接手操船為止。）

19. Too many accidents are caused by watchkeepers simply neglecting to look out of the window regularly, or to use radar properly.

（有太多的事故只是單純的肇因於當值駕駛員疏於定時瞭望駕駛臺窗外的情境，或不當使用雷達。）

20. Most information needed for the safe conduct of a ship comes through the eyes.

（安全航行的資訊主要來自目視瞭望。）

21. The use of navigational aids is not a substitute for maintaining a visual lookout.

（航儀的使用無法替代保持目視瞭望。）

22. To ensure the safety of navigation, it is imperative that the shipping community acknowledge that the training and experience of watch-keepers are critical factors in mitigating the risk of collision and groundings.

（爲確保航行安全，海運界必須認知到，當值者的訓練與經驗才是降低碰撞風險與擱淺的最重要因素。）

23. Do not use a mobile phone or any other portable electronic device while on watch.

（當值時不得使用手機或是任何手提電子裝置。）

24. Do not let others draw your attention away from keeping a proper lookout.

（不要因任何外務讓您自保持適當瞭望的工作中分心。）

25. You should know how to operate your electronic navigational aids properly, and you should be well aware of their limitations.

（您必須知道如何適當地操作您的電子航儀，以及注意到它的限制。）

26. By the time target ship was discerned, there was often insufficient

time to react.

（等辨別出目標船，已經沒有充分時間因應了。）

27. Unfortunately, shipowners and managers tend to neglect the important contribution the watch-keepers make towards the sustainability of the mercantile business.

（很不幸的，船東與經理人仍依舊忽略當值者的貢獻是支撐海運事業永續性的重要因素。）

28. In too many cases, a shipowner treats a watch-keeper as an expense item rather than as an asset who can add value to the business.

（有太多的案例顯示，船東傾向於將當值者視爲多餘的支出項目，而非具附加價值的企業資產。）

29. The safety and sustainability of shipping will always rely on a stable and competent workforce.

（海運的安全與持續經營永遠值基於穩定與有能力的工作力。）

30. To build a ship is easy; to build a pool of proficient seamen is not.

（要造一艘船很容易，但要養成一批熟練的海員不容易。）

31. Whatever technology or concepts are introduced for the future, crews will still need to use the equipment properly and the equipment will still need to be maintained properly

（無論未來科技與觀念如何發展，船員仍需要適當地使用航儀，而且航儀仍須適當的保養。）

32. Technological improvements have reduced the workload of the crew to great extent.

（科技化的改善已大幅減低船員的工作負荷。）

33. Good situational awareness requires the continual checking of complementary positioning systems and the intelligent application of common sense.

（良好的情境警覺需要持續比對支援定位系統，以及善用〔專業〕常識。）

34. Never rely on a single means of fixing the ship position.

（切勿依賴單一定位方法。）

35. The widespread availability of GPS, is increasingly encouraging mariners of all classes to navigate either closer inshore or close to dangers, sometimes doing so in conditions of darkness and reduced visibility.

（GPS的廣泛使用使得船員愈來愈大膽的敢於貼近岸邊或危險物航行，有時黑夜與能見度受限時亦如此。）

36. With the visibility conditions changed, in an otherwise similar situation, the vessels need to take a totally different series of actions.

（隨著能見度的改變，船舶可能要採取一系列完全不同的動作。）

37. The OOW has an even more intensive duty to monitor the vessel's position and progress.

（當值駕駛員的最重要責任是要審視船位與進程。）

38. Monitoring the speed and distance of the vessel being conducted to ensure the operation remained within safe limits required the constant attention of watch officer at the radar.

（當值駕駛員要持續注意雷達顯示，並監督本船的船速與距離，以確保本船保持在安全界限內運轉。）

39. OOW must avoid making assumptions on scanty information.

（當值駕駛員必須避免依賴不實資訊擅做假設。）

40. Navigation at night requires special care. It is essential to be able to see other vessels and ensure they see you.

（夜間航行需要特別注意。而最重要的是，不僅要看到其他船舶，更要確保讓他船能夠看到你。）

41. It is difficult to judge distances at night and not all navigation hazards will have lights indicating their position.

（夜間不容易判斷距離，而且並非所有航行險阻都有燈光顯示其所在位置。）

42. Shear your knowledge!

（分享您的知識！）

43. Mentoring is key. Experienced mariners should take time to help fellow mariners master positioning techniques.

（經驗相授最為重要。資深海員應多花點時間教導資淺同仁精通定位技術。）

44. Many officers have said there was no additional and appropriately qualified person available for lookout duty from sunset to sunrise on their vessel other than the OOW.

（許多船副常埋怨自日落至日出期間，除了當值駕駛員外，沒有額外且適當的適格人員可充當瞭望員。）

※STCW公約有關客船船員訓練的規定

In accordance with STCW 95 Chapter V, all Masters, officers and ratings serving on board passenger ships engaged on international voyages shall have completed training related to assisting passengers in an emergence situation before they are assigned shipboard duties.

（依據STCW95第五章規定，服務於國際航線客船上的所有船長、甲級船員與一般船員在被派上船前，必須完成有關在緊急狀況下協助旅客的完整訓練。）

All crew members on board the passenger ships shall have completed training in crowd management which includes training in passenger safety, cargo safety and hull integrity.

（所有被派往客船服務的船員必須完成群眾管理的訓練，包括旅客安全、貨物安全與船殼完整性的訓練。）

In brief, this training should cover：
（簡而言之，訓練課程應包括：）

1. Awareness of life saving appliance.
   （救生器具的認識。）
2. Ability to assist passenger en route to muster station.
   （協助旅客前往求生集合站途中的能力。）
3. Mustering procedure.
   （求生站集合程序。）
4. Communication with passenger in emergency.
   （緊急狀況下與旅客的聯絡方法。）
5. Crisis management and human behaviour training.
   （危機處理與行為能力訓練。）
6. Passenger safety, cargo safety and hull integrity.
   （旅客安全、貨物安全與船殼的完整性維護。）

第二節　船舶因素（Ship's factor）

1. Today advanced technology is found in all sectors of the shipping industry.

   （今天在海運業的每一個區塊皆可看到先進科技。）

2. Technology has fundamentally altered the role of seafarers.

   （科技已基本上改變了海員的角色。）

3. Many people see technology as a solution to most of the problems that exist on our planet.

   （許多人將新科技視爲解決地球上現存大部分問題的良方。）

4. The introduction of new technology onboard merchant ships has the potential to improve the efficiency and effectiveness of watchkeeping and to improve the safety of operations.

   （船上新科技的引進，具有改善瞭望效能與當值的有效性的潛能，進而改善作業安全。）

5. The fundamental nature of marine navigation has altered over the last decade as result of the reliable, with accuracy of 1 m or better.

   （由於過去十餘年來航儀的可靠性發展至精確度小至1公尺或更小，因而改變了海上航行的基本特質。）

6. Modern technology is a very useful tool but the advantage and benefits are minimized if proper knowledge and training are not part of it.

   （新科技是非常有用的工具，但如果沒有適當的知識及訓練，將使

其好處與優點降至最低。）

7. Advances in navigational technology are not always matched by advances in navigational ability.

（航行能力的進步常常無法跟進航行科技的進展。）

8. The first step in maintaining navigation technology in good operating condition is to monitor its performance.

（欲保持航行科技處於良好的作業情況的第一步就是監督其運作。）

9. A modern ship's bridge is equipped with an impressive array of integrated, state-of-art navigational and communications equipment, designed to enhance navigational safety.

（新式船舶的駕駛臺配置令人讚嘆的全套整合式航儀與通訊設備，期以提升航行安全。）

10. Modern electronic navigation systems have unquestionably improved vessel navigation safety and reduced accidents.

（現代化的電子航行系統無疑地已改善船舶的航行安全並減少事故的發生。）

11. It's true that technology can be used for good, but with new developments come new challenges.

（毫無疑問的，科技可以被好好利用，但是新的發展卻也常帶來新挑戰。）

12. Undoubtedly, technology can sometimes have an adverse effect.
（毫無疑問地，科技有時亦會有負面效應。）

13. New technology in the maritime industry is to be welcomed. However, it brings an element of risk because of unfamiliarity.

（新航儀當然受海運業歡迎，然而其亦會因爲不熟悉而帶來風險元素。）

14. The serious shortcomings with the navigation on board the vessel had not been identified during the vessel's recent audits and inspections.

（船上許多有關航行的嚴重缺失未能在最近的稽核與檢查中被發現。）

15. In any event, mariners are strongly advised not to use single aids to navigation systems in isolation but to use all alternative means available to information received.

（強烈建議在任何情況下，駕駛員不應只依賴單一導航系統航行，而需使用所有替代方法交叉比對所收到的訊息。）

16. Several recent maritime accidents suggest that modern technology sometimes can make it more difficult for mariners to navigate safely.

（最近幾起海難事故發現新科技有時是造成船員安全航行更爲困難的主因。）

17. Officers on the watch can find their heads turned (in the wrong direction) by an abundance of modern gadgets

（裝置過多新式航儀常會造成當值駕駛員疲於奔命或被誤導。）

18. The failure to do so will compound the likelihood that their vessels will be held liable in the event of a casualty that could have been prevented by the use of all the resources and equipment available to

them.

（若疏於此，將可能導致其船舶被判決負有事故的責任，而此一責任原本只要使用所有可用的資源與設備即可避免的。）

19. The technical limitations of the radar equipment mean that changes of course and/or speed by the target vessels may not be readily apparent on the radar screen.

（雷達設備的技術上限制可能導致目標船航向與船速的變化無法及時顯示在雷達螢幕上。）

20. GPS is an invaluable aid to navigation. However, the exclusive use of GPS in coastal or confined waters may not always be appropriate and is often a contributory factor in ship groundings.

（GPS是一種極為重要的助航儀器，但在沿岸或受限水域單獨使用GPS並不一定適當，而且經常是造成船舶擱淺的主因。）

21. AIS will provide you with the luxury of more information, but will not tell you what to do.

（AIS可以提供您豐富的訊息，但卻無法告訴您要如何避讓船舶。）

22. The speed of progress and navigational advances can be astonishing, but there is still much that can be learnt from the past.

（航儀的快速精進發達雖令人驚訝，但我們仍可從過去的種種學習到很多技藝。）

23. Ship collisions, sometimes involving loss of life or damage to the marine environment, unfortunately continue to occur.

（船舶碰撞，有時涉及生命的喪失或造成海洋環境的損壞，但很不幸的，事故依舊發生。）

一、不當使用航儀的責任與分析

1. A vessel involved in a casualty has the burden of establishing that any failure to properly use its navigation equipment did not contribute to the casualty.

   （一艘涉及海難的船舶負有舉證其疏於適當使用航行設備並非促成海難的原因之責任。）

2. ECDIS與國際海上避碰規則第五條的關係
   - Rule 5 of the COLREG:

   "Every vessel shall at all times maintain a proper look-out by sight and hearing, as well as by all available means appropriate in the prevailing circumstances and conditions, so as to make a full appraisal of the situation and of the risk of collision."

   （第五條 瞭望：「各船應經常運用視覺、聽覺及各種適合當前環境所有可使用之方法，保持正確瞭望，以期完全了解其處境及碰撞危機。」）

3. Analysis of most ECDIS-assisted accidents suggests the causes are not system design failures, but are more likely to be due to operational failures, such as:

   （分析大部分與ECDIS直／間接有關的事故得知，事故原因並非系統設計缺失，大多屬於操作缺失造成的。諸如：）

   (1) Improper voyage planning, not using or incorrectly setting safety depth, safety contour or watch vector alarms or wrong inputs of vessels' data, such as draught.

   （不當的航行計畫。未使用或不正確的設定安全深度、安全等深線或航向監視警報，或是船舶資料的錯誤輸入，諸如水呎。）

(2) Using inappropriate scale or display mode.

（使用不適當的比例尺或顯示模式。）

(3) Not using the automatic route check facility.

（未使用自動航路核對功能。）

(4) Not carrying out visual checks or lookout.

（未進行視覺核對或瞭望。）

(5) Using ECDIS as an anti-collision tool; it is not a means for this purpose.

（利用ECDIS作爲避碰工具，但它並不能作爲此用途。）

(6) Not ensuring that ENCs are up-to-date, due to navigators not being clear on the automatic and/or manual updating procedure.

（因爲航行員不清楚自動或手動更新程序，致未確保所使用的電子海圖是最新更正的版本。）

(7) Improper use of radar and/or AIS overlay.

（雷達的不當使用或將AIS資訊鋪蓋在上面。）

(8) Inability to plot visual and/or radar fixes.

（沒有能力畫出目視或雷達定位。）

(9) Improper use of source data check on ENCs.

（從電子海圖核對的資訊來源的不當使用。）

(10) Not being aware of contingency procedures for hardware and/or software failures.

（未注意到軟硬體失常的應變計畫。）

第三節　環境因素（Environmental factors）

1. The sea is still the same dangerous place but since the days of sail, the inevitable march of progress has forced the industry to acknowl-

edge new challenge, dangers and lifestyles while at the same time reducing accident rates and introducing safer working practices throughout.

（自從帆船時代起海上即一直充滿風險，因而業界在推展業務無可避免地被迫面對新的挑戰與生活型態的同時，更要不斷找出降低肇事率並引進更安全的工作實務。）

2. Economic difficulties for the ship owner and/or flag state may lead to dangerous compromises and reduced safety standards.

（經濟不景氣使得船東或船旗國可能走向危險的妥協，並降低安全標準。）

3. In costal waters or in traffic separation schemes, the restricted nature of the available sea room, and the high density of traffic, necessarily reduces the margins of safety. In these situations, it becomes particularly important to consider all the options available. If in doubt, err on the side of safety, or slow down.

（在沿岸水域或在分道航行區，可用水域空間的限制特質，以及高密度的交通，勢必會降低安全邊際。處此情況下，考量所有可用的選項變成非常重要。如有任何疑慮，寧可選擇過於安全謹慎也不要冒險犯錯的措施或降低船速。）

4. The harbor approach, fairway and harbour operations form a large part of the risk profile of any voyage.

（進／出港航路、航道與港口作業勾勒出船舶每一航次的風險概況。）

5. Close monitoring of external factors such as currents, windage, shallow water effects on the <u>vessel's manoeuvrability</u> must be carried

out.

（密切監督影響<u>船舶操縱性</u>的外在因素，諸如流、受風面，淺水效應等。）

6. The increasing development of offshore <u>aquaculture fish farms</u> gives rise to increasingly crowded coastal waters with competing interests that impact on the safety of navigation in specific coastal areas.

（近岸<u>水產養殖場</u>的快速發展所帶來的利益競爭使得沿岸水域更趨擁擠，當會衝擊到特定沿岸水域的航行安全。）

7. <u>Risk assessment</u> should take into account every realistic hazard.

〔<u>風險評估</u>應考慮所有眞（現）實的危險。〕

8. A detailed risk assessment should be carried out before entering <u>areas of restricted sea room</u> and plans for contingencies must be in place.

（在進入<u>受限水域</u>之前，必須做詳細的風險評估，並備妥應急計畫。）

9. Superfluous or persistent bridge system alarms are distracting-and may result in the alarms being in appropriately disabled, so they do not sound when they are needed

（過多不必要或持續的駕駛臺系統警報都會造成當值人員的分心，而且可能導致正常的警報失靈，致無法在眞正需要時示警。）

10. A large tanker passed our vessel, causing it surge and sway away from the jetty by about two meters.

（一艘大油輪通過本船，造成本船前、後進動，以及水平左右搖擺離開碼頭約2公尺。）

11. A key objective of Aids to Navigation is to meet the requirements for safe marine transport and protection of the marine environment.

（助導航設施的主要目的之一是滿足海上運輸安全的要求與保護海洋環境。）

12. As the harsh realities of climate change become ever more apparent, there is a noticeable shift towards increased renewable energy generation. One of the most popular renewable energy sources is wind power.

（由於全球氣候變遷的嚴酷事實變得更為明顯，導致人們加速轉向再生能源的開發，而風力發電就是最普遍的再生能源。）

13. Significant technological advancements – as well as improved installation, maintenance and decommissioning strategies – have particularly boosted the reliability of offshore wind farms (OWFs) and driven down the associated levelized cost of energy.

（科技的精進已使得風力發電設施的設立、保養與退場策略的相關技術大幅改善，進而提升海上風場的可信賴性，並降低能源的平準化成本。）

14. A crucial topic often discussed in the context of environmental impacts is the interaction between OWFs and maritime activities. This multi-dimensional interaction is often viewed as a marine spatial conflict, with both industries vying for adequate space in marine areas that may be already over-crowded with other multiple uses.

〔有關環境衝擊最重要亦常被討論的議題就屬風場與海上（商業）活動之間的相互影響。此一多方面的相互影響常被視為海上空間衝突，而上述兩個產業競相在原本已被其他多元使用的過度擁擠海域爭取足夠空間。〕

15. In addition to the technical and cost-related challenges, further barriers to the continued growth of the offshore wind industry ironically stem from the environmental impact of OWFs.

（除了技術與成本相關的挑戰之外，離岸風電產業欲持續成長的進一步壁壘竟是源自其本身對環境造成的衝擊。）

16. Of all the different impacts related to OREIs (Offshore Renewable Energy Installations), the navigational safety risks are perhaps the most concerning for stakeholders.

（所有關於這些離岸風力發電設施的不同衝擊，航行安全風險乃是所有相關關係人最為關切者。）

17. The presence of an OWFs, for instance, means that:

（離岸風場的存在表示：）

- There more obstacles in the water which ships have to avoid.

（離岸有更多船舶必須避開的障礙物。）

- OWFs may also restrict the navigable space available to ships, leading to increased traffic density, and an increased risk of collision.

（離岸風場可能限制船舶可利用的航行空間，導致交通密度的增加，進而增加碰撞的風險。）

- It is also well established that OWTs may interfere with ships' onboard navigation equipment such as radar and other radio-frequency devices.

（離岸風電設施已被確定會影響船上的航行儀器，諸如雷達與其他無線電頻率設備。）

All these factors, and more, can be detrimental to navigational safety.

（以上所列因素，勢必會影響航行安全。）

18. In most coastal states, there are stringent processes requiring OWF owners/developers to demonstrate that they have thoroughly assessed the maritime risks and implemented adequate risk management measures.

（大部分的沿海國，都會嚴格要求風電廠商提出證明其已完全評估海上的風險，並採行充分的風險管理措施。）

第四節　開船前船長與引水人交換資訊內容（Master and Pilot Exchange）

1. Trim condition.
   （船舶吃水狀況。）
2. Two Bow Thruster/Two Stern thruster.
   （艏、艉橫向推進器的功率。）
3. Two propeller Inboard/Two rudder.
   （俥、舵配置；雙俥俥葉內旋或外旋。）
4. Pilot/Captain doing the manoeuvre.
   （由船長或引水人執行操船。）
5. Close loop/aloud/Raise your hand in emergency.
   （緊急狀況時的警示方法。）
6. Weather condition well/bad.
   （天候狀況良好／不良。）
7. Everything is functional.
   （所有機具航儀運作正常。）

第五節　引水人與引航 （Pilots and Pilotage）

1. Definition of the Pilot （引水人的定義）
   - Persons qualified to take charge of ships entering, leaving, and moving within certain specific navigable waters.
     （引水人係指有資格在特定可航水域內負責引領船舶進、出港口，或在該水域內的移動的人。）
   - Is a man or woman who is hired to conduct her into or departure from port where she ought to discharge/loading.
     （係指一位被僱用引導船舶進出其裝、卸貨港口的先生或女士。）

2. Why are Pilots engaged? （為何要僱用引水人？）
   - For their expertise in navigating in close proximity to land and in narrow channels.
     （借重其航行於沿岸與狹窄水道的專業技術。）
   - For their ability to anticipate accurately the effects of currents and tidal influences.
     （能夠準確地預測潮流與洋流的影響的能力。）
   - For their understanding of local traffic.
     （了解當地交通狀況。）
   - For their ability to work effectively with the local VTS.
     （具備與當地船舶交通服務中心有效合作的能力。）
   - For their language ability when dealing with shore services.
     （具備處理陸上相關業務的語言能力。）
   - For their expertise in handling tugs and linesmen.
     （指揮拖輪與纜工的專業。）
   - To support Master and relieve fatigue.
     （支援船長業務並解除其疲憊。）

- To provide an extra person or persons on the bridge to assist with navigating the ship.

  （爲駕駛臺團隊提供增額人員以協助船舶航行。）

- A Pilot onboard improves both the safety and efficiency of operation.

  （引水人登輪改善作業的安全與效率。）

一、如何質疑引水人 ? How to challenge pilot?

1. Pilot, we are 2 cables off the charted track, Is there any special reason for this?

   （引水人！我們偏離既定航路0.2浬，請問有何特殊原因嗎？）

2. Pilot, we are at ... distance (3 miles)... From... (the bearing of ... is ...). Is that correct?

   （引水人！我們與……距離3浬，方位……請問這樣恰當嗎？）

3. Pilot, what should be the bearing/distance of ... When we must started turning?

   〔引水人！我們位於（特定目標）方位……距離……處，請問我們何時開始轉向？〕

4. Pilot, what distance must be pass off ... (buoy, light)?

   （引水人！請問我們要以多少距離通過浮標／燈塔？）

5. Pilot, what is your intended rate of turn?

   〔引水人！請問你（妳）想要的迴轉角速度爲何？〕

6. Pilot, what is the number/name of the next buoy?

   （引水人！請問下一個浮標的號碼／名稱爲何？）

7. Pilot, do you think we should increase speed/ reduce speed?

   （引水人！請問我們應該加速或減速呢？）

8. Pilot, how are we going to clear that vessel?

   （引水人！請問我們該如何避讓那艘船？）

9. Pilot, what distance must be pass off ... (buoy, light)?

（引水人！請問我們應該與浮標、燈塔保持……距離通過？）

10. Pilot, what was the conversation with Tug's Master about?

（引水人！請問您與拖船船長交談內容為何？）

二、船長／引水人的角色 The role of the master / pilot

1. Over the years there has been a steady increase in both the number of vessels and their tonnage. Large container vessels and VLCCs are commonplace and, with a number of ports now being able to accommodate the world's largest vessels, the problems of the captains and pilots have increased and the role of the pilot hasbecome absolutely essential.

（過去多年來，無論在船舶艘數與噸位都呈穩定成長。航行海上的大型貨櫃船與超級油輪極為尋常，而且很多港口也陸續新建或拓建以容納此等世界上最大的船舶，使得船長與引水人面對的問題愈多，任務也愈趨艱鉅，尤其引水人的角色變得更為重要。）

2. The master is responsible for the safety of the ship, her cargo, the environment and everyone on board, as well as all phases of ship operations in port and at sea.

（船長須為船舶的安全、貨載、環境、船上的每一個人，以及船舶在港內或在大洋的所有操作過程負責。）

3. Pilotage service does not substitute for the ship's own safe navigation, but complements it.

（僱用引水人提供引航服務，並不表示可以確保船舶的安全航行，但卻可輔助其不足處。）

4. Notwithstanding anything in any public or local Act, the owner or master of a vessel navigating under circumstances in which pilotage is compulsory shall be answerable for any loss or damage caused by the vessel or by any <u>fault of the navigation of the vessel</u> in the same manner as he would if poilotage were not compulsory.

（儘管已有公法與當地法規所訂的任何規定，但航行於強制引水區的船舶，其船東或船長仍必須爲其船舶或<u>船舶的航行疏失</u>所造成的任何損害與損失負責。在非強制引水區亦同。）

【註1】
answerable：負有責任的。

5. Despite the duties and obligations of a pilot, his presence on board does not relieve the master or officer in charge of the watch (conduct) from their duties and obligations for the safety of the ship. The master and the pilot shall exchange information regarding navigation procedures, local conditions and the ship's characteristics.

（不論引水人的責任與義務爲何，其登船並不解除船長與當值駕駛員對於船舶安全的責任與義務。船長與引水人必須交換關於航行程序、當地狀況與船舶特性的資訊。）

6. The fact that a pilot has been given control of the ship for navigational purposes does not mean that the pilot has superseded the master.

〔即使引水人實質上因航行需要被（船長）賦予操縱船舶的作爲，但並不表示引水人可以取代船長。〕

7. The master should be fully aware of any problems on board the ship, navigation equipment, anchors, machinery, shiphandlig difficulties

and be frank in mentioning any defects to the pilot or VTS.

（船長必須完全了解本船的任何問題，包括航行設備、錨具、機器、操縱困難等，而且要坦白地將任何缺失告知引水人或VTS。）

8. Always maintain close communication with the pilot and be fully aware of his intentions, particularly when communication between pilot nag tugs and shore are in a local language.

（船長應隨時與引水人保持密切溝通，並充分注意其企圖，特別是當引水人與拖船，或岸際人員以當地語言喋喋不休做聯絡時。）

9. It is the master himself who decides whether or not to enter the port and one can say that is dangerous and should be avoided.

〔船舶是否進港由船長自行決定。但有些船長（或公司）認為那是危險的做法，應避免之。〕

10. It is recognized that each pilotage situation is different, weather, vessel size and manoeuvrability, channel constraints and currents, among other, all influence the way the operation will be conducted.

（我們必須認知到每一個引航情況都是不同的，如天候、船舶大小及操縱特性、航道限制及潮流等皆會影響操船的方式。）

11. Because of the specialized nature and handling characteristics of some ships, the shipmaster can anticipate better than the pilot the outcome of certain maneuvers. The need for team work on the bridge then become essential.

（因為某些船舶的特質與操縱特性，船長本較引水人善於預測某些操作帶來的後果，故而對於駕駛臺團隊合作的需求至為重要。）

12. The place where pilots join the ships should be defined as "pilot

boarding area or ground" rather than a single point, to allow more flexibility in passage planning and give more manoeuvring room.

（引水人登船處應被定義為「引水人登船區」而非單一定點，唯有如此才允許航程計畫較有彈性，並保有更寬闊的操船空間。）

13. The worst case scenarios include arriving on the bridge to find:

（引水人抵達駕駛臺最不想見到的場景如下：）

(1) The vessel in a dangerous situation.

（船舶陷於困境。）

(2) The bridge team not having a clue where they are.

（駕駛臺團隊對本船所在位置毫無概念。）

(3) The vessel on the verge of breaking down or already broken down. （船舶瀕臨失控或已經失控。）

(4) Half the bridge and navigational equipment out of order.

（駕駛臺團隊成員有一半以上未進入狀況，以及駕駛臺內有一半以上的航儀失常。）

14. We must understand those delicate points and make sure that not only will pilots do their best for the safety of navigation in the pilotage area, but also master and crews.

（我們必須了解許多微妙特點，並確實體認船舶在引航區內的航行安全不能單靠引水人，更要船長與船員配合。）

15. The "one man band pilot" should not be the norm but unfortunately is unavoidable on many ships today.

（讓引水人一人在駕駛臺唱獨角戲絕對不是標準模式，但很不幸的，今天仍有很多船舶無法避免。）

16. The master is responsible for his own professional competence, in-

cluding having sufficient knowledge and experience to be able to judge the pilots' performance and recognize significant pilot error.

（船長必須爲其自身的專業能力負責，包括有足夠的知識與經驗判斷引水人的作爲，並指出引水人的重大錯失。）

17. The master's authority is never completely in abeyance even while a pilot has immediate charge of the ship's navigation.

（船長的權力絕不中止，即使船舶在引水人直接操控下亦同。）

18. As mariners (pilots), we are very aware of the importance and necessity of the proper verbal confirmation of orders given on the navigating bridge.

〔作爲海員（引水人），我們必須高度警覺到在駕駛臺所下達指令之正確口頭確認的重要性與必須性。〕

【註2】
目前普遍採用的方式就是「Closed loop communication」，亦即發信者必須確認所發指令爲所有駕駛臺團隊成員明確收到並複誦。

19. Orders that are misinterpreted or not heard can spell disaster very quickly when a vessel is manoeuvring in close proximity to dangers such as within the pilotage phase of the voyage.

（當船舶運轉於接近危險物或水域的所在，諸如進入引航區，設若指令未被聽到或是被誤解常會迅速地帶來重大災禍。）

20. All information exchanged should be concise, prioritized and mutual understanding and intentions clearly acknowledged by every member of the bridge team.

〔所有資訊交換要簡潔，依輕重緩急列出優先順序，並確認相互了

解，而且（自己的）企圖要讓所有駕駛臺團隊成員知道。〕

21. When the pilot comes on to the bridge he (she) should be fully informed of the condition of the ship's propulsion machinery and navigational equipment.

（當引水人來到駕駛臺時，應被詳細告知船舶推進機器與航儀設備的狀況。）

22. The courts always tend to take the view that the "advice" of a pilot is advice that the master should follow on account of the pilot's specialized local knowledge and special skill, but that is not to say that the master is bound to follows the pilot's advice implicitly if it would appear in the master's deliberate judgement to involve danger to the ship.

（法院經常傾向採信引水人的「建議」，只是本於引水人具備專業的當地水文知識與特別技巧，是船長應當遵循的「建議」，但這並不隱含著如果船長憑著其專業判斷認定船舶將涉及危險，船長亦必須遵循引水人的建議。）

23. Each of the European Pilots carries a Potable Pilot Unit (PPU) when boarding a vessel. For safety reasons they do not depend upon the ship's electronics alone. Instead, they carry their own hardware and software. Because they carry the same equipment every day, they are familiar with how to use it, its accuracy, and its limitation.

〔每一位歐洲引水人登船時都會背著攜帶式引航裝備（PPU）上船。因為基於安全考量，他（她）們不能只相信船上的電子航儀。為此他（她）們攜帶本身的硬體與軟體上船，因為他（她）們每天攜帶相同的設備上船，非常熟悉設備的使用方法、精確性與其限制。〕

24. If in doubt, query his intentions, and in case of disagreement, ensure that conflicting intentions / interpretations are resolved before continuing with the operation.

〔如有任何疑慮，應即詢問其（引水人）意圖，又遇有意見不一時，應在採取下一動作前確認衝突的意見或解釋已經化解澄清。〕

25. The pilot exercises his judgment in electing to come into port with a few inches of water under the keel, because he believes it to be safe, but also because he knows it is expected of him.

（引水人運用其專業判斷選擇船底餘裕（海底距龍骨之間的水深）只有幾吋的情況入港，是因為其認為這是安全的，同時也是其所希望的。）

26. Should such a situation develop suddenly with no time to order a pilot the master would be fully justified to carry out this operation himself to avert disaster.

〔如果情況突然發展至來不及僱用引水人，船長為避免災難而自行操船（進港）是完全合理的。〕

27. You can't blame it all on the pilot. There were other people on the bridge and they were not saying anything.

〔事故的發生不能完全歸咎於引水人，因為還有其他人在駕駛臺，而且他（她）們未曾提出任何意見。〕

28. Maintain communication by walkie-talkie between the pilot ladder and the bridge when the pilot is boarding or leaving.

（當接、送引水人時，引水梯現場與駕駛臺之間必須利用對講機保持聯絡。）

第五章　船舶操縱

第一節　船舶操縱的本質（The essence of ship-handling）

1. Ship manoeuvring has been, for centuries, the epitome of good seamanship, carried out with pride and excellence. But, sadly, following the reduction of practical exercise, the traditional seamanship skills associated with ships have disappeared as well.

（幾世紀以來，「操船」一直是操船者利用卓越技術所表現，並引以自豪的優良船藝縮影。然遺憾的是，隨著實務練習機會的減少，連帶地使得傳統船藝技術亦隨之消失。）

2. The marine environment is intrinsically a set of variables that are part of an equation which cannot be solved by the linearity of a traditional mechanical model.

（海洋環境本質上即是一套變數，其乃方程式的一部分，根本無法利用傳統力學模式的線性程式解決。）

3. Science can't tell you how to manoeuvring a ship to docking alongside.

（科學無法教您如何操縱船舶泊靠碼頭。）

4. You must know those you conduct before you can be a proficient maneuver.

〔要成為一位精通熟練的操船者之前，必須先了解你（妳）所欲操縱的船舶。〕

5. Any <u>prudent ship handler</u> should expect the <u>unexpected</u> in advance.
（任何一位謹慎的操船者必定會預先防範突發（非預期）事件的發生。）

6. Good ship handling is anticipation, not reaction.
（優質的操船術貴在採取動作前的預為防範，而非後期的補救因應。）

7. Nor could we sit by idly and watch out profession being kicked in the head without a response.
（我們的專業不容許我們保持沉默不做回應。）

8. Ships do not behave in a totally random way, so provided there is enough time to respond in accordance with the COLREG there need be no collision.
（船舶的運動不會全然任意隨機，倘若有足夠時間依據避碰規則的規定採取行動因應，就不會發生碰撞事故。）

9. The skill can only be acquired from experience.
（操船技術只能從經驗習得。）

10. While this is acceptable in theory, it is not entirely practical.
（理論上是可以接受的，但實際上並不盡然。）

11. More haste, less speed（=Haste makes waste）
（欲速則不達、忙中有誤。）

12. A professional is never in a hurry to do anything aboard ship.
（一位專業海員在船上絕不匆促行事。）

13. Any accident or problem situation is the result of an unfortunate mix of different parameters at a given time.

（任何事故或困境都是許多不同參數在同一時間不幸的匯合所造成的。）

第二節　影響操船的因素（Factors affect ship-handling）

1. Maneuverability refers to how easily the operator can maneuver and manipulate the ship, or whether the operator can maneuver the ship as he please.

（「操縱性」意指如何能讓操船者輕易的操縱船舶，或是讓操船者可以依照本身喜歡的方式操船。）

2. Positioning is essential for navigation and manoeuvring: to ensure you have situational awareness; know where you are in relation to navigational hazards.

（「定位」是航行與操縱領域最重要的；因為唯有透過「定位」才能確保自身的情境警覺；掌握本船與航行險阻的相對關係。）

3. Close monitoring of external factors such as currents, windage, shallow water effects on the vessel's manoeuvrability must be carried out.

（必須密切進行監測影響船舶操縱性的外在因素，諸如水流、受風面、淺水效應等。）

4. Ships must be built with appropriate maneuverability so the they can

overcome <u>unfavorable external factors</u> like the tidal currents, oceanic currents, wind, and waves and be operated safely.

（船舶建造必須具備適當的操縱性，如此才能使操縱者得以克服<u>不</u><u>利的外部因素</u>，諸如潮流、洋流、風及波浪等因素，也唯有如此才能安全操縱船舶。）

5. The drift of <u>wind-driven currents</u> in the open ocean approximates in knots 2% of the wind velocity in miles per hour.

〔在開放大洋中，<u>風吹流</u>的流速約爲風速（節）的2%。〕

6. The set of wind-driven currents in open ocean areas is about 40° to the right of the wind direction in the Northern Hemisphere and 40° to the left in the southern hemisphere.

（在北半球開放大洋中，風吹流的流向約介於風向的右側40°左右，南半球則位於左側40°左右。）

7. Cruise vessels, container vessels and LNG carriers are becoming much larger and require specific attention during pilotage because of their large windage.

（客輪、貨櫃船與瓦斯運送船愈來愈大，故而在引航過程中需特別注意其廣大的受風面積。）

8. Remember that the wind force on the ship increases by the square of the wind speed.

（必須牢記吹襲到船上的風力是隨著風速的平方增加的。）

9. The longitudinal wind area, when taking into account five-high containers (although nine containers high is possible), will be approximately 12,000 m² at a draught of 13.5 m. This requires approxi-

mately 100 tonnes <u>bollard pull</u> with a crosswind of Beaufort Force 5(10m/sec), not taking into account the bow and stern thrusters.

〔假設甲板裝載5層高的貨櫃（也有可能裝到9層），其縱向受風面積在吃水13.5公尺時約可達12,000平方公尺。如未計入艏、艉橫向推進器，則在蒲氏風力5級橫向風時約需要100噸的<u>纜樁額定拉力</u>。〕

10. Bulk carriers and oil tankers have not grown much in size during recent years. However, cruise vessels, container vessels and LNG carriers are becoming much larger and require particular attention during pilotage because of their large <u>windage</u>.

（最近幾年散裝船與油輪在船舶噸位上並無太大的成長。但是客船、液化瓦斯船及貨櫃船則愈造愈大，而因爲其<u>受風面積</u>巨大，所以在引航過程時需特別注意。）

11. For all ships with a <u>large windage</u>, one should always be aware of wind gusts, which can be predicted but not the exact location and movement they will attack the ship.

（對所有具有<u>巨大受風面積</u>的船舶而言，人們必須經常注意強陣風，它們雖可預測，但卻無法準確地預測其將吹襲到船上的眞正位置與動態。）

12. When coming closer to the berth, as the speed and its steering capability decreases, the wind forces tend to become the predominant factor and tugs have to operate to their full capabilities.

〔當船舶接近碼頭時，由於船速及操舵性能的降低，此時風力將成爲主導操船的因素，故而拖船必須盡全力運轉。〕

13. In the real world, any alterations of course for shipping, imprecise

steering and the effects of the tidal stream/current and/or leeway will inevitably mean that the vessel will wander off track.

（實務上，只要用舵轉向、不精確的操舵、受到潮流／洋流或是風壓差的影響，船舶終將偏離預定航路。）

第三節　船舶操縱（Ship handling/Mamoeuvring）

1. The principles of the science of ship handling can be learnt from books or instructors, but the art of handling a ship in restricted water or in heavy seas can be acquired only after practical experience.

（船舶操縱的科學原理可以從書本或講師處習得，但是在限制水域，或在惡劣天候情況下的操船技藝只能從實際的經驗中去獲取。）

2. In the preparation for the forecast poor weather.

（為惡劣天氣預報做準備。）

3. The navigator must have a good knowledge of the manoeuvring capabilities of the vessel.

（航行員應該具備有關船舶運轉能力的豐富知識。）

4. The aspiring ship master should waste no opportunity of watching intelligently, and taking note how the experienced and expert pilot handle his (her) ship.

〔一位有抱負的船長絕不會錯失任何機會去用心注意有經驗的專業引水人如何操縱他（她）的船舶。〕

5. Navigation in the confined waters has traditionally been conducted using visual pilotage techniques.

（傳統上，航行在受限水域要採用目視引航技術。）

6. Face in the direction of ship movement – if going astern fact aft, its' where the action is.

（操船時永遠要面對船舶運動的方向，如倒俥時，要面朝船艉方向。）

7. We might expect ship-shaped with larger block coefficient to suffer from severe swing of the bow when engine running astern.

〔我們亦可預期方型係數較大（寬胖型船體）的船舶在倒俥時，船艏將會發生嚴重的偏轉。〕

8. Remember to conduct the ship to stem the current at all times, if conditions permit, thus offering a much greater margin of safety, greater controllability of the vessel and more time available to assess an unplanned event.

（如情況允許，記得隨時都要保持頂流航行，以便獲致較大的安全餘裕，較好的船舶操縱性，以及爭取較多評估非預期事件的時間。）

9. We care about safety and many experiences have taught me that "fast", in many cases, is almost the opposite of "safe".

（我們在意的是安全，而從許多經驗學習到，「快」在許多案例中幾乎都是不安全的。）

10. The speed factor is probably at the root of the majority of all marine disasters.

（速度因素常是大多數海上事故發生的主因。）

11. One of the most important things to remember in shiphandling is to make sure that you do not have too much way on the vessel. Speed through the water is very deceiving.

（操縱船舶最重要者就是船速不要太快。船舶對水速度是不易捉摸的。）

12. The speed should give them better sea-keeping and manoeuvring characteristics.

（適當的船速始能獲致較佳的適海性與操縱性。）

13. As per the passage plan, speed was to be reduced to below 12 knots to minimize the effect of squat on under keel clearance.

（依據航行計畫，將船速降低至12節以下以減少因龍骨下船底水深不足引起的「艉蹲」效應。）

14. Failure to control the initial astern movement.

（疏於控制初始倒退運動的慣性。）

15. The major difference between the neophyte and the experienced shiphandler is the speed ay which they work. The less experienced shiphandler generally works too fast.

（有經驗的操船者與菜鳥操船者最顯著的差別在於其操船運轉的速度，經驗較淺者通常有船速偏快的傾向。）

16. The OOW should not hesitate in reducing speed to avert collision if circumstances so require and should also be guided by Rule 8 (e) of the Colregs.

（如環境或情況需要，而需減速避讓時，當值駕駛員切勿猶豫依照避碰規則第八條規定採取行動。）

17. Though reducing speed and stopping propulsion would be fully correct according to the rules, they may not be the best action to take in the given scenario as they may not be readily apparent to the other vessel.

（雖然依據規定，減速或停俥是完全正確地，但在某些情境下，減速或停俥並不是最好的行動，因為這兩個動作在特定情境下都不易被他船明顯看出。）

18. Another good reason for going slow is the many things that may happen suddenly and unexpectedly due to human or mechanical failure.

（減緩船速的另一個好理由是有許多事故是起因於人為因素或機械缺失等無法預期而突然發生的。）

19. The astern movement on the main engine was ordered much too late.

（倒俥的指令下得太晚。）

20. When ahead thrust is applied with port or starboard helm, the ship's stern moves in a direction opposite to the intended direction of turn due to the aft location of the propeller and rudder.

（當對前進中的船舶施以左舵或右舵，因為俥、舵位處船艉，所以船艉會向意圖轉向一側的反向移動。）

21. Turning on the spot, or nearly on the spot, is only possible with the high lift rudders.

（只有配備高揚力舵的船舶才可能施行原地調頭或接近原地調頭。）

22. Twin screw ships are much more manoeuvrable than single screw ships. They can turn on the spot without making headway and can easily manoeuvre straight ATERN. Turning can be done by reversing one propeller and setting the other for ahead while applying helm in the intended direction.

（雙俥船較單俥船易於操縱。其可在不會產生前進運動的情況下進行原地調頭，而且可以簡單地進行直線倒退。調頭轉向時，只要一俥前進另俥倒退，並將舵板扳向欲轉向的一舷即可。）

23. How fast will the ship turn at full speed with maximum helm? To what speed will the ship slow down during such turn?

（在全速狀態下用滿舵轉向，其轉向角速度有多快？採行此種轉向模式，船速會降落多少？）

24. Occasionally ship masters feel pressured to move vessels, even though there are not enough tugs to do so, which has an impact on safety levels.

（有時候船長因迫於開船壓力，雖拖船艘數或馬力不夠仍執意為之，此勢必對安全水準產生影響。）

【註1】
船舶安全不容妥協。

25. Several serious incidents have occurred due to excessive use of rudder moves by ship's handler.

〔很多嚴重事故是因為操船者下達太多舵（俥）令所造成的。〕

26. The number of manoeuvres is limited by the volume of starting air available.

〔操縱船舶的俥令（次數）受到可用啓動空氣量的限制。〕

第四節　狹窄水道與限制水域（Narrow and restricted waters）

1. Sailing in narrow waters entails increased risks of collision or grounding. Therefore, prior to commencing a passage in confined waters, a risk analysis should be carried out (or consulted) as part of the SMS in order to verify that back-up systems are instantly available.

〔航行於狹窄水道勢必會增加碰撞與擱淺的風險。因此，作為船舶安全管理系統的一部分，船舶在進入受限水域之前，為了確保作為（替代）腹案的系統隨時可派上用場，必須進行風險評估。〕

2. When navigating in confined waters it is essential to maintain a visual lookout with frequent visits to the bridge wings on both sides of the ship.

（航行於受限水域最重要的是要保持目視瞭望，而且要經常至駕駛臺兩舷外之翼側瞭望。）

3. Navigation in the confined waters of the Keelung has traditionally been conducted using visual pilotage techniques.

（傳統上，航行於類似基隆港的受限水域，就須採取目視引航操船的技術。）

4. The term "middle" does not necessarily always mean on the center line between the banks, but can also mean the middle of the best

available water where the banks are irregular.

（「中央」一詞所指的未必是兩河岸之間的中央線，例如在不規則狀彎曲河道中，則指最佳可航水域的中間部分即是。）

5. Prohibit overtaking in and around all precautionary areas and in places where the lanes are narrow.

（禁止在狹窄的航行巷道與所有警戒區及其附近追越他船。）

6. We have recognized meeting and passing another vessel in a confined channel is almost the ultimate in ship-handling technique. It involves bringing ships very close together, within very fine limits where the margin for error is small.

（我們體認到在受限航道與他船相遇或通過他船時，是展現操船技術的最高境界。其意味著船舶在極度受限水域內相互緊密接近，致容許犯錯的空間極小。）

7. All the time when in narrow waters watch the helmsman when altering the course, and see that the wheel house doors are open so that he can hear.

（航行於狹窄水域轉向時，務必一直注意舵工操舵是否正確，而且要保持駕駛臺的門開啓著，以便聆聽外部動態。）

Be sure he repeats each order. What with a foreign pilot and foreign sailors, each speaking a different brand of foreign English, anything can happen.

（確認舵工複誦每一個舵令，因爲在不同國籍的引水人與水手操著不同腔調的外國英文互動的情境下，什麼事情都可能發生。）

8. I really did not want to go any shallower with a draught of 13 m.

（本船吃水13公尺，我不想航往任何淺水區。）

9. A warning whistle signal of 5 short blasts was sounded by own vessel to alert the approaching ship of the perceived danger.

（本船用汽笛鳴放5短聲警告接近中，且認爲有危險的他船。）

第五節　進／出港口、錨地、離／靠碼頭（Entering and leaving ports、Anchorage/Berthing and unberthing）

211

一、進／出港口

1. The convenience of a direct course and a shorter transit time must not justify the selection of a route that plainly contravenes the Colregs.

（爲圖方便抄短路、走捷徑而公然違反避碰規則並非合理的航路選擇。）

2. At all times and under all conditions. Both anchors are ready to be dropped, if require, with not more than one shackle in the water.

（隨時隨地備妥雙錨，如有需要拋錨時，錨鏈鬆出不要超過一節。）

【註2】
拋雙錨鬆出短鏈拖行，旨在增加錨具對地的（滾動）摩擦力，而非想要抓著力，唯有如此才能減緩船舶的前進慣性。

3. The timing of the passage was planned for high water at the habaour entrance beacons to maximize the available depth of water.

（計畫於高潮時通過港口入口信標，以利用最大可用深度的效益。）

4. Therefore, it is better to keep the engine at dead slow, to correct any unwanted change in heading immediately by appropriate rudder angle.

（因此，最好保持主機微速運轉，以便藉由適當的舵角立即修正任何非預期的艏向變化。）

5. Stopping and waiting till visibility improves would be the safest thing to do.

（停俥等候視界好轉再進出港是最安全的作法。）

6. During the passage of that area, her stem enters the slack water (shelter water) while her stern is caught by the tidal current on one of her quarters, making her bow either turn away from the intended heading.

（當船舶通過防波堤時，其船艏已進入堤內的無流區，但是船艉翼側卻遭受潮流的作用，使得船舶會自預期艏向偏轉至左舷或右舷。）

7. To counter a sheer, it is preferable to take drastic steps first and then ease those steps.

〔為制衡（前項所述的）突然偏轉現象，應立即採取果斷的操船動作，（待偏轉控制後）再逐步回復正常操作。〕

8. When there is still ample room on the axis of the entrance, One should not be frightened by this (said) phenomenon to reduce the speed (to stop the engine) at any cost, especially not at the cost of losing steerage, or worse, losing control over the ship's heading.

〔當港口進口的軸線上仍有足夠水域時，操船者切勿因為上述現象而驚慌失措，而不計後果地去減速（或停俥），尤其是不能以喪失操舵能力或失去船艏向的控制作為代價。〕

9. Anticipate any tendency to deviate. If necessary, apply propeller thrust to the rudder.

（預估前述偏向趨勢，必要時應及時加俥以提升舵力。）

10. When manoeuvring in a harbour both anchors should always be ready for letting go immediately.

（當船舶在港內運轉時，雙錨應備便隨時可拋下。）

11. Keep in mind that it is movement over the bottom that's important when letting go, not speed through the water.

（切記！拋錨時要注意的是對地速度，而非對水速度。）

213

二、錨泊術語 Anchoring terms

1. Weighing anchor 起錨
   起錨是將錨從海底拉起，直到完全離開海底為止。此一錨離開海底的狀態稱作「錨離地」（Anchor aweigh），而船舶即可由其錨位處離開，雖然在IMO英文內無此一字彙。但在一般實務上卻經常使用。在IMO中與其相當之用語為「My anchor is clear of the bottom.」。

2. Let go ... anchor 下……錨（後面跟隨欲使用錨之名稱）
   如「Let go starboard anchor.」（拋下右錨）。
   當船舶到達錨位而必須拋錨時，即下達此命令。如船舶進港靠泊碼頭，如果衝向岸壁速度太快時，引水人也會下達緊急之拋錨口令，此時下錨之行動必須快速，以免導致危險。

3. Shorten cable 絞短錨鍊
   例：「You must shorten your cable to three shackles.」（你必須將

錨鏈絞短至3節。）

亦即指必須起錨直到只有三節錨鏈留在水中，此種指令通常是引水人欲將船舶由錨地帶領進入港口時，為縮短起錨作業時間，於登船前由引水站所下達的。

4. Slip anchor 錨滑脫

   例：「I have slipped my anchor in position ... 」（本船的錨已滑脫掉在……）

   即考慮將某一卸扣（Shackle）拆掉，以切斷錨鏈，使錨或整個錨鏈滑脫掉入水中。在緊急狀況時，例如當有他船漂流經過擁擠的錨區而威脅到本船時，本船可將錨鏈滑脫盡速駛離現場，以避免碰撞或造成更大損壞。實務上，因滑脫錨鏈費工費時不可行。建議動俥配合調整錨鏈長度較為有效。

5. Dredging anchor 拖錨

   「拖錨」一詞乃指船舶將其將錨具沿著海底拖行的航行狀態。

6. Dragging anchor 走錨

   「走錨」一詞，係指船舶因其所拋出的錨在不可抗力或外力作用下，已無法（確實抓住海底）防止船舶之移動，而導致錨在海底移位。

7. Anchor position 錨位

   錨位乃指船舶已下錨或欲下錨的地方。

8. Foul anchor 錨障

   錨與錨鏈互相絞纏，或是纏住其他海底或水中障礙物。

9. Forward! Bridge. How about the chain direction and tension?

（船頭！駕駛臺。請問錨鏈方向與吃力狀況？）

10. Your message broken. Say again.

（你的信號不清楚，請重複。）

11. Chain leading two O'clock and tension.

（錨鏈方向2點鐘、吃力。）

12. Two shackles on deck , chain up and down.

（二節甲板，錨鏈垂直。）

13. For the time being, we...

（我們暫時……）

三、進／出錨地、離／靠碼頭

1. It is a known fact that more collisions occur in anchorages than anywhere else.

（眾所周知，船舶在錨地發生碰撞的機率較其他水域大。）

2. One should not assume that the nearby anchored vessels keep proper anchor watches nor act according to maritime best practices.

（不能假設他船都會按照海運最佳實務輪值錨更，並據以採取行動。）

3. When traffic or weather make it necessary, the engine should be kept at short notice at anchor to ensure the possibility of immediate picking up the anchor.

（當交通或天候狀況變得有需要時，主機應隨時備便，以便在最短時間內可以立即起錨。）

4. The Master decided to keep the main engine fully manned and on stand-by.

（船長決定全員備俥因應。）

5. Before arrival, the Master (Pilot) have to conduct a meeting to brief officers on the mooring plan and the constraint at the port.

〔抵達港口前，船長（引水人）必須針對帶纜計畫與在港期間的限制事項對船副進行簡報。〕

6. At certain times of the year, the weather conditions can change rapidly in the short time between making the fairway and docking.

（在一年中的某些時候，天候狀況在航道航行與離、靠碼頭之短暫時間內會產生急遽變化。）

7. In deep anchorages many an anchor with its entire cable has been lost through attempting to let go with the usual brake control as in shallow water.

〔在深水錨地拋錨，如果一如在淺水區採取通常的錨機剎車片控制方法，常會造成錨及整條錨鏈流出（喪失）的後果。〕

8. In depths of 10 fathoms or more an anchor should never be let go by the run, especially so should there be some way on the vessel over the ground.

〔在水深深度超過10噚的水域拋錨，絕不可採自由落體（鬆開剎車）方式拋錨，特別是當船舶仍具有對地速度時。〕

9. Lower the anchor with the windlass in gear to within a few fathoms of the bottom, and then let go under brake control.

（利用錨機將錨絞出至離海底數噚處，再利用控制〔鬆開〕刹車片方式拋錨。）

10. The force required to stop a vessel by means of the cable or a mooring line varies directly as the square of the ship's speed, and, by this rule, at 2 knots 4 times the more stress is necessary to bring the ship rest in a given distance that at 1 knot.

（欲利用錨鏈或纜繩將船停住，所需的制動力與船速的平方成正比。依此法則，在相同距離內，欲將船速2節的船舶停住，則所需的制動力要比船速1節的船多4倍。）

11. Use the propulsion system to manoeuvre a vessel to relieve tension in the anchor chain before "heaving in", and stop the windlass as soon as any significant tensioning is observed or difficulty is experienced.

（在起錨前，可利用主機微進以減緩錨鏈的張力，又一旦發覺錨鏈有任何過度張力或作動困難時應立即停止錨機絞錨。）

12. Closely monitor the predicted weather and sea conditions and ensuring that the anchor is recovered in good time, before the conditions make this difficult to achieve.

（密切注意天候與海況預報，並應確保在天候海況變惡劣，起錨不易之前，有足夠時間起錨駛離困境。）

13. After the anchor was clear of the water, the anchor party could not fully house the anchor in the hawsepipe, as a twist in the cable between the gypsy and the guide roller prevented the anchor from ori-

entating properly.

（當錨出水時，船頭拋錨人員發現介於鏈輪〔絞盤〕與防止錨鏈絞入方向翻轉的導引輪之間的錨鏈扭轉而無法完全收入錨鏈筒內。）

14. At wind force 4 Beaufort, everybody is confident that the anchor will not drag or the chain will not break. However, at wind force 10 Beaufort, nobody can guarantee that the vessel will not drag or lose the anchor.

（我們都知道蒲氏風力4級風不會流錨或斷鏈。然而，風力達蒲氏風力10級時，就無人敢於保證船舶不會流錨或斷鏈。）

15. Advise that in the event of any vessel fouling a pipeline, the anchor or gear should be slipped and abandoned without attempting to get it clear. Any excessive force applied to a pipeline could result in a rupture, in the case of a gas pipeline, could cause serious damage or loss of the vessel.

（遇有錨鏈勾纏到管線時，建議切斷錨鏈離開而非企圖強行起錨離開。任何過度施力可能造成管線破裂，如果是瓦斯管線，即可能造成船舶嚴重的損失或損壞。）

16. The ship approached the berth at an angle of about 30 degrees and, with her bow close to the jetty, the forward spring line was sent ashore and belayed on a bollard.

（船舶以近30°的角度趨近碼頭，讓船頭接近碼頭，再送出前倒纜，並挽於纜樁上。）

17. No sideways movement of a single screw ship is possible.

（單俥船不可能做側向運動的。）

18. Assisting steering is achieved by the stern tug sheering to port or starboard.

〔可藉由船艉拖船向左或向右偏轉，達到協助操船（轉向）的效能。〕

19. The stern tug was fast with a line led through the center lead aft and the pilot ordered it to pull the ship astern.

（拖船在正船艉帶拖纜，而且引水人命令拖船將本船朝後拉。）

20. The ship overshot this (bridge) mark and it was now required to move the ship back by about 5 meters.

（船舶位置超過駕駛臺位置的標誌，現在必須將船再往後移動約5公尺。）

21. The pilot explained that he had ordered the after tug to push the tanker on the transom stern in order to move ahead.

〔引水人解釋為了要使船前進，其已下令船艉拖船推頂油輪的正船艉（平面船殼板）。〕

圖5.1　船艉橫材（平面船殼）

22. Realizing that the transom stern was not a designated "tug pushing" area, the master overrode this order.

〔船長意識到正船艉（平面船殼板）不是指定「拖船推頂區」，所以拒絕這項指令。〕

23. The tanker was warped ahead safely and correctly positioned by heaving on the after backspring.

（油輪是利用絞進後倒纜，將船安全的移動至正確的位置。）

24. Ships have to keep the maximum distance possible from crowded anchorages. This will allow the bridge team sufficient response time in case any vessel leaves anchorage suddenly.

（船舶在擁擠的錨地應盡可能與他船保持最大的距離，以便讓駕駛臺團隊有足夠時間因應任何突然自錨地離開的船舶。）

25. The effective of a tunnel thruster is not high when the ship has speed ahead.

（當船舶有前進速度時，橫向推進器的效能不高。）

26. The containership probably had a working bow thruster but as soon as a ship gathers headway, the effect of the bow thruster decreases fast.

（貨櫃船或許設置有運作正常的船艏橫向推進器，但只要前進速度增加後，船艏橫向推進器的效能亦會很快的下降。）

27. The propeller wash of tugs towing on a line may hit a ship's hull and decrease pulling effectiveness. This can be influenced to a certain extent by correct towline length and towing angle.

（拖纜帶得太短，會因為拖船俥葉的排出流衝擊到被協助船的船殼上，而降低拖曳效用。此可藉調整拖纜的施力方向，以及拖纜長度

達致某種程度的改善。）

28. In the event of strong winds, securing tugs may take even longer than normal.

（在強風狀況下，繫帶拖纜可能要比正常情況花費更多時間。）

29. All those who are involved in mooring operations are to be reminded of the need to keep as well clear as practicable of any danger area.

（所有參與繫纜作業人員應被提醒盡可能遠離任何危險區。）

30. The risks in conducting mooring operations must be assessed rigorously and safe working practices developed.

（繫纜作業的風險應先嚴加評估，再行安全作業實務。）

31. Mooring accident are all too frequent, and can lead to delays, loss of time, income, injury, and ultimately, loss of life.

（帶纜引發的事故時有所聞，常導致船期延遲、浪費時間、營收、受傷，乃至人命喪亡。）

32. The mooring crew/squads should be aware that a small omission or error can have serious consequence, especially when the conditions on the mooring stations are difficult.

〔船頭船艉的帶纜（組）人員務必警覺到任何小疏失或錯誤都會帶來嚴重後果，特別是船頭船艉的現場處於艱困的情況下，如強風、降雪等。〕

33. Second mate's chief concern aft is to see that nothing fouls the propeller, and never signal all clear until you see the lines are aboard and all actual is clear.

〔船艉二副最要注意的是，確認俥葉不要糾纏到任何東西，直到你（妳）確實看到所有纜繩收回到船上，以及全部清爽後，才能報告駕駛臺：「船艉全部清爽（Aft all clear！）」。〕

34. If you want to keep out of trouble you must see to things yourself, as the responsibility is yours, and that is why you are given authority to give orders.

〔如果你（妳）想避開麻煩，你（妳）就需親自檢視，因為負責任的是你（妳），這也是為什麼你（妳）被賦予發號施令的權限的原因。〕

35. The number and locations of fairlead and bollards onboard vessels may be such that the tugs cannot operate in the best and most effective positions.

（大船上導纜器與纜樁的位置與數量，可能導致拖船無法在最有效與最佳的位置作業。）

36. Ship bollards and fairleads may even not be strong enough for powerful tugs.

〔大船上的纜樁與導纜器（的強度）可能沒有足夠強度供大馬力的拖船拖拉。〕

37. A urgent order was given to the tug to pull the vessel apart, but this sudden stressing of the towline resulted in it parting and the vessel coming into contact.

（突然下達拖輪拖開船舶的指令，造成拖纜驟然受力而斷纜，船舶因而撞上碼頭。）

38. Each ship must (Almost need to) execute a 180 degree turn inside the harbour and this maneuver is generally done before (sailing) berthing.

〔幾乎所有船舶在港內都要做180°轉向，此一操作通常要在泊靠碼頭（或開航）之前完成。〕

39. Remember to leave yourself in a position where you can always come ahead for you cannot always come back.

〔切記！永遠將船的位置置於讓你（妳）有「進俥」機會的所在，因爲你（妳）不一定有後退或重來的機會。〕

四、進、出港與離、靠碼頭常用指令

1. 繫纜作業（Mooring Operation）相關名詞

圖5.2 船舶繫纜名稱

(1) Head Line 艏（頭）纜
(2) Forward breast line 艏橫纜
(3) Forward spring 艏倒纜
(4) Aft spring 艉倒纜
(5) Aft breast line 艉橫纜
(6) Stern Line 艉纜
(7) Take to 帶上（纜繩）
　 Take tug's towing line to capstan (winch)...
　 將拖纜由拖船帶到被服務的大船絞盤（絞俥）上，當絞盤（絞俥）起動時，纜繩可由船上拉住。
(8) Capstan/Winch 絞盤
　 可纏繞纜繩及鋼纜之機械圓盤。
(9) Make Fast 繫住纜繩
　 ... then make fast on starboard quarter.
　 在右後舷繫住纜繩，即將纜繩繫在纜繩樁上，如此可防止打滑。通常麻繩纜或鋼纜，皆纏繞在繫纜樁上以繫緊。
(10) Let go (XX) Line 解掉（XX）纜
　 Let go fore and aft.
　 解掉艏、艉所有各纜。（除非已提及某特別的纜繩不解開）。
　 fore and aft 即 forward and aft 船艏與船艉之意。

2. All station；各局（かっきょく）どぅぞ！
   （呼叫所有繫、帶纜人員！）

3. 2nd (3rd) Mate! Make fast the tug (tow) line center lead Forward (Aft).
   〔二（三）副！正船頭（艉）帶拖船纜。〕

4. 2nd (3rd) Mate! Connect the tug (tow) line center lead Forward (Aft).
   〔二（三）副！正船頭（艉）帶拖船纜。〕

5. Make 10 degrees Rate Of Turn to Port (Starboard)!
   〔保持迴轉率向左（向右）10°！（AZI POD推進系統操船指令）。〕

6. Please shift the control to the Starboard wing (bridge wing).
   （請將控制系統轉至右舷翼側操控。）

7. Take engine; Take thruster
   （請將主機轉過來；請將側推轉過來。）

8. I have the engine, I have the thruster.
   （主機與側推的控制已經轉到右舷翼側來了。）

9. Don't let heaving line be thrown until you are certain they will reach!
   〔確認撇纜可以丟到岸上前不要拋出你（妳）的撇纜！〕

10. You can run the heaving line (ashore)!
    〔你可以拋出你（妳）的撇纜到岸上！〕

11. Fore and Aft proceed with heaving line!
    （船頭、船艉拋出撇纜！）

12. First spring on the bollard!
    （第一條倒纜帶上纜樁！）

13. The forward and after backsprings were already on the shore bollards.
    （前、後倒纜都已帶上纜樁。）

14. One ship's length to go!
    （船頭、船艉！前進一個船長！）

15. 35 meters to go.

（船頭、船艉！向前移動35公尺。）

16. Forecastle, slack one meter.

〔船頭！纜繩鬆出1公尺。〕

17. Second , Proceeding 6 and 2!

〔二副！帶6（條艉纜）2（條倒纜）！〕

18. Second, run your spring!

（二副！鬆出你的倒纜！）

19. Running spring aft!

（船艉！鬆出你的倒纜！）

20. Bridge! Weighing the spring aft!

（駕駛臺！船艉絞倒纜！）

21. Weigh on your spring!

（將你的倒纜絞緊！）

22. Forward station! good position? Position good.

〔（郵輪的）船頭（大副）位置可以嗎？位置很好。〕

23. We are in position!

（我們到位了！）

24. I will keep the ship in position!

〔船到位了（各纜絞緊）！〕

25. Nothing astern!

（船到位了，不要再退了！）

26. Fore and Aft we are in good position!

（船頭、船艉我們到位了！）

27. Put good weight on the breast!

（將橫纜盡量絞緊！）

28. Forward station! You can tight the spring and then hold.

〔船頭（大副）你可以絞緊倒纜，並鎖緊打住。〕

29. Stand by to check spring!

（準備將倒纜剎住！）

30. Aft! Check your spring!

〔船艉！將倒纜打（剎）住！〕

31. Aft! don't give too much weight!

（船艉！不要絞太緊！）

32. Put weight on the tow line.

（拖纜帶力！）

33. Security! You can open up the side door.

〔（郵輪的）梯口警衛！你們可以打開邊門了。〕

34. Let me know when we are two and two, guys!

〔夥伴們、帶好2（條頭纜或艉纜）2（條倒纜）時告訴我！〕

第六節　大型船舶操縱難處與應注意事項

1. Today, as ships become larger, faster and more complex, a troubled or an uneasy relationship can have devastating consequences.

（今日船舶愈造愈大、船速愈快而且更複雜，任何一個麻煩或是一個不合諧的關係皆能造成毀滅性的後果。）

2. However, it is very important to remember that most larger vessels manoeuver slowly, speed changes can be slow to materialize and, importantly, to be detected.

（無論如何，要切記！大多數巨型船舶運轉緩慢，速度的變化慢到難以具體的觀察出。）

3. The manoeuvre of large ships, with very high sides, is more delicate and the consequences of accidents are almost unimaginable.

（操縱高乾舷的大型船舶，需要特別謹慎，因其發生事故的後果難以想像。）

4. The ship-handler must maintain constant awareness of the relative dimensions of very large vessels compared to harbor basin size, and the dead angles closed by the dimensions.

（操船者必須隨時注意超大型船舶與港池幅員的相對空間，以及因船體尺寸過大所造成的死角。）

227

5. As ships have become bigger in size and forced to operate in relatively smaller port or harbor areas, more precise and skilled manoeuvring is needed. The traditional concept of the pivot point is no longer accurate enough for these purposes.

（隨著船舶愈造愈大，迫使其不得不在相對較小的港區操作，因而船舶操縱需要更精確與更高超的技術。為此，迴轉支點的傳統觀念已不再能夠精準地適用於操船目的上。）

6. It must also be taken into account that a larger ship takes longer to lose speed than a small one. When reducing speed sharply, it is important to keep an adequate amount of way on to maintain manoeuvrability, unless it is intended to stop the ship completely, and keep a vigilant lookout for any ship coming up astern.

（必須考慮大船減速較小船慢。除非企圖將船完全停止，否則不能降速過快。最重要的是要保持足夠速度，以保持操縱性，並密切瞭望任何來自後方的船舶。）

7. The length and height of container vessels, cruise ships and gas carriers can present difficulties in ship handling, particularly in high winds.

（貨櫃船、郵輪與瓦斯運送船的超長與超高特質，常造成操船上的難度，特別是在強風的情況下。）

8. There have been nemeraous accidents involving large vessels, possibly linked to the lack of space in some places, strong winds, inadequately adopted tools (tugs, bollards, etc) or inadequate knowledge of their particular characteristics.

〔有太多事故涉及大型船舶，其可能與某些操船水域的空間不足、強風、裝備工具（拖船、纜樁）不足，或是與欠缺涉事船舶的操船特性知識有關。〕

9. The feeling of gigantic size is heightened by blind angles, which are in front of the ship as well as behind it.

（操縱超大型船的感覺會因為視覺盲角更為凸顯，其不僅存在於船艏方向，船艉方向也是如此。）

10. The ship's handler must consider the large overhanging bow and stern and the small flat area at the sides of the large container vessels.

〔操船者必須考慮到大型（流線型）貨櫃船的船艏與船艉部的大幅度（曲率）外展，以及船舶舯段船殼平面區域較小的特質。〕

【註3】
限縮拖船的協助作業範圍。

11. There is an increasing need for these more expensive powerful tugs, especially in the bigger ports, but depending on the traffic and the type of service that needs to be provided.

（港區愈來愈需要昂貴的大馬力拖船，特別是在大港口。但仍需視港口的交通狀況與所提供的服務而定。）

12. In cases where more power was needed for certain large ships, more tugs were ordered.

（當遇有某些大型船需要更大的拖船馬力時，就需要增雇拖船協助。）

13. It was not uncommon to have up to 6 tugs assisting a ship.

（僱用6艘拖船協助一艘大船的情況亦時有所聞。）

14. Although tug capabilities have increased considerably during recent years, even modern tugs have limitations.

（近幾年來，雖然拖船的能力已大幅改善，但即使再現代化的拖船亦有其限制。）

15. Some of tugs which were pushing on the ship's side experienced difficulties due to the swell causing them to skid and to be unable to apply full power.

〔湧浪太大，致使部分在舷側協助推頂的拖船遭遇到自身無法保持既有作業態勢（滑開）的困難，也因而無法施出全力推頂。〕

16. Tug performance in wave conditions decreases, often due to the fact that a tug captain does not want his towline parted and/or will try to avoid hitting the ship with too much force.

（拖船在有波浪的狀況下作業，其效能會降低，通常是起因於拖船船長不願讓其拖纜斷裂，或是避免其拖船過度用力撞擊被協助船的船殼。）

第七節　其他

1. What would you do in such a situation?
    （在那種情況下您該如何自處？）

2. We are under obligation to do so.
    （我們有義務如此做。）

3. This is contrary to current practice.
    （此有違現行實務。）

4. We have 3 boats in the water.
    〔（客船開航前仍有）3艘接駁船尚未回收。〕

附錄

　　以下為被服務船舶的船長與引水人在拖船協助運航情況下，透過對講機雙方溝通或下達指令的常用語句。

被協助船的船長（引水人）與「拖船1號」間的無線電話聯絡用語	
船長／引水人	Tug 1, stnd by to pull on stbd quarter. 拖船1號！準備在右船艉拖拉。
拖船船長	Tug 1 ready to pull on stbd quarter. 拖船1號已準備在右船艉拖拉。
船長／引水人	Tug 1, 15 tons pull on stbd quarter. 拖船1號！請用15噸的拉力朝右船艉方向拖拉。
拖船船長	Tug 1 pulling 15 tons. 拖船1號正以15噸的拉力拖拉。
船長／引水人	Tug 1, increase to 20 tons. 拖船1號！請將拉力增加至20噸。
拖船船長	Tug 1 pulling 20 tons. 拖船1號正以20噸的拉力拖拉。
船長／引水人	Tug 1, ease to 10 tons；Pull 10 tons on stbd beam. 拖船1號！請將拉力減至10噸，改向右舷正橫方向拖拉。
拖船船長	Tug 1 pulling 10 tons on stbd beam. 拖船1號正以10噸的拉力往右舷正橫方向拖拉。
船長／引水人	Tug 1, Stop. 拖船1號！停俥。
拖船船長	Tug 1 all stop. 拖船1號完全停俥。

被協助船的船長（引水人）與「拖船2號」間的無線電話聯絡用語	
船長／引水人	Tug 2, stnd by to pull on port quarter. 拖船2號！準備在左船艉拖拉。
拖船船長	Tug 2 ready to pull on port quarter. 拖船2號已準備在左船艉拖拉。
船長／引水人	Tug 2, 10 tons pull on port quarter. 拖船2號！請用10噸的拉力朝左船艉方向拖拉。
拖船船長	Tug 2 pulling 5 tons. 拖船2號正以5噸的拉力拖拉。
船長／引水人	Tug 2, increase to 10 tons pull. 拖船2號！請將拉力增加至10噸。
拖船船長	Tug 2 pulling 15 tons. 拖船2號正以15噸的拉力拖拉。
船長／引水人	Tug 2, ease to 5 tons; Pull 5 tons on port beam. 拖船2號！請將拉力減至5噸，改向左舷正橫方向拖拉。
拖船船長	Tug 2 pulling 5 tons on port beam. 拖船2號正以5噸的拉力往左舷正橫方向拖拉。
船長／引水人	Tug 2, Stop. 拖船2號！停俥。
拖船船長	Tug 2 all stop. 拖船2號完全停俥。

第六章　船務管理

第一節　船長職責（Master's obligation and responsibility）

1. As master you are the direct representative of your company and, in some chartered vessel, the representative of the charterer as well.

   〔作為一名船長，你（妳）必須直接對公司負責；在租傭船情況下，同時要對租船人的代表負責。〕

   You are responsible for all damage and accidents which happen on board, not only through your own personal fault or negligence of your crew.

   〔不論是你（妳）個人錯誤或是船員的疏失，你（妳）都必須對船上發生的所有損壞與事故負責。〕

   You are responsible for all events and incidents occurring on board which may affect the interests of your company; for the safety of your vessel, her cargo, all gear and equipment; for all persons legally on board and, in some cases, even those illegally on board.

   〔你（妳）必須對船上發生，以致影響公司利益的所有事件與事故負責；同時也要對船舶安全、貨物、所有機具與設備、所有合法在船人員，有時甚至連非法登船的人員負責。〕

2. The seaworthiness of the vessel is your responsibility as is the proper loading and discharging of the cargo, even though in most trades the loading, stowage and discharging of cargo is in charge of the chief officer.

   〔即使大部分航線（船舶），貨物的裝、卸與堆積是大副的責任，

但在適當的裝、卸貨物狀況下確保船舶的適航性依舊是你（妳）的責任。〕

3. A prudent shipmaster will not hesitate to listen to suggestions made by his officers or chief engineer but will always bear in mind that he alone is responsible for the safe navigation of his/her vessel and is held accountable, as well, for all incidents and accidents aboard his / her ship. If he/she requests advice on any matter from his home office, agent, or others, including surveyors, and acts on that advice, the responsibility for any occurrence resulting from such action is entirely his own.

（一位謹慎的船長從不會猶豫聽取船副們與輪機長的建議，而且會謹記只有自己須為船舶的安全航行負責，而且需要為船上的所有事件與事故承擔法律責任。如果船長尋求總公司、船務代理或其他人，包含驗船師的建議，並依照建議行事，則亦須為因此作為所衍生的任何事故負起全責。）

第二節　駕駛臺航行守則（General Orders）

The following General Orders are given as a guide. They can and should be changed to sit the vessel and trade. A copy of the General Orders should be attached to the Night Order Book.

〔下列航行守則常被用作駕駛臺當值指南，但可依船舶與航線做適當修正，此守則的副（影印）本應附著於夜令簿上。〕

1. The orders listed below must be read by each deck officer before taking his first watch on the bridge. He/She must sign on the appro-

priate line on the last page indicating that he/she understands these orders.

〔每一駕駛員於首次在駕駛臺當值前，應詳讀下列守則。他（她）必須在最後一頁的適當處簽名以示其已了解本守則。〕

2. When alone on the bridge you should always keep in mind that the time for taking action for the vessel's safety is while still time to do so.

〔當駕駛臺只有你（妳）一人當值時，必須經常謹記採取行動確保船舶安全的時機，就是及早為之。〕

3. An officer should be on the bridge at all times when the vessel is under way and he must not leave the bridge until properly relieved by another officer or myself.

（當船舶處於航行中的狀態下，駕駛員絕對不能離開駕駛臺，而且必須直到其他駕駛員或本人正式接替其職務後始能離開駕駛臺。）

4. Before relieving the watch, the relieving officer will sign the Night Order Book, acquaint himself/herself with the vessel's position, course and speed, weather conditions and obtain any pertinent information the officer being relieved may have to pass on.

（交班前，接班駕駛員必須在夜令簿上簽名，了解船位所在、航向與速度、天候狀況，以及交班駕駛員所傳達的任何相關資訊。）

5. As watch officer of this vessel, you are, when on duty, expected to keep a good lookout. Unnecessary conversation with the man at the wheel, or with the lookout on the bridge, is not conductive to keeping a proper watch.

（作為本船的當值駕駛員，值班時務必保持充分瞭望。與舵工或駕

駛臺瞭望員閒聊無助於保持適當瞭望。）

6. When visibility becomes poor or if you anticipate that visibility may become poor because of fog, rain, snow, or any other reason, call me.

〔當能見度變差，或如果你（妳）認為能見度將因霧、雨、雪或任何其原因降低時，請呼喚我。〕

7. Be sure your lookout is thoroughly familiar with his duties and that he keeps alert. He is not to be assigned to other duties.

〔確認你（妳）的瞭望員徹底了解其職責，並能保持警戒。而且不能指派他（她）擔任其他任務。〕

8. Call me at any time in doubt-but do it in ample time-better to soon than too late.

（有任何疑慮時，必須及早呼叫本人，寧早勿晚。）

9. Whenever you think it will be necessary to slow down, try to notify the engine room in advance. But in an emergency do not hesitate to slow down, stop or go astern. Try to call mee in time to get to the bridge.

〔無論何時，當你（妳）認為有需要降低速度時，須預為通知機艙。但在緊急情況下，切勿猶豫減速、停俥或倒俥。並嘗試及早呼叫本人至駕駛臺。〕

10. Give passing vessels a good berth in ample time. Don't try to bluff the other vessel out of his right of way. Let the other vessel know in plenty of time what you intend to do.

〔避讓他船必須及早為之，而且要保持充分距離通過。切勿（仗

著本船性能優越）逼迫他船進而剝奪其航路權。讓他船及早了解你（妳）的企圖。〕

11. At sea keep at least 3 miles off passing vessels when possible; more if you think it necessary. Let me know when you have a meeting or crossing situation less than 3 miles.

〔在海上如果可能，與過往船舶保持至少3浬通過；如果你（妳）認為有需要還可更遠。當你（妳）遇有須與他船在3浬內相遇或橫越的情勢時，請讓我知道。〕

12. Watch out for small craft and fishing vessels on fishing banks and along the coast. Many do not carry proper lights.

（注意漁場與沿岸航行的小船與漁船。許多未能展示適當號燈。）

13. If using the short-range function of the radar, be sure to switch to the long-range and intermediate ranges frequently so that a target won't show up on the screen.

（如果使用雷達的短距程功能，應經常定時轉換至長距程或適當距程以免漏失目標在雷達螢幕上的回跡顯示。）

14. Check the course on the ECDIS/Chart every time there is a change of course on your watch. Let me know immediately if there is an error or the course will lead the vessel into danger.

〔在你（妳）值班時每次轉向後，請核對電子海圖顯示系統的航線。如果航線有誤並將導致船舶趨近危險物時，請立即通知我。〕

15. This vessel is to be put in hand-steering all the time the telegraph is on "Stand-By", when a pilot has the con, and when you, as officer on watch, may think it necessary.

〔一旦俥鐘搖至「主機備便」位置時，當主導操船的引水人或是作為當值駕駛員的你（妳），只要認為有需要，必須隨時改採手操舵。〕

第三節　船長夜令簿（Night Order Book）

The Night Order Book, you are expected to sign, when read and understood, and then carry out to the letter（嚴格按照字句）. Usually, contain but not limit to:

〔夜令簿是你（妳）被要求詳讀與了解後簽名，進而遵照施行的船長書面指令。通常包括但不限於下列：〕

1. Never hesitate to call the captain when in doubt, or to slow down immediately, or start fog signal on your own initiative.

   （如有疑慮切勿猶豫呼叫船長，或立即減速，或自行決定啟動霧號。）

2. Remain on the bridge at all times when under way unless properly relieved by a licensed officer.

   （除非有持照駕駛員正式接班，船舶在航行中務必隨時留在駕駛臺。）

3. Before taking over the watch, read and sign the night orders, check position and verify the course laid off to see that it is safe and that it is being steered.

   （接班前，請先詳讀夜令簿並簽名，核對船位，以及確認當下航行

的航向是否安全，而且操舵無誤。）

4. Fix position by radar as directed; more frequently if in doubt.
（依據指示利用雷達定位；如有疑慮時應更頻繁定位。）

5. Do not call upon he look out to perform any other duties.
（不可指派瞭望員擔任其他職務。）

6. Commence taking bearing when the target was sighted. If the vessel will pass within 1 mile notify the captain immediately.
（當目標可以看見時，就應開始觀測其方位。如果目標會在1浬內通過時，請立即通知船長。）

7. Obey the rules of the road; give all vessel a wide berth and make any course changes ample and definite.
（遵守航路規則；讓船必須以充分距離通過，任何航向的改變必須充分且明確。）

8. Shift Autopilot from automatic to hand while still 2 miles from the other vessel.
（當其他船舶距離2浬時轉換自動舵至手操舵。）

9. Call the captain when an aid to navigation is sighted, or if it is not sighted at the time expected.
（當助導航設施可以見到，或是在預期可見的時間點仍未見到時，請呼叫船長。）

10. Make no erasures in the log or bell book；initial all changes.
（請勿擦掉或刪去航海日誌或傳鐘記錄簿上的紀錄，如有任何改變

必須簽名以示負責。）

第四節　開船前船長廣播（Master's Before-Departure announcement）

一、藍寶石公主郵輪船長航前廣播

- Good afternoon Ladies and Gentlemen.

  This is your Captain speaking from bridge, my name is Paolo

  On behalf of Princess Cruise and the entire Officers and crew of Sapphire Princess I would like to extend a warm welcome on board to all of you.

  First of all thank you all for attending our Mandatory Safety Drill, I hope that you can now start enjoying your vacation discovering our beautiful ship and her features.

  （各位女士、先生午安！這是船長自駕駛臺發言，本人名為Paolo，謹代表公主郵輪公司與藍寶石公主號所有幹部與船員熱烈歡迎各位搭乘本輪。首先，感謝各位配合參與法定安全操演。本人希望從現在開始各位就可藉由探索這艘豪華的郵輪與其特質享受您美好的假期。）

- This itinerary will bring us visiting three very interesting Ports in Japan. The islands of Okinawa, Miyakojima and Ishigaki. We really hope to make the journey special and memorable to all of you.

  （此一航程將帶領我們灣靠3個非常有趣的日本港口，沖繩島、宮古島與石垣島。我們衷心希望能帶給各位一趟美好與值得記憶的旅程。）

- Please be reminded that when calling to Miyakojima and Ishigaki we will use Ship's <u>Tenders to shuttle</u> you ashore and back on board the Ship. Tender Operations require a very good organization dispatching groups and independent Passengers. It is therefore very much important that you will listen and follow instructions that will be broadcasted on these days.

（各位旅客請注意，郵輪抵達宮古島與石垣島時，我們會使用<u>接駁船</u>接送您上岸與返船。運作接駁船需要所有乘客、旅行團的合作與配合，才能確保接駁船順利作業。因此，請您在這兩天務必仔細聆聽以下的廣播並遵照指示，以便讓所有乘客能盡快上岸遊玩。）

- Please be reminded that your Safety onboard is always our priority. Pay very much attention when exiting to any Open Deck as we may experience strong winds. Make good use of handrails particularly in Stairways as the ship may experience rolling or pitching movements due to Sea conditions.

（請注意，您在郵輪上的安全是我們的首要責任，在進出開放甲板時請特別注意強風，以避免發生危險。郵輪在航行期間可能會有顛簸起伏，請您在上下樓梯時務必抓緊扶手，避免摔倒。）

- For the ones of you smoking, please strictly observe our smoking policy, smoking only in the areas which are allowed and indicated. Smoking is not allowed in any Passenger Cabin and Balcony. It is very important for everyone safety that you strictly follow these instructions.

（為了郵輪全體人員的安全著想，請吸菸的乘客嚴格遵守吸菸規則，並在指定吸菸區吸菸。乘客的艙房及陽台為禁菸區域。）

- All passengers Cabin are equipped with very sensitive Smoke Detectors. Please be reminded when taking a shower to keep the bathroom door closed as the steam coming from the shower would activate the Fire Detector.

（所有的乘客艙房皆配置有煙霧感測器，洗澡時請確保浴室門緊閉，以免蒸氣誤引煙霧警鈴。）

- If you are travelling with small children please be very careful and look after them at all times, particularly if you occupy a Cabin with a Balcony.

（若有孩童與您同行，特別是居住在配置有露台客艙的乘客，請隨時注意孩童的安全。）

- Presently our departure time is set for 17:00 from Keelung Passenger Terminal. Exiting manoeuvre will take approximately 45 minutes as we have to back and turn in quite a tight basin. As we come out of the Port the ship may experience some unusual listing caused by very strong current which are present in the waters adjacent and North of Keelung Port.

（目前我們預計於晚間5點離開基隆港客運碼頭。離港過程約45分鐘，我們會先行倒退，並在一個極為狹窄的水域迴轉，隨後朝北離開基隆港。離港過程中我們預計會遇到一個較強的流水，屆時郵輪可能會有些許不尋常的傾斜，請各位乘客小心行走。）

- Speed to our next Port Okinawa is approximately 18.5 Kts. Sea conditions on the way to Naha, Okinawa are expected to be good.

（我們預計以時速18.5節前往下一個港口──沖繩。預測前往沖繩途中海況良好。）

- One more reminder!

  Ship's clock will be set 1 hour Forward (Advanced) at 2 am tomorrow morning to adjust o Japan Local Time UTC +9.

  （再次提醒您！爲配合日本當地時間，今晚凌晨2點，郵輪內所有時鐘會撥快1小時。）

- Weather forecasts tonight are: Wind-Southerly 10-15 kts; Temp -27°C; Sky partly cloudy.

  （天氣預測：今晚天氣多雲，氣溫27°C，風速爲南風10—15節。）

- Ladies and Gentlemen, we wish a very enjoyable time on board Sapphire Princess enjoy the rest of your evening and have a great vacation.

  （女士先生們！感謝您的收聽，敬祝您在藍寶石公主號有美好的一晚與美好的假期！）

二、太陽公主郵輪船長航前廣播

- A very good afternoon ladies and gentlemen, this is Captain Wxxx speaking from navigational bridge, and on behalf of the entire ship's company & Princess cruise, I would like to welcome you all onboard.

  （各位乘客午安，這是船長Wxxx來自駕駛臺的廣播。在此謹代表公主郵輪歡迎您登輪。）

- All our pre-departure checks are now complete; therefore, Sun Princess is ready in all respects to proceed to sea. Very shortly we will still start to let go our lines, and once our final clearance from port control has been received, we thrust clear off the dock prior to moving astern to the swinging basin. Once we have completed our swing, the pilots will disembark, and we will increase speed to leave the port of Keelung passing between the breakwatrers. We will transit a short traffic scheme before altering course to starboard and coming onto an Easterly heading towards our first port of call, Okinawa in Japan.

（駕駛臺團隊已完成所有的啓航預備作業，太陽公主號即將出海。很快我們會收回所有纜繩，一旦得到港口交通管制中心同意，我們會離開泊位，並倒俥退到迴船池，完成調頭轉彎後，引水人將會離船，我們也會加速離開基隆港的防坡堤。進入短暫的交通航道，隨後右轉開始向東航往我們航程的首站——日本沖繩。）

• I expect to embark the Okinawa Pilot at 10:30 tomorrow morning to be berthed alongside by 11:30.

（我們預計於明天早上10:30讓沖繩引水人上船，並在11:30將船停妥。）

• The weather forecast for this evening is for a Fresh Breeze of 15/20 knots from the South-South-West and cloudy skies, with S'ly swell of 1.5 mtr. The temperature is expected to reach a low of around 28°C. Sunset tonight: 18:34.

The weather for tomorrow in Okinawa is for Mostly sunny skies, a Gentle Breeze from the South-South-East and an outside temperature expected to reach a high of 28°C. Sunrise tomorrow morning will be at 05:49.

（天氣預報：今晚南南西風15—20節，多雲，浪高約1.5公尺。氣溫約爲28°C。

今晚的日落時間爲下午6點43分。

明天沖繩天氣晴朗，南南西風微風，氣溫約爲28°C；明天早上的日出時間爲05:49時。）

- Tomorrow morning at 02:00 the ships clock will move 1 hour forward.

Ladies and Gentlemen, I wish you an enjoyable evening on board Sun Princess and wish you an excellent cruise.

（在此提醒各位乘客，爲配合日本時差，今晚凌晨2點所有時鐘會撥快1小時。

各位女士先生、祝您在優質郵輪太陽公主號有一個美好的夜晚，謝謝！）

三、鑽石公主號抵達基隆港船長廣播

- 皆樣おはようございます、基隆へようこそ。

本船ダイヤモンドプリンスは基隆に到著致しました。

（各位旅客早安，歡迎到基隆來，本輪鑽石公主號已抵達基隆港。）

- 下船の手順（てじゅん）につきましてはグループ毎にご案内いたしますので、下船についてのお手紙をご參照くださいませ。

現在、基隆のお天氣は晴、北東から風速10メートルの風、外の氣溫は25度でございます。本日の日のいりは 18：10です。

（有關各旅行團下船順序的安排，請參閱下船説明書。現在基隆天氣是晴天，東北風風速每秒10公尺，室外溫度爲25°C。今天的日落時間是18：10時。）

- 改めましてこの度はダイヤモンドプリンスにご乘船いただきまして、誠にありがとうございます。素晴らしいクルーズをお過ごしいただけたら幸（さいわ）いでございます。

（再次衷心感謝各位搭乘鑽石公主號，並以提供各位愉快的郵輪假期深感榮幸。）

- 私キャプテンをはじめ、乗組員一同船上にてきた皆様にお会できる日を、心よりお待ち申し上げております。どうぞ、お氣をつけてお帰りくださいませ。

  （船長暨所有船員衷心期待與各位在船上再相會！返家途中請注意安全哦！）

- また、お客様のご協力は勿論のこと、乗組員一人一人の尽力がなくては最終日まで迎えることは出來ませんでした。下船される前に乗組員に勞いのお言葉をお願いいたします。

  （此外，除了各位旅客的協助外，船員們以客爲尊的努力直至各位離船的最後一天，希望各位下船時能夠給予船員嘉勉的致意。）

- 尚、連續乗船のお客様は午後4時までにお戻りくださいませ。それでは皆様、基隆にて素敵な日をお過ごしください。

  （此外，繼續搭乗本船前往下一港口的旅客請在下午4時前回船。敬祝各位在基隆度過愉快的一天。）

第五節　客船航前操演廣播（Boat drill onboard cruise）

A very embarrassing necessity for many officers is the talk to the passengers regarding the boat drill. Something along the following line is suggested:

（要如何向乗客廣播救生操演是許多船副的困擾，特列述下文作爲參考：）

- In complying with the rules and regulations for the safety of life at sea, we are having a fire and boat drill, which is for the benefit of all. Please cooperate by wearing your lift belts, which are to be found under the lower berth in your cabin. If you are not familiar with the adjusting of life belts, a member of the crew, locate at your boat station, will assist you. You will also find a card in your cabin with the number of the boat to which you are assigned.

〔爲遵守海上人命安全公約規定，並顧及所有人的權益，本輪即將舉行滅火與求生操演。敬請配合穿起你（妳）的救生衣，救生衣放在房間內的下舖床底下。如果你（妳）不知如何調整救生帶，一位位於你（妳）的登艇集合站的船員將會協助你（妳）。同時你（妳）將可在房間內找到一張卡片，上面印有你（妳）被指定前往的救生艇號碼數。〕

• After acquainting yourself with the number of your boat go to B deck. If your has an odd number you will find it stenciled overhead on the starbard or right side; if an even number, on the port or left side. The six short and one long blast if the whistle will be the call to boat stations. The three short blast will terminate the drill.」

〔當你（妳）知道被指定的救生艇號碼數後，請前往B甲板。如果你（妳）卡片上的號碼是單數，你（妳）將會在右舷找到該編號的救生艇，如果是雙數則在左舷。當汽笛鳴放6短聲1長聲表示：「你（妳）應立即前往救生艇集合站。」3短聲表示：「操演結束」。〕

第六節　當值駕駛員的接班要求（Requirements of the relieving officer）

1. Section A-VIII/2 of STCW requires the relieving officer to ensure his vision is fully adjusted to the light conditions before taking over

the watch. In practical terms this means that during the hours of darkness an officer or rating (lookout) must come up to the bridge at least 10 minutes before their watch begins.

（STCW的Section A-VIII/2要求接班駕駛員在其接班前必須確保其視覺完全調整至適應夜間狀況。實務上的意義就是表示其必須在接班前10分鐘抵達駕駛臺以適應夜間視覺。）

2. This section also stipulates that prior to taking over the watch the relieving officer shall:

（此章節同時規定接班駕駛員接班前必須：）

(1) Be satisfied of the ship's estimate true position;

（確認船舶的估計真實位置。）

(2) Confirm it's intended track, course and speed;

（確認船舶的預期航路、航向與船速。）

(3) Shall note any dangers to navigation expected to be encountered during their watch.

（必須注意值班期間預期遭遇的任何航行險阻。）

(4) Learn the Standing orders and other special instructions of the master relating to navigation of the ship thoroughly;

（詳讀船長對於安全航行的安全守則與其他特別指示。）

(5) Prevailing and predicted tides, currents, weather, visibility and the effect of these factors upon course and speed;

（當下與預期的潮流、洋流、天候、能見度等狀況，以及此等因素對航向與船速的影響。）

(6) Acquaintance with the procedures for the use of main engines to manoeuvre when the main engines are on bridge control;

（熟悉主機轉換至駕駛臺操控時的主機使用操縱程序。）

(7) Check the error of gyro compasses;

（核對電羅經的誤差。）

(8) Recognize the possible effects of heel, trim, water density, and squat on under-keel clearance.

（確認船體傾斜、俯仰差、海水密度與船艉下蹲造成龍骨下間隙變化等現象的可能影響。）

第七節　進出船塢注意事項（Precaution during Dry-Docking）

1. No free liquid surfaces in tanks, etc.
   （槽櫃內不得有自由液面。）

2. Vessel trimmed to an even keel.
   （調整俯仰差至平正狀態。）

3. Shift no weight, cargo or water while docked.
   （進塢期間禁止移動重物、貨物或水。）

4. Make connections between ship and yard fire lines.
   （連接船岸之間的滅火管線。）

5. All closets, drains should be shut off.
   （所有排水孔必須堵住或鎖緊。）

6. Check bottom plugs, underwater cocks and valves, zinc protectors, and note when removed and when replaced.
   （檢查並記錄海底塞、水下旋塞或閥門、防蝕鋅板何時拆下與何時更替回復。）

7. Examine bottom cleaned and painting works.
（檢查船底清潔與油漆作業。）

8. Look for corrosion along whole shall plating.
（檢查全船船殼板的銹蝕處。）

9. After undocking, look for leaks where repairs have been made.
（出塢後檢查曾經修理處有無裂痕。）

第八節　紀律（Discipline）

1. The sailing time should be known and posted on the board for all to see.
（開船時間必須公布於所有人都能看見的處所。）

2. Alcoholic beverages depress the body's central nervous system and affect vision, judgment, and motor skills.
（酒精飲料會降低人體中央神經系統，並會影響視覺、判斷與運動神經技能。）

3. Drinking could result in a momentary lapse of judgement. And only one incident of this nature need occur over the course of 10 years for a rating's or officer's good name to be besmirched and career to be shattered.
（飲酒可能導致瞬間失去判斷，一世英名毀於一旦並且斷送前途。）

4. To minimize risk to yourself, your passengers and other boaters, remember that you are in command on your creational boat and you should not drink and drive.

〔為降低你（妳）本身、旅客與其他在船人員的風險，切記當你（妳）在操控你（妳）的休憩船艇時，你（妳）就是不能飲酒並操縱船艇。〕

5. Individuals vary in their ability to cope with stressful situations, workload and long hours but a dominant factor in many accidents has been accumulated sleep deprivation.

（每一個人對抗壓力狀況、工作負荷、長時間工作的能力不同，但許多事故的發生主因卻是睡眠不足所累積的。）

6. There was no active management of the use of mobile telephones while on the bridge.

（有關在駕駛臺使用手機並無積極管理。）

7. The cell phone, in the hands of any member of the bridge team, is indeed becoming a menace.

（駕駛臺團隊任一成員手中握有手機無異是安全的最大威脅。）

第九節　其他（Others）

Treatment of Officials 港口招待

　　In all ports, domestic and foreign, all officials should be treated courteously and with consideration. Above all, do not cross them or argue with them. Generally, they have the last word and they may turn out to be an expensive one for your company and a troublesome one for you.

〔無論在國內或國外的所有港口，必須禮貌與尊敬的招待公部門官員。最重要的是，切勿與其起爭執。基本上，凡事都是他（她）們說了算，與其爭執可能給公司帶來昂貴的代價，以及你（妳）個人無盡的困擾。〕

第七章　海事文書

第一節　報告與陳述書的差異（Difference between The Report and Statement）

1. Statement is a declaration or remark while report is a piece of information describing.

   （陳述書是一種陳述與聲明，報告則是資訊的敘述。）

2. A statement is usually given in response to something and are often quite short, compared to a report. Statements can be written or spoken. Reports are always written, and can be between 1-1000 pages.

   （相對於報告，陳述書通常是本於對某一事件的回應，內容較短。陳述可以用書面或口頭表達。報告則幾乎都採書面為之，從一頁至上千頁都有。）

3. The report should be in detail no matter how minor the accident, bearing in mind that the recipients will be many miles away and all they can go by are your reports.

   （無論事件多麼微小，報告都需詳述。切記！收件者位於數千里之外，其會完全遵照你的報告行事。）

4. When writing your own statement be sure to include all pertinent details, but don't make it too long-winded. A clear, absolutely truthful statement will be of greatest assistance to your company's insurance department.

（當你在書寫陳述書時，務必確認將所有相關細節納入，但不能過於冗長。一份清楚、完全真實的陳述將爲你公司的保險部門提供最大的協助。）

第二節　海事報告的意義（Meaning of Sea Protest）

1. When any casualty occurred in relation to operation of a vessel, the master is obligated to submit Sea Protest to the authorities concerned under Article 19 of the Seamens Law.

（當發生任何有關船舶運航的意外事故，船長就有依據船員法第19條規定向主管機關提出海事報告的義務。）

2. Sea Protest has significance that it is one of the documents to decide as to whether or not the carriers are liable under conditions of Bill of Lading. It also serves as a supporting document when claim is filed with insurance company under hull insurance and Protection and Indemnity insurance.

（海事陳述書爲決定運送人是否遵守提單所載條件責任的重要文件之一。同時也是向船體保險與船東互保協會保險提出索賠的證明文件。）

※ Point for attention（注意事項）

In your statement or report, refrain from comment on the possible incompetence of your pilot. Rest assured that the master of the other vessel and the opposition lawyers will take care of that! And don't let them talk you into saying your pilot was incompetent and not on the job.

〔在你（妳）的報告書或陳述書中，<u>避免批評所僱用的引水人不適任。勿庸掛慮</u>！那是對造律師不會放過的辯駁利基。而且不要被誘導說出引水人不適任或不盡職。〕

第三節　海事文書範本（Paradigm of report/statement）

一、Stevedore's damage report 碼頭工人損害報告

M. V. "XXX"

Yokohama, Japan,

NOV 22,2021

The Manager

JJJ Stevedore Company

Damage Report

（損壞報告）

Dear Sir:

We wish to inform you that after discharging cargo, we found some damage as follows:

（我藉此通知貴公司，本輪於貴港卸完貨物後，發現下列損壞：）

1. GGGGGG

2. KKKKKK

The above-mentioned damage was caused by Stevedore's improper handling machine while discharging the cargoes.

（上述損壞乃因碼頭工人於卸貨時的不當操作機具所致。）

Please arrange the repairing work and replacement of it as soon as possible.

（敬請盡速安排修理替換工作。）

Kindly take this matter up with the stevedore company and hold them liable for the damage sustained.

（請就上述本輪遭受之損壞與碼頭裝卸公司洽談並課以其毀損責任。）

Very Truly Yours,

Capt. OOO

Master of M.V. "XXX"

二、Notice of Readiness 船舶完成準備通知書

M.V. "XXX"

Yokohama, Japan,

NOV 22,2021

The Manager

JJJ Stevedore Company

Notice of Readiness

（完成準備通知書）

Gentlemen:

Please be advised that the subject vessel, under my command, arrived at this port at 0100 hours on the 10th October , 2021 and in all respects ready to commence loading/discharging your cargo of 10,000 Long Tons Raw Sugar in bulk.

（敬啓者：茲通知上述船舶在本人指揮下，已於2021年10月10日0100時抵達本港。並完成所有裝/卸貨準備，隨時可開始裝/卸貴公司託運的10,000長噸散裝粗糖。）

In this connection, we hereby formally tender to you this Notice and beg your acknowledgement accept this by signing on this space provided thereon

（就此，本人正式藉此提出裝/卸貨完成準備通知書，敬請認知並簽收。）

Gratefully Yours,

Notice of Readiness tendered

（提出完成準備通知書）

Notice of Readiness accepted

（接受完成準備通知書）

三、Encounter Bad Weather、Deck cargo on fire 遭遇惡劣天氣、甲板貨失火

M.V. "Mayflower"

Yokohama, Japan,

NOV 25, 2021

Marine Note of Protest
（海事抗辯陳述書）

I, Captain. XXX Master of Motor Vessel "Mayflower", which registered under the Government of the Republic of Liberian, Official No.2222, Gross Tonnage of 15,000 units, which sailed from Keelung, Taiwan, on the 9th SEP 2021, with a cargo of Hydraulic Crane on deck, was bound for European Ports and arrived at Antwerp, Belgium on the 24th day of SEP 2021, and declare:

（本人，XXX船長，「五月花」輪船長，僅陳述賴比利亞籍「五月花」輪、官方註冊號碼第2222號、總噸位15,000，於2021年9月9日甲板上載運油壓起重機，從台灣基隆港航往歐洲港口，並於2021年9月24日抵達比利時的安特衛普。）

That, during the voyage, from 15th day of SEP to 17th day of SEP, at this near position, Lat 16°30' Long 100°20' the vessel encountered with typhoon "Beauty", it had very rough weather, rolling and pitching heavily, shipping seas on deck all the times, and at the time 0345 hours 16th, one Hydraulic Truck's control room was smoking, we extinguished immediately.

（航程中，自9月15日至9月17日，本輪在緯度16°30'經度100°20'附近遭遇颱風「美麗」，天候異常惡劣，船體縱搖與橫搖劇烈，海水經常打至甲板上。約在16日0345時，一部油壓起重機的控制室冒煙，船員迅即撲滅。）

Now fearing any damage to the vessel or cargo owing to the above-mentioned weather and smoking, hereby enter this Marine Note of Protest against all losses, damages caused therefrom reserving the right to extend it if need be.

（於今擔憂上述惡劣天候與起重機的冒煙，恐對本船與貨載造成損壞，藉此提出海事陳述書以作為抗辯為此所衍生的損壞與損失，並保留本人的法律權益。）

Capt. XXX

Master of M.V. "Mayflower"

第四節　常用文書詞彙

1. Amazingly, ...（不可思議的……）

2. among other things, ...〔除了……外（還），除其他因素之外〕

3. And as we all know, ...（眾所周知，……）

4. a short while later, ...（稍後）

5. As a consequence, ...（結果……）

6. As I have written, ...（如同本人在文中所述，……）

7. As mentioned above, ...（如上所述，……）

8. as a result of a lack of...（因缺少……的結果）

9. Assuming all else went reasonably according to plan, ...（假設一切條件依計畫合理發生，……）

10. As the situation developed, ...（然隨著情勢的改變，……）

11. At first glance, ...（乍看之下，……）

12. Attached please find the report of the meeting.（隨函附上會議報告，請查收。）

13. At the risk of ...（冒……的危險）

14. At the earliest available opportunity ...（盡可能地早）

15. at his (master's) disposal...〔任其（船長）自行處置〕

16. Be causative of ...（成爲……的原因）

17. Because of this, ...（正因如此，……）

18. Be entitled to ...（有……的權力）

19. Be liable for ...（需負起……責任）

20. By contrast, ...（兩相比對，……）

21. By so doing ...（如果那麼做……）

22. Coming into force on (Saturday) ...〔即將自（星期六）起生效〕

23. Consequently, ...（結果，……）

24. Despite this ..., ...（不計……）

25. Difficulty was experienced in...（在……過程中遭遇困難）

26. Earlier this year, ...（今年稍早，……）

27. Eventually, （最後／終於，……）

28. Exercise due diligence（盡最大努力）

29. Force majeure（不可抗力）

30. For safety reasons, ...（爲安全計，……）

31. Generally, ...（一般地／通常，……）

32. Hence we have to ...（因此我們必須……）

33. However, on this occasion, ...（處此情形，無論如何……）

34. If this is true, ...（果眞如此，……）

35. In consequence, ...（結果／因此）

36. In consequence of ...（由於……的結果）

37. In fact (In reality), ...（事實上，……）

38. In other word, ...（換言之，……）

39. In particular, ...（特別是，……）

40. In regard to ...（關於……；通常置於句首）

41. In summary, (In brief,) ...（簡單言之，……）

42. Interestingly, ...（有趣的是，……）

43. In the context of ...（在……領域裡／背景下……）

44. in the preparation for the...（預爲準備）

45. In this connection, ...（關於這一點，……）

46. In this way, ...（以此方法，……）

47. It is reported that ...（根據報導，……）

48. It must be borne in mind that ...（必須謹記……）

49. Laissez faire（放任主義）

50. Make sense of ...（了解……的意義、理解、懂得）

51. Meanwhile, ...（於此同時，……）

52. Obviously, ...（很明顯地，……）

53. Of no consequence.（不重要的；通常置於句尾）

54. On this occasion, ...（處此情形下，……）

55. On rare occasions, ...（在極少的情況下，……）

56. Over the last few decades, ...（在過去幾十年，……）

57. Prevent ... from ...〔防止……不會（遭受／被）……〕

58. Prima facie（表面證據的）

59. Rather, ...（猶有甚者，……）

60. Shortly after, ...（稍後，……）

61. Similarly, ...（相同地，……）

62. Since that ...（因爲那……）

63. Statistics indicate that ...（依據統計顯示，……）

64. The details are ...（細節爲……）

65. Therefore, ...（因此，……）

66. This should have been taken into account.（這必須列入考慮。）

67. Thus, ...（因此，……）

68. Unfortunately, the results are disappointedly.（很不幸地，結果是令

人失望的。）

69. Until recently, ... （直到最近，……）

70. We have considered the various options. （我們已考慮許多不同方案。）

71. With regards to the ... （關於……）

第五節　海事報告相關詞句

1. If damages caused by our negligence or our error of judgment could result in court proceeding, why are we not referring to basic rules and concepts of courts which deal with negligence and liability?

（如果損壞是因爲我們的疏失或錯誤判斷所造成，則在訴訟過程中，勢必會面對爲什麼我們不遵從法庭處理疏失的基本規則與觀念行事的質疑。）

2. While the collision regulations are-or should be-clear, the way in which they are used to apportion fault in court is sometimes less so.

（儘管避碰規則寫的非常清楚，但是法院在判決分攤過失責任時，常不是如此的。）

3. If the vessel breached a collision regulation, it was presumed she is guilty unless she could prove otherwise.

（如果船舶違反避碰規則，除非其能證明有必要，否則即被推定爲有罪。）

4. Unless the vessel could show that the circumstance of the case made departure from the regulations necessary.

（除非該船舶能夠證明當時的環境必須背離規則的規定。）

5. The burden of proof is considered heavy, as a great deal of material evidence is required, and the defense has been successful in only a few cases.

（舉證的責任是相當重的，因為需要許多具體的證據，而且答辯成功的只有少數幾個例子。）

6. If the perilous situation was caused through the defendant's own fault, this defense is not available.

（如果危險的情況是因被告本身的過失所造成者，則抗辯將是無效的。）

7. All available evidence suggests that no avoiding actions were taken by the yacht and no look out was being maintain by her prior to the collision.

（所有可靠證據顯示，該遊艇於碰撞前，既未保持瞭望，也未採取任何避碰措施。）

8. Both vessels had been observing each other approaching.

（兩船在趨近時都有看到對方。）

9. No action was taken by either vessel until they were within 0.2 nm of each other.

（直到兩船接近至0.2浬時，兩船都未採取行動。）

10. STCW Convention requires that the OOW "shall take frequent and accurate compass bearings of approaching ships as a means of early detection of risk of collision". However, this requirement is often ig-

nored.

（STCW公約要求當值駕駛員必須經常且準確地觀測接近船舶的羅經方位，作爲及早探知碰撞危機的方法。但此要求常被忽略。）

11. If you do need to take avoiding action to avoid risk of collision, you have a number of tools available.

（如果你有需要採取避碰動作去避免碰撞危機，你有許多方法可採用。）

12. The collision could have been averted if one or both vessels had reduced speed in good time.

（如果其中一船或兩船能及早減速，則碰撞或可避免。）

13. As the squall passed, own vessel started to drag anchor.

（當暴風雨通過時，本船開始走錨。）

14. During this period, nobody was observed on the bridge or the deck of the cargo vessel; only upon impact did crew members appear.

（碰撞當時，貨船駕駛臺與甲板上看不到任何人，直到碰撞發生後船員才出現。）

15. The tanker sustained only minor scuffing damage on her bow.

（油輪僅船艏遭受輕微擦傷。）

16. It is probable that collision would have been avoided in such situation if She had been instructed to made fast the tugs.

（如果該船有被指示拖船繫帶拖纜或許可以避免碰撞。）

17. Passage plan did not take into account local navigation warnings.

（航行計畫未考慮當地航行警告。）

18. The heading marker was not being switch off occasionally to check for obscured targets.

（未不時關掉雷達船艏輝線顯示功能，致無法辨認出適被輝線掩蓋的目標。）

19. The 3 cm (X) band radar provides better definition which can improve the accuracy of the bearings and ranges used for position fixing.

〔3公分（X）頻帶雷達可提供較佳的解析度，其可改善目標方位與距離的正確性，故應作為定位時使用。〕

20. Radar range scale and tuning (gain、sea clutter、rain clutter) should be regularly adjusted throughout the watch in order to detect weak radar targets.

〔整個值班過程中，雷達距程與調諧控鈕（增益、雨浪回跡濾波）都要定時調整，以免失去掃到微弱目標回跡的可能。〕

21. The most common reason for vessels to be found at fault is defective appreciation of the situation on the radar.

（大部分船舶最容易犯過失的原因就是對雷達上的情況做錯誤的判斷。）

國家圖書館出版品預行編目資料

實用船藝與海技英文／方信雄著. －－初
版.－－臺北市：五南圖書出版股份有限公
司, 2021.03
面；　公分
ISBN 978-986-522-449-3（平裝）

1.英語　2.航海　3.航務　4.讀本

805.18　　　　　　　　110000708

5I55

實用船藝與海技英文

作　　　者 ─ 方信雄

發 行 人 ─ 楊榮川

總 經 理 ─ 楊士清

總 編 輯 ─ 楊秀麗

副總編輯 ─ 王正華

責任編輯 ─ 張維文

封面設計 ─ 王麗娟

出 版 者 ─ 五南圖書出版股份有限公司

地　　　址：106台北市大安區和平東路二段339號4樓

電　　　話：(02)2705-5066　　傳　　　真：(02)2706-6100

網　　　址：https://www.wunan.com.tw

電子郵件：wunan@wunan.com.tw

劃撥帳號：01068953

戶　　　名：五南圖書出版股份有限公司

法律顧問　林勝安律師事務所　林勝安律師

出版日期　2021年3月初版一刷

定　　　價　新臺幣350元

經典永恆・名著常在

五十週年的獻禮──經典名著文庫

五南，五十年了，半個世紀，人生旅程的一大半，走過來了。

思索著，邁向百年的未來歷程，能為知識界、文化學術界作些什麼？

在速食文化的生態下，有什麼值得讓人雋永品味的？

歷代經典・當今名著，經過時間的洗禮，千錘百鍊，流傳至今，光芒耀人；

不僅使我們能領悟前人的智慧，同時也增深加廣我們思考的深度與視野。

我們決心投入巨資，有計畫的系統梳選，成立「經典名著文庫」，

希望收入古今中外思想性的、充滿睿智與獨見的經典、名著。

這是一項理想性的、永續性的巨大出版工程。

不在意讀者的眾寡，只考慮它的學術價值，力求完整展現先哲思想的軌跡；

為知識界開啟一片智慧之窗，營造一座百花綻放的世界文明公園，

任君遨遊、取菁吸蜜、嘉惠學子！